THE TASTE OF
MURDER

THE TASTE OF MURDER

Joanna Cannan

Dover Publications, Inc., New York

This Dover edition, first published in 1987, is an un-
abridged, unaltered republication of the work first published by Victor Gollancz, London, 1950, under the title
Murder Included (first U.S. publication by William Mor-
row, New York, 1950, under the title *Poisonous Relations*).

Manufactured in the United States of America
Dover Publications, Inc., 31 East 2nd Street, Mineola,
N.Y. 11501

Library of Congress Cataloging-in-Publication Data

Cannan, Joanna, 1898–1961
    The taste of murder.

    Previously published as: Poisonous relations.
    I. Title.
PR6005.A483P6   1987   823'.912   86-23999
ISBN 0-486-25296-5

THE TASTE OF
MURDER

CHAPTER ONE

FROM the depths of a shabby leather armchair Ronald Price looked round the Chief Constable's study, noticed the hunting prints, the photographs of polo teams, the shelves of books, the blue-and-red Turkey carpet, the golden cocker spaniel just now dislodged from the very chair he was sitting in and sent to its basket. Colonel Blimp . . . he thought, and: dog's hairs all over my blue suit . . . and: stinks of dog, this room does . . . and: whatever would Valerie say to all those books? – regular dust-traps. . . . The Chief Constable, standing on the worn hearthrug with his back to the fire, said, 'Well, good hunting,' and gulped down half his whisky-and-soda, and Price heard the lips of the Superintendent smack as he himself took a sip of gin-and-orange.

The Chief Constable said, 'It's not lack of self-confidence that made us apply to the Yard, Inspector. The Superintendent and I have solved many a knotty problem, eh, Treadwell? It's just that we're too near to these people – first thing I said was, well, we can count out Sir Charles – he was at school with me, and a moment later Treadwell comes out with, well, there's no need to question Miss Pat – I knew her as an infant. It's the same with the servants. Neither Treadwell nor I can remember a time when we didn't know Benson – he's the butler. Beatrice Blythe, the head housemaid, is Treadwell's aunt, and Kate the kitchenmaid is his cousin. Nanny, of course, was born on the place – at the south lodge – she was old John Toomer's daughter. Mrs Capes, the cook, comes from farthest afield: she's from Aston-on-the-Green, five miles away. The under housemaid, Sylvia Spencer, comes from the Home Farm – her grandfather farmed it and, I believe, her great-grandfather. The first Lady d'Estray was a cousin of mine and I'm Hugo's god-father, so it's altogether rather an impossible situation, eh, Treadwell?'

'That's what baffles me, sir,' owned the Superintendent, a round-faced man with unblinking china-blue eyes. 'Question Sir Charles after all he's done for my grandmother I could not. Of course, there's not all that need to bother the Family – it must be one of those paying guests or an outside job. I don't mean by that the outside staff, Inspector. They're all well known to us – in fact Perry, the head-gardener, is my brother-in-law.'

'And the deceased?' Price asked. 'Was *she* related to either of you?'

His sarcastic tone went unnoticed. 'Well, actually,' said the Chief Constable, 'Miss Hudson, being a distant cousin of the d'Estrays, must have been a connexion of mine. I've known her for many years. She used to stay at the Park every year for a fortnight or three weeks to get some hunting, before they started this paying-guest business.'

'And when did they start it?'

'Another drink?' asked the Chief Constable.

'No, thank you, sir. When . . . ?'

'Treadwell?'

'Well,' said the Superintendent, 'just a thimbleful.'

Price fidgeted while Colonel Rivett-Bankes refilled the Superintendent's glass and then his own. Arriving by car at the county town of Harborough, Price had expected to find himself promptly in conference at the Police Station, but the Sergeant on duty there had informed him that a police car was waiting to run out a further ten miles to the Chief Constable's home, where Superintendent Treadwell would meet him. Price was a Londoner; he was Left Wing; he had no fancy for doing his work in the dog-and-flea-ridden 'studies' of retired Colonels. He had kept silence as a loutish local constable drove him through the October dusk over hills to wrought-iron gates, yew hedges, and Elizabethan gables. A doddering parasite of a butler had shown him into this large, over-crowded, shabby, so-called study, where Colonel Blimp, after nearly wringing his hand off, had turned 'Susie – little woman' out of a chair and expected him to sit down in it. Now, fussing about with cut-glass decanter and silver cigarette box, he was doing his best to turn an important conference into a cosy chat. Price repeated his question.

6

The Colonel set down the decanter, flung a log on the already extravagant fire, caught the spaniel's eye, and said, 'There's a good bitch,' whereat she leapt from her basket and he roared, 'Get back, Susie, get back.' Susie got back; he settled himself in the chair opposite Price, stretched out his long legs in their muddy corduroy trousers, drank some whisky and at last came to business.

'The paying guests didn't start till Sir Charles married his second wife about eighteen months ago. Like all the rest of us, the d'Estrays are hard up. Charles was thinking he might have to sell the place and that would have been an awful thing for everyone. Towards the end of the war an old aunt of his had died out on the Riviera and left him her villa. He went out to see about selling it and brought home his second wife – Bunny. Now I come to think of it I don't know what her real name is – everyone calls her Bunny. Well, Bunny,' said the Chief Constable, his voice growing drier, 'is made of different stuff from the d'Estrays. Instead of moaning about selling the place, she said, why not turn it into a guest house and hunting stables, she and Sir Charles running the house and Pat the stables. The family hung back at first and Sir Charles still loathes his "guests", but, to give her her due, Bunny's worked hard and she's made a go of it.'

'And Miss Hudson was one of the guests?'

'Yes, but *she* was a welcome one. As I told you, she had stayed there on and off for years and she worshipped the place and was delighted at the chance of living there. Sir Charles and Hugo and Pat were always tremendously fond of her – Hugo, by the way, is out of the army and looking round; there was some talk of him starting a dairy herd, I believe, but it needs capital. In the meantime he's hunting the Badgemoor. Now the paying guests . . . '

'May we finish with the family first? Is that all of them?'

'Oh no. There are two younger children, Simon and Iona. Fourteen or fifteenish – nice kids, very popular with the village. Then there's Bunny's child – Lisa.'

'The second Lady d'Estray was a widow?'

'Widow of some French chap,' said the Chief Constable.

7

'I've never got hold of her name, I'm afraid – he was a writer fellow. She's in that line herself – writes books about Siamese cats and children.'

'And did she get on with Miss Hudson?'

'As far as I know quite amicably. Thought her a bit of an old battle-axe, I expect, not having been brought up with her like the d'Estrays. I thought her that myself, as a matter of fact – I don't care for these excessively horsey women.'

'And the other paying guests – did they like Miss Hudson?'

'If I know her, she put 'em in their place and kept 'em there. But I never heard of any unpleasantness.'

Price got out his note-book. 'And their names?'

'I've got 'em all down,' said the Chief Constable, and, putting on a pair of horn-rimmed spectacles, he took a crumpled envelope from the pocket of his checked hacking coat, turned it about and read, 'Mr Rose. Well, Mr Rose is a type that I daresay you're familiar with, though it's not common, thank the Lord, down here. A few years back his name was Rosengarten or Rosenberg, I daresay. He's a man of fifty odd, with a fancy to be a country gentleman; talks about buying a place but hasn't found one to suit him yet; goes up to town twice a week and the rest of his time his business – whatever it is – is managed by his son, Howard. Howard comes down Friday nights and goes up Sunday evenings as a rule. Both of 'em ride to hounds, and Pat finds them very trying. Mrs Rose seems a nice little woman.'

'The servants don't care for her,' put in Treadwell.

'Oh well, they wouldn't,' said the Colonel. 'She's what they call round here a "lady left on the wrong doorstep". But there's no harm in the woman.' He referred to his envelope. 'Mr and Mrs Scampnell – now I bet she's liked by the servants. She was a General's daughter, and she was first married to a chap in the Indian Army, who left her quite well-off. Scampnell's in some family business – goes up to the Midlands to directors' meetings once a month or so. Mrs has a daughter by her first husband, a nice-looking girl but getting on. Mrs Scampnell's the horsewoman of that party – rides astride but sits well back, quite good in the old-fashioned

8

style.' He glanced again at the envelope. 'Flight-Lieutenant Marvin. Air Force bloke,' he added unnecessarily.

'Ah,' said Treadwell.

'He's Treadwell's fancy,' said the Chief Constable, smiling, 'but I'm afraid he's going to floor us with a cast-iron alibi. Treadwell fancies him because, unlike the other p.gs., he's known Miss Hudson for some time and she introduced him here. He got shot up in the war, I gather, and she started him riding as a sort of cure for nerves. A good-looking fellow . . .'

'They had a name for them in the 1914 war,' said the Superintendent, 'Temporary gents.'

The Chief Constable said, 'Oh, you're a snob, Treadwell. It runs in your family. I remember – '

Price interrupted, 'What's this alibi?'

'You'll see it in Treadwell's notes,' said the Chief Constable. 'He interviewed several of the p.gs. this morning. According to Marvin and everybody else he was in London. From the doctor's report it seems certain that the poison was taken last thing at night and Miss Hudson kept the where-withal for a nightcap – whisky and water – in her bedroom. What's his name – Marvin – went up to town with Howard Rose on Sunday evening, so if he'd done the tampering, Miss Hudson would have drunk the fatal dose on Sunday night. Beatrice and Sylvia both remember taking a dirty glass down from the bedroom on Tuesday morning as usual, so we know she didn't give her nightcap a miss on Monday. Of course all that may be immaterial. It's not yet confirmed that the poison was in the bottle. Incidentally the only finger-prints we found on it were those of Miss Hudson.'

'Finger-prints are not what they were. Everyone knows too much,' said Treadwell.

'Their absence is significant,' said Price. 'If there's only one set of the deceased's finger-prints, it is obvious that prior to her retiring for the night the bottle had been wiped clean by the murderer. Otherwise there would have been a mass of superimposed prints – her own and the domestic helps' – when they dusted.'

'If they dusted properly there wouldn't have been,' said

Treadwell. 'They would have dusted the bottle every morning when they did the bedroom. And I bet Beatrice did too. I've always heard that she's an excellent servant.'

It was natural, thought Price, for Colonel Blimp to use the word 'servant' but he couldn't understand Treadwell using it, especially of his own aunt, was it? or cousin? These country chaps . . . he thought. They're years behind the times . . . don't they realize we've done away with masters and servants? To teach them better he said, 'I presume the domestic helps can enlighten us on that subject. Now with reference to the glass – was that tested for finger-prints?'

'It was taken down and washed up before even the doctor got there. Of course it never occurred to Beatrice, who had taken in the morning tea, that Miss Hudson had died other than naturally. Nor to Nanny, who was next on the scene – called in by Beatrice. Nor to Lady d'Estray, called in by Nanny. I can quite understand that Beatrice's instinct was to tidy up for the doctor. He told them, too late, not to touch anything. He suspected that the old girl – Miss Hudson, I mean – had taken an overdose of some sleeping draught. He didn't know her – she was as tough as a moorland pony and had absolutely no use for doctors or drugs. I went to the Park before lunch – I found a message from the Superintendent when I came in. The general opinion was that, what with cub-hunting twice a week and dragging people out for ten-mile walks the rest of the time, she'd overdone it, getting on for seventy she was – I should never have thought it, would you, Treadwell? When I heard that she was full up with oenanthotoxin – whatever it may be – you could have knocked me down with a feather. Treadwell and Sergeant Blow went up at once and started questioning the servants, that's to say Beatrice, who took in the tea, and Nanny, called in by Beatrice, and Benson. None of the others, of course, would know anything.'

'With the possible exception of the kitchen help who, presumably, washed up the glass.'

'The glass wouldn't go to the kitchen,' said Treadwell.

'Where would it go then?' asked Price a little irritably.

'To the pantry, of course,' said Treadwell.

A gong rang then and Treadwell got up and said, 'Well, sir, that will be your dinner.' The lady-dog jumped out of her basket. Though there were still questions that Price wished to ask, the conference, if such it could be called, was plainly over. Price got out of his chair and picked golden hairs from his coat sleeve. The lady-dog was wriggling and whining at the door.

'Have to dine early now,' said the Chief Constable. 'We've only got Mrs Witts in the kitchen, and she likes to get washed up and finished.'

'Too bad, sir,' said Treadwell.

'Oh well,' said the Chief Constable, and Treadwell knew what he meant and thought, not for the first time, how well they were taking it, these doomed and done-for ladies and gentlemen; but Ronald Price thought, dine early! It would do him good to get his own dinner and wash it up too, the old bastard. 'I suppose you'll be going up to the Park first thing tomorrow,' said the Chief Constable. 'You won't want me under your feet, but I'll be at home all day if I can help you. Astonleigh 96. Incidentally it takes longer to get through than it does to walk across the d'Estrays' park and up my spinney.'

Out in the drive the Superintendent said, 'I'll send my car back and come along with you, Inspector; then I'll see you get fixed up at the Red Lion and hand over my notes – you might like to glance through them.' And, 'This is Aston-leigh,' he said, as the car turned into the highroad. 'I was born here. It's supposed to be one of the prettiest villages in England. Well kept up too,' he continued, peering into what seemed to Price the total darkness. 'The Colonel owns what doesn't belong to Sir Charles and both of them are good landlords.'

Price said, 'Landlords are, or should be, an anachronism.'

'I suppose,' said Treadwell, 'you're in favour of Council houses. We don't care for them here – all as alike as two peas – rules and regulations – no end of a rigmarole if you want anything done in the way of repairs; while Sir Charles's or the

11

Colonel's tenants have only to mention it next time they run into them in the village. It's pleasanter too if a chap gets behind with the rent to be dealing with one of their sort, instead of a lot of yapping Rural District Councillors. However, we can't all think alike, can we?'

Price said, 'In the case of thinking men, there are some subjects on which there can be no difference of opinion.'

'Well, I suppose we all agree that the world's round and a few things like that,' said Treadwell. 'But otherwise – well, it's always fascinated me to study both sides of a question. That's why I take two papers – the *Mail* and the *Herald*. The Chief Constable does the same, only of course he takes the *Times* instead of the *Mail*, and the *Spectator*.'

'I should have thought *Country Life* or the *Field* were about his mark,' said Price. 'I don't suppose that he actually reads the *Herald*. Trying it must be for you chaps to have to work with these old buffers.'

Treadwell gasped. 'I'd sooner work under the Colonel than – well, anybody. D.S.O. and bar and a lieutenant-colonel at thirty in the old war and ran our Home Guard in this: a wonderful horseman and everybody's friend for miles round – you ask anyone you meet in this village. Well, not this village,' he amended. 'This is Aston Common; pretty enough once, I daresay, but spoiled by bungalows run up by retired Harborough tradesmen. We get a lot of trouble here – no crime, of course, but a mass of petty complaints about dangerous dogs and mischievous kids and crowing cockerels.'

'I don't blame people,' said Price. 'We all require our night's rest and recuperation. Recently I have been compelled to complain about some neighbours of mine in Finchley. If once householders commence to keep chickens, a locality quickly deteriorates. In addition to the fact that recuperative slumber becomes impossible, a view of hen-runs, where lawns and rose-beds were intended, detracts considerably from the amenities.'

'Well, I must say I like a nice egg for my tea,' said Treadwell. 'I'd sooner any day see a nice brown egg than a bed of roses.'

Price said, 'I don't deny that I'm partial to an egg myself, but the present allocations are sufficient to keep us in health, and the amateur poultry-keeper is merely attempting to secure for himself a luxury unobtainable by his neighbour.'

'Well, that's human nature, isn't it?' said Treadwell. 'And here we are at the Red Lion,' he continued thankfully. 'You stay where you are for a moment, Inspector, and I'll pop in and see what Mrs Dawes can do for you . . . '

And later in the evening he said to his wife, 'I almost wish we hadn't called in the Yard. That chap Price, with his long words and his third-hand opinions – he'll get on the wrong side of everybody,' but at the same moment, in the Residents' Lounge at the Red Lion, Ronald Price was writing to Valerie:

We in the towns have no conception how time has stood still in rural localities. These country bumpkins are living in the Middle Ages and liking it, and as for their complacent lords and masters I anticipate the necessity of reminding those with whom I may come into contact during the course of my investigations that a few years have passed since we did away with the feudal system! Fancy, the owner of the Guest House where the fatality occurred is a Bart!! I shall meet him tomorrow!!

CHAPTER TWO

SINCE she had come to the Park, Bunny had grown accustomed to waking with a load on her mind: after the first few weeks it had been plain to her that her step-children not only resented their father's second marriage but unanimously disapproved of her. Hugo, whom she thought very handsome and charming, had been ready enough to talk to her on general subjects, but had answered off-handedly any questions she had asked him about himself or his brother and sisters; Patricia, whom she thought handsome but 'faultily faultless, icily regular, splendidly null' and still, at heart, the Senior Prefect at St Olaf's, treated her with the disinterested courtesy which one member of a family accords to another member's school friend; Simon and Iona had been sullen, hanging their heads and muttering monosyllables in reply to her painstaking enquiries about their pets. Lisa, banished for the first time in her life to a schoolroom, called them 'those uncouth children', and within a week the noise of an altercation between her and Patricia had penetrated to Sir Charles's study. 'I ticked her off,' said Patricia in explanation. 'Well, don't tick her off. It's not your job,' said Sir Charles, glancing at Bunny. 'I expect she needed ticking off,' said Bunny with equal generosity. 'Actually she did,' said Patricia. 'I happened to go into the schoolroom when they were having supper and she was mopping her plate up in the most disgusting way with a piece of bread – quite revolting.' 'Oh dear,' said Bunny, 'I'm afraid one does that in France.' 'So she said,' said Patricia, 'and she was jolly cheeky about it.' 'Well, you must be tactful,' said Sir Charles. 'You can't treat Lisa quite as you treat Iona.' 'That's obvious,' said Patricia. 'Iona's a little beast, but she knows how to take a ticking off – she's learned that at St Olaf's.' 'Well, perhaps Lisa will, if she goes there next term,' said Sir Charles. 'But in the meantime you just be particularly tactful. I'm sure you can, old lady.'

Bunny hadn't been so sure and, reproached in the privacy

of the large cold room where Sir Charles had tenderly furnished a Chippendale writing-table for his author-wife,
accustomed to lie on her stomach under an olive-tree and
doodle with chewed pencil-stubs on the backs of envelopes,
Lisa had replied that she was always anxious to learn, but not
from one whose mental and emotional age was twelve and
who had never heard of Baudelaire. However, she had
promised to be tactful and to remember how awkward it all
was for Bunny.

And there had been no more open trouble until Lisa and
Bunny together had committed the indiscretion of buying an
ill-used pony from Harborough cattle market, into which they
had strayed while shopping. Simon and Iona each had a
pony, and Patricia had her hunter, Huntsman; Sir Charles
had several times spoken of a pony for Lisa, and Bunny and
Lisa had been particularly pleased that, in addition to
rescuing from further blows of fate an obviously unfortunate
animal, they had secured it for the small sum of seven pounds,
in contrast to the sixty and seventy guineas which had been
given for Iona's Champagne and Simon's Brandy. Having
named her pony Romanée Conti, so that he would be sure not
to develop an inferiority complex in his relations with the
d'Estray ponies, Lisa had ridden him home, as she had ridden
her donkey in Provence, bareback and in a halter, and the
storm had burst when Patricia had greeted her with, 'What
an awful old thing. I wouldn't be seen dead on him. He had
better go straight to the kennels.' Later, Sir Charles, while
admitting that tact wasn't Pat's strong point, had explained
that she was bitterly disappointed: she had been negotiating
for a neighbour's well-known gymkhana winner, which Iona
could have ridden in shows until Lisa became proficient.
'But Charles, that would have cost the earth,' cried Bunny.
'Lisa and I – at least we have made an economy.' Charles
had replied, 'I may be hard up, but I like to see my family
well mounted,' and this had been his last word on the subject, but Patricia had continued to speak of Lisa's screw and
Lisa's crock and, though now the pony was sleek and fat and
Lisa had cub-hunted him with such success that Lord Badge-

moor had been heard to say that that mad-looking girl, whom the d'Estrays had brought out, was the only member of the Field whose horse was under control, Patricia still at intervals affirmed that he was a disgrace to her stables. Lisa was naturally sweet-tempered, but until she had come to England she had lived almost entirely among adults; she had no armour against the jibes of her contemporaries, and an observer of a noisy scene in the d'Estrays' stable yard was more apt to blame the screaming little fishwife than her cool, contemptuously smiling adversaries.

It would be untrue to say that it was solely for Lisa's sake that Bunny, in her forties, had accepted Charles d'Estray's proposal. She had asked for forty-eight hours in which to think it over, and was still hesitating when Charles, immaculate and cold sober, had left her party at midnight; the others – Justin and Ferdinand, Oscar, Gabriel, and their women – had stayed on and on, endlessly talking, endlessly drinking. Towards dawn Ferdi had been missing, and Bunny had found him slumped on the bathroom floor and Lisa, in her nightgown, dosing him with black coffee. Ferdi was a genius, Justin was world-famous; they were all talented people and her dear friends, but, remembering her own decorous English childhood, Bunny had thereupon decided that this was no *milieu* in which to bring up a young girl. Charles had told her that he wasn't rich, but she hadn't wanted riches for Lisa: after the shock of seeing her daughter at the age of twelve expertly reviving a drunk, she had wanted for her a decent English background and nice little friends. Next morning, creeping downstairs in a dressing-gown towards noon, seeing herself tousled and tawdry in the mirror at the foot of the stairs, seeing the shambles of the *salon*, the dirty and the smashed glasses, the smeared plates, the scattered cigarette ends, the indecent, if lovely, drawing which Ferdi, before he had passed out, had executed in charcoal on the wall, she had wanted a decent English background and nice friends for herself, too, and when Charles had come for his answer she had promptly accepted him. Since then, on most mornings, *I made a bargain and I must stick to it*, or, *I made my bed and I must lie*

on it were the thoughts that drifted across her mind as she
wakened, for though she adored Vanbrugh's great house
dreaming among its cedars and deeply respected the handsome d'Estrays and the simplicity and severity of their design
for living, she had quickly realized that she could never be
one of them, that though you can learn you can't un-learn,
though you can sharpen your wits you can't dull them, that
among these honourable, dutiful, and witless people she
would always feel a bit of a cad. After six months at the Park
(she thought of it in those terms rather than as having been
married to Charles), she had realized, too, that the d'Estrays
were heading for bankruptcy. It had been a difficult job to
persuade Charles, who was no business man, to look financial
facts in the face, for his family had been established since the
Conquest and a sense of unshakeable security seemed to be
bred in him. Like most of his kind, he was no lover of money
or high-living; it was the simple love of his house and fields
that would break his heart if he had to leave them. Very
humbly he had apologized for having dragged Bunny into
the mess that she had opened his eyes to, but the helpless little
woman, whom he had thought to protect, laughed, arranged
mortgages, sold some pictures he had never liked much but
which were apparently Corots, and some glass knick-knacks
he had never noticed in the spare bedrooms, and casually
declared during dinner that only six wash-basins, two bath-
rooms and lavatories and a little rearrangement of the
furniture were needed to transform the Park into a perfect
guest house. Sir Charles had looked pained but resigned;
Hugo, calling on his Maker, had left the room; Iona had
uttered irritating schoolgirlish groans and Simon had sulked,
but the worst opposition had come from Patricia: she had
definitely refused to keep horses to be mucked up by mutton-
fisted beginners. Bunny had bided her time, and behind Sir
Charles's back had mercilessly revealed to Patricia the full
horror of his financial position, adding in excuse, as she
thought, that as a business man the poor sweet was con-
genitally incapable. Patricia thought her disloyal to Daddy
and compared her very unfavourably with Mother, who

had never allowed the slightest criticism of her husband to pass her lips; but aloud she said, 'Very well, Bunny. I will,' and Bunny, aware that in spite of all their faults and foolishness the d'Estrays possessed the supreme virtue of keeping their word, had handed over to Patricia (after a sharp skirmish with Charles, who wanted it to buy an annuity for an idle old gamekeeper) the five hundred pounds for which two pieces of the Ravenscroft glass had sold at Christie's. Hugo began to talk of farming, Iona of leaving St Olaf's and helping Patricia; no one spoke any more of a good school for Lisa; Bunny arranged morning lessons with a retired school-mistress in the village and Lisa gladly agreed to get the rest of her education in her stepfather's library.

The first person to reply to the announcement of the advantages and amenities of life at Aston Park Guest House and Hunting Stables had been Elizabeth Hudson, and Sir Charles had promptly declared that he couldn't take money from Elizabeth, and, after some argument, that he couldn't, at any rate, make a profit out of her. Patricia had felt the same, and Miss Hudson's enormous Roman-nosed hunter, Brutus, occupied, for a price that barely fed him, the largest box in the stable and, entirely free of charge, was groomed and waited on by Patricia. Bunny was careful to send no more prospectuses even to the d'Estrays' most distant relations; she sent them to total strangers, and when the Roses came to look over the Park and Sybella called the drawing-room 'the lounge' and her coat and skirt her 'costume' Sir Charles said that he considered seven guineas a week *most* reasonable.

Bunny had had no difficulties with the servants. Before a rumour of her plans could reach them, she had explained the situation to them with perfect frankness: they adored Sir Charles; they loved and shared his great house – my silver, said Benson; my kitchen, said Mrs Capes; my nurseries, my babies, said Nanny – and they understood the plight of the squirearchy. Bunny was fully aware that to them she would never be Lady d'Estray: in absent-minded moments Mrs Capes called her 'duck' and Nanny, 'my lamb'; but Bunny, who was five feet two inches in height and as thin as a rake, with curly yellow hair, amber eyes, and a face which seemed to be made of indiarubber, had known at first glance that it would be worse than useless to try to fill the place vacated by the queenly figure in black velvet and diamonds, whose classic beauty, painted by Sargent, hung a little oppressively, thought Bunny, trying to be gay on wet Sundays, above the fireplace in the dining-room.

When the Roses and the Scampnells and a family on leave from the East had made definite bookings, Bunny had stored the great mahogany dining-table in the old laundry and had fetched a round table from the morning-room and set it in the south window; there the d'Estrays were to take their meals, while smaller tables, rather thinly disposed about the immense room, were provided for the paying guests. Sir Charles said that the place looked like a station hotel and exchanged a glance with the portrait of his first wife, and Bunny, fit to drop, said sharply that beggars can't be choosers, whereat he apologized with a meekness that tore her heart, and thanked her for all her trouble. 'The Roses, the Scampnells, the Malay people . . . ' he had calculated. 'Then who's to sit at the little round table over there?' 'Miss Hudson. Pat says she never feels the cold and I'm sure the Malay people will, so I put them near the fire, and the Roses, who must have come from the East originally, have the radiator.' Charles had replied, 'Oh, but Elizabeth's a cousin – she must sit at our table,' and what with fatigue and pity for him, Bunny had been in no mood for argument. For a twelve-month now Elizabeth Hudson, horse-faced, high-collared, hair-netted, had laid down the law at the d'Estrays' table. 'One day,' Bunny had told Lisa, 'I'll poison that woman . . . '

For there was something fundamentally and unalterably opposed in those two natures. Bunny couldn't make head-way with Patricia, but admired her beauty and her integrity and blamed the rest on St Olaf's and the English climate: she disliked Sybella Rose for her pretentiousness, her complacent ignorance and meanness, but a slipshod kind of intimacy grew up between them: cosily they discussed dress and diseases, menstruation and men. But there wasn't, it seemed, an inch of common ground where Barbara d'Estray and Elizabeth Hudson could walk together. Bunny had few principles and they were all open to revision: from time to time she was amazed and ashamed to realize that she was more than half-way through life and had not yet made up her mind. But Elizabeth Hudson had been born knowing all the answers, and with *bosh! tripe! I happen to know,* and *the fact is* could put you right on any subject under the sun. In her dealings with her sometimes difficult guests, Bunny strove to use tact and courtesy: Elizabeth accused her of 'smarming' ... tell 'em to go to hell and have done with it! Having known and loved the house since childhood, she resented Bunny's changes: if Cousin William – Sir Charles's father – had been able to walk two hundred yards to his bath, why the hell couldn't the Roses? ... the dining-room looked like a desert studded with toadstools ... poor dear Hermione would turn in her grave if she could see her drawing-room. On the subject of food she was particularly trying. She liked it good and plain: porridge, kedgeree, a cut off the joint, stiff rice puddings. Mrs Capes had been trained by a French chef, imported by Sir William, a *bon viveur*; her talents had lain dormant under the economical rule of Hermione, who had been brought up very plainly in a Scottish castle, and the young Patricia's healthy disinterest, and, rather to Bunny's surprise, she had responded enthusiastically to tentative suggestions of *sole Mornay* and *soufflé surprise*. 'I can't understand what's come over Capes,' said Elizabeth Hudson, loud enough for Benson to hear. 'She used to be a dam' good plain cook – now she's doing her best to poison us with these filthy French messes. ... '

Elizabeth was certainly no Francophile. At the age of eighteen she had passed a week in Paris and could assure you that it was dirty, disorderly, unmannerly, and immoral; yachting in the Mediterranean, she had spent an evening at Monte Carlo, and the fug in the Casino and the awful old vultures round the tables had turned her stomach: she couldn't conceive how Bunny could have chosen to live on that coast like cardboard scenery from a senseless musical comedy, among croupiers and card-sharpers, tarts and gigolos, frauds, failures, and the filthy French. Bunny had left France owing to what she believed was a change of heart, but now feared was a mood: fits of nostalgia, not only for the country and for her villa, but for the people she had lived among, were becoming more frequent and more painful, and she was finding it more and more difficult to treat with the indifference it deserved Elizabeth's opinion of France and the French. Ferdi and Oscar, Justin and Lili, little Margaret Lyall, old T. H. Teviot – how tiresome they'd been with their never-ending see-saw between despair and mad gaiety, humility and vanity, drink and devotion, industry and idleness, the mud and the stars . . . but they'd never been – and their very inconsistency made it impossible for them to be – dictators. . . . 'One day,' Bunny had told Mrs Capes, 'I'll murder that woman.'

In the stables Patricia, long disciplined by St Olaf's, allowed Miss Hudson to rule her. Elizabeth's authority was only questioned by Mrs Scampnell, and between these two ladies, who had both, as they put it, been born on horses, there was constant bickering, especially in the evenings after hunting. 'Where the deuce did you get to, Cecily? I hardly saw you all day. I suppose you were hopelessly lost with the rest of the dam' silly Field?' 'Good gracious, no, Elizabeth. As a matter of fact I kept on wondering where *you* were. I felt sorry for you in that awful scrum – there's more room in the front, I always find.' . . . But Mrs Scampnell and Miss Hudson were in agreement on the day when Bunny went riding. She had been taught to ride in France by a Dutchman on a Hungarian Arab; she had ridden in the Nice Horse Show for a manufacturer of cosmetics, but with scornful laughter Miss Hudson corrected her for facing her horse's head when she mounted, for unduly long stirrups, for descending into the wood without leaning back and sticking her legs out, for jumping a log with her bottom right out of the saddle. Bunny had heard and believed the traditional fiction of the superiority of English horsemanship and she did not protest when Elizabeth told Sir Charles, 'I daresay your wife shone among comic French horsemen, but she's not yet ready for the hunting field.' Nevertheless, as Beatrice pulled off her boots, 'I could wring that woman's neck,' said Bunny.

And now she had no time for riding. There were accounts to do, bills to pay and render, and to relieve the busy Beatrice she had taken over the care of the linen cupboard. Lisa helped her with that and had obligingly volunteered to 'do' the flowers, but was soon involved in a series of scenes with Elizabeth, who was a keen gardener and criticized both Lisa's spoliation of the borders and her unconventional arrangement of the blooms. 'You pig, you cow, you Hitler! You ought to be painlessly destroyed,' screamed Lisa, and was heard by everybody. There was unending friction, too, over the Sallusts' dog, a Boxer bitch, which had been released from quarantine shortly before Elizabeth's arrival. Though the d'Estrays disliked it, disapproving on principle of foreign breeds, of champion-bred dogs, of non-sporting dogs, of allowing dogs on your bed, of providing them with coats in cold weather, of giving them silly names like Babette and hanging up stockings for them at Christmas, they heroically forbore from criticism except in the absence of the owners, when even Sir Charles referred to Babette as that great ugly useless brute. Elizabeth Hudson, however, did not hesitate to speak her mind. Introduced by the doting Lisa, she exclaimed, 'What a monstrosity! It's a nightmare. Take it out of my sight, child, for goodness' sake,' and when, with considerable difficulty, it had been proved to her that Babette wasn't, as she insisted, the offspring of a bull bitch which had gone astray, she lost no opportunity of pointing out the disadvantages of owning fashionable foreign freaks instead of decent English terriers and gundogs. When Babette ailed, it was no wonder, with that short nose and mis-shapen jaw: 'If she pegs out,' said Elizabeth to the distracted child, 'I'll get you a dog that is a dog and will be some use to you.' 'Babette is of use to me – she guards me,' said Lisa. 'What from?' asked Elizabeth with scornful laugh. 'You *are* a little sissy to need to be guarded. With a decent

23

terrier you could go ratting and rabbiting.' Lisa stamped. 'I don't want to rat and rabbit. I'm not like you – always wanting to kill things. It would be poetic justice if you were tossed by a bull. And I hope you will be,' she added beneath her breath, but loud enough for Patricia to hear her. 'You shouldn't mutter things that you're ashamed to speak aloud,' said Patricia. 'I'll speak it aloud, then. I hope that Cousin Elizabeth gets tossed by a bull,' Lisa shouted.

Elizabeth Hudson's death stunned rather than grieved the d'Estrays. She had been for so long in their lives that they had accepted her without asking themselves what they had felt for her. Sir Charles said, 'Good old Elizabeth! We were all children together. She was the eldest and our leader in every-thing.' Hugo, who had been her favourite among the present generation, said, 'It'll seem queer without her.' Patricia said, 'It'll be rotten at Christmas.' But when, in the evening, Sir Charles called his household together and announced that Miss Hudson's death wasn't natural, wasn't suicide, might possibly have been an accident or – though he couldn't bring himself to believe it – something very much worse, and hoped that everyone would do everything in his power to help the police in their enquiries and not be offended by the routine questioning, which would no doubt be necessary, Hugo and Patricia waited until the door had shut behind the paying guests and the servants and then Patricia burst out with: 'It couldn't have been an accident. Cousin Elizabeth never had any sleeping drugs or medicines. She wouldn't even take aspirin. All she ever took was those old-fashioned senna-pod things. Some devil's poisoned her,' and Hugo more quietly said, 'Whoever it was, we'll hang them.' 'We'll do our best,' said Sir Charles. 'To the guillotine!' cried Lisa from the window-seat, where she had been unnoticed. 'What's that child doing here?' asked Sir Charles. 'It's no place for her, Bunny.' 'Lisa, go and make daisy chains or something,' said the distracted Bunny.

It had been a dreadful day. She had been awake and was thinking: another day . . . well, I made my bed and I must lie on it . . . but hadn't opened her eyes when someone had

24

entered her bedroom, and since there was no chink of china or
smell of coffee she had realized that something was wrong
before she heard an urgent whisper, 'Wake up. Come along
– wake up, my lady.' Then she had opened her eyes and seen
Nanny in her blue print dress and white apron, and Nanny
had said, 'Miss Hudson's gone,' and Bunny had said,
'Where?' Nanny replied, 'I mean, she's dead, Beatrice
found her. You'd better come and have a look at her.' She
held out Bunny's dressing-gown of cherry corduroy and
Bunny dived into it and they hurried along the corridor and
across the gallery at the head of the stairs to Miss Hudson's
room, which, since she didn't care a dam' if her bedroom
faced north, south, east, or west, faced north and looked
between Palladian pillars, across the sweep of the drive to
the deer park. Beatrice, a plump woman of middle age,
with faded frizzy hair and china-blue eyes in a placid
countenance, was standing at the door of the bedroom; she
led the way in and there was Elizabeth Hudson, staring,
quite horribly, from beneath a muddled heap of bedclothes.
'Oh lord,' said Bunny. Her first husband, the gifted but
difficult Raoul Sallust, had died of tuberculosis of the lungs
in a chalet in Switzerland, and he had died when the sun
was setting behind the snow-peaks and the cows were coming
in from pasture, and, bored by his sickness and knowing
that he had left immortal lines behind him, he had died
readily and peacefully, and Bunny, pulling down the blind,
had thought, *after life's fitful fever*. . . and *the sweetest canticle is
nunc dimittis* . . . and *the setting sun and music at the close*. . . .
In the little Mediterranean port, on the outskirts of which
she had built her small villa, she had become – how or why
she never clearly understood – the friend and confidant of
several of the poorest families, and more than once she had
been with the grandmothers and the great-grandmothers
when they died, and that had been *well and good*, the folding
up of the garment at the end of day. But Elizabeth Hudson
had died convulsed and frightened, struggling and vomiting.
. . . 'What *could* have been wrong with her?' said Bunny, and
then, 'I'll call Charles.'

Sir Charles was slow to waken and then embarrassed because he hadn't got his teeth in. 'Something wrong with Elizabeth – well, surely you can ring up Hope-Johnstone without rousing the entire household.' 'But she's dead,' cried Bunny. 'Nonsense,' said Sir Charles. Bunny said, 'Oh Charles, don't be silly. I know a corpse when I see one.' 'Wait a minute,' said Sir Charles and turned aside and there was a click and he'd got his teeth in. 'Hand me my dressing-gown. I expect it's all your imagination.'

In Elizabeth's room Nanny and Beatrice had set the bed to rights, but Charles turned very quickly from the body and said he would ring up the doctor. 'What do you think she died of, Nanny?' Nanny hadn't liked Elizabeth and had always deplored her visits: she had taken the children for long walks and rides and overtired them, and she had encouraged them to make collections of pressed wild flowers, which littered the nurseries. 'A heart attack, I should think, racing round like she did at her age.'

Bunny went away and dressed, and Sylvia, the under-housemaid, brought in her breakfast and Lisa's: Bunny, anticipating Simon and Iona's opinion that to breakfast in your room was a disgusting French habit, had insisted that in the holidays Lisa should descend fully dressed to the schoolroom, but this was October and Simon and Iona were back at school. Lisa, small for her age and slight, with smooth brown hair, hazel eyes, and a clear pale skin, an insignificant figure among the tall handsome d'Estrays, was still in her pyjamas, but knew that Miss Hudson was dead and seemed inclined to a philosophical discussion; Bunny had barely got rid of her before Hope-Johnstone came and, after spending what seemed to Bunny, as she waited in the corridor, hours in Elizabeth's bedroom, told her to lock the door and not let anyone touch anything, and then went down to the study, where he remained for some time closeted with Sir Charles. After he had gone, Sir Charles called Bunny and, carefully closing the door, tactfully broke it to her that Hope-Johnstone was unable, without a post-mortem examination, to sign a death certificate, that he suspected an accident or

26

suicide, and that the Superintendent from Harborough would be coming along and, later, an ambulance. Bunny said, 'He must think she took an overdose of something. There *was* a glass on the bedside table when Nanny fetched me this morning, but Beatrice may have taken it down when she tidied up the room for the doctor.'

This she repeated later to Superintendent Treadwell, who then held the view that Miss Hudson wasn't, probably, as tough as she liked to make out, was in the habit of taking some kind of sleeping draught and had overdone it, 'though what baffles me is that there's no sign of any sort of medicine in her room,' he admitted. He saw Beatrice and Sylvia, who confirmed Bunny's supposition about the fate of the glass and were able to tell him that it was Miss Hudson's invariable habit to take a nightcap of whisky and water, and that a long tumbler was placed in her room every evening when the bed was turned down. Refreshed by elevenses in the housekeeper's room, Treadwell went back to the police station; the police ambulance arrived; Sir Charles and Benson took charge and Elizabeth Hudson went out of the house on a stretcher down a secondary staircase. Shortly afterwards Colonel Rivett-Bankes called, stayed some time with Sir Charles and exchanged a few words in the drive with his godson, Hugo. Bunny kept out of his way. She never knew what to say to him.

At luncheon, when the guests were seated at their tables, Sir Charles, with his back to the fire, addressed them simply and solemnly, was sorry to tell them that his cousin, Miss Hudson, had died suddenly, was afraid that, as she hadn't seen a doctor for many years, there would have to be an inquest, but could assure them that they would suffer no inconvenience. Before he could reach the family table, where Bunny was looking out of the window at the light drizzle, Lisa was making bread pellets, and Hugo and Patricia had their eyes on the table-cloth, Mr Rose got to his feet and was sure that he was speaking for all in expressing his deepest sympathy for their popular host in the loss he had sustained. 'Those of us who had the great good fortune to meet her in the hunting field,' said Mr Rose, 'were particularly impressed by her courage and good sportsmanship.'

Sidney Rose, dark-haired and high-coloured, was wearing riding-breeches and a hacking coat of chestnut-brown Harris tweed; his yellow tie was adorned with foxes' masks and hunting whips, a handkerchief to match was in his breast pocket and he wore a yellow waistcoat. His cable-stitch stockings matched his coat. His suede shoes looked and were hand-made. Henry Scampnell, who, as Rose sat down, twisted himself into a position that was neither sitting nor standing, was dressed neither for country nor for town. He wore a rather thin grey tweed suit and a stiff collar with a silk tie. His most distinguished features were his thick grey hair and deep-set blue eyes. In his light voice and with the grammar-school accent that Iona imitated, he said, 'I should like to second Mr Rose's remarks. I'm sure we all feel for Sir Charles and the family in their sudden loss.' Across the table his desiccated, ladylike wife frowned at him and he subsided.

Sir Charles said, 'Thank you. Thank you very much,' and sat down to his rapidly cooling tomato soup.

After luncheon Bunny retired to her little sitting-room up-stairs. She had contrived to vacate the morning-room on the ground that it was needed as a writing-room for the guests, and, in spite of Sir Charles's protest that it wasn't fit for her, had established herself in an erstwhile sewing-room in the west wing. Sir Charles, with *The Times* under his arm, joined her there and, having announced that it was useless to discuss Elizabeth's death until the result of the post-mortem was known, discussed it until four o'clock, when Benson came in to tell him that Superintendent Treadwell was in the study. 'Don't come down,' Sir Charles told Bunny. 'Since I married you, I've dragged you through one sordid affair after another. Let me spare you this,' and Bunny assented, for, since only goodness knew what was in front of them, it would be wise, she felt, to seize the smallest opportunity of allowing Charles to protect her.

He was soon back. Treadwell wanted the whole household called together, and Sir Charles was to hint at what Treadwell believed – that Elizabeth had been murdered. For the post-mortem had revealed that she was full up with some vegetable poison. 'I'll tell you about it later,' said Sir Charles. 'I think the drawing-room would be best – more room. Benson's told the servants to come in and he's collecting the others. I've sent Hugo to fetch Pat from the stables.' 'And I suppose,' said Bunny at the head of the stairs, 'that, while you're speaking, that imbecile Treadwell will be watching for guilty faces. I do hate policemen.' Sir Charles, going down the stairs, turned and gave her a look. Treadwell was standing in the hall below them.

Bunny watched him while Sir Charles spoke. His expressionless eyes did indeed move from face to face, and then quite unexpectedly met hers, and she felt herself blushing and at the same moment remembered saying to someone that she would like to strangle – was it? or poison? – Elizabeth. Please God, I said it to Lisa or someone who doesn't matter, she thought in a panic, and then: Lisa . . . that scene over the flowers . . . she yelled and screamed, you beast, you pig, you cow, I'd like to kill you, and everybody heard her, everybody. . . . Sir Charles, having finished hoping that everybody would do everything in his power to help the police in their inquiries, was speaking to Treadwell, and then he nodded to Benson and the servants went out and, as though he were at a party, Sir Charles said, 'Mr Rose, this is Superintendent Treadwell, who's going to clear up this business for us . . . and Mr and Mrs Scampnell and Miss Margot, and here's Flight-Lieutenant Marvin. Our only absent guest is Mr Howard Rose, who comes down at week-ends from London.' Treadwell said, 'Well, ladies and gentlemen, there are some routine questions that I should ask – just for form's sake,' and Sir Charles said, 'I'm sure everyone will be glad to do everything they can. My study's at your disposal, Treadwell. Would you like me as your first victim?' Treadwell looked embarrassed and said, 'I can talk to you any time, Sir Charles,' and Sir Charles said, 'Well, what about Hugo?' 'I can always find Mr Hugo,' said Treadwell. 'One of the guests, perhaps . . . ' and then Sidney Rose said, 'Take us in order of seniority: then we can't be jealous. I think we came here a few days before the Scampnells,' and, 'You're the big noise in Harborough, I suppose,' he said chattily, as he left the room with Treadwell.

At dinner, while the d'Estrays ate in silence, the paying guests gossiped, calling from table to table. Treadwell had been sweet to Sybella Rose, but Cecily Scampnell thought him dense and doubted if he would ever find out anything; Henry Scampnell pointed out that he had not been trained as a detective; Sidney Rose believed that these country-bred chaps had an enormous amount of common sense, partly inherited from their forebears, who for generations had lived near to Nature, and Nature couldn't suffer fools, and partly acquired by living near to Nature themselves; and this common sense was often sounder, if slower, than the sharpness of the townsman. To support his contention he recounted a conversation he had had with a philosophical hedger, which Mrs Scampnell capped with the sagacities of an Indian *syce*.

It was not until late that evening that the Chief Constable telephoned to tell Sir Charles that, after a lot of consideration, he had decided to call in Scotland Yard. Sir Charles, as he told Bunny afterwards, had been a little stiff about it, and pointed out that it wasn't going to be very pleasant, having outsiders butting in. But the Chief Constable besought him to consider Treadwell's point of view: 'He has known you and been taught to look up to you since he was a nipper – how can he ask you where you were on Monday at eleven pip emma?' 'I shouldn't care if he did – he'd only be doing his job,' Charles argued. 'I don't suppose you would care,' said the Chief Constable, 'but Treadwell would. Awkward for me, too, Charles. By and large I'm a tactless blighter, and I'd hate to endanger a long and, may I say, a very pleasant friendship.' 'You'd have to be very tactless to do that, old man,' said Sir Charles. But, sitting on the edge of Bunny's bed as he told her, 'Sounds as if he saw himself arresting me!' 'I think he's right in a way,' said Bunny, lighting a cigarette and remembering too late that Charles didn't like to see women smoking in bedrooms. 'He'd have to keep an open mind, wouldn't he? And it's rather awful to keep one's mind open about one's friends.' 'I don't see any difficulty in that,' said Sir Charles. 'Well, of course, men don't,' said Bunny. 'They throw chaps out of clubs because they cheat at cards and afterwards they cut them in Piccadilly.' 'Well, naturally,' said Sir Charles. Under the lace of her French nightdress, Bunny shrugged her firm thin shoulders and then she changed the subject. 'What do you suppose he'll be like – the Scotland Yard detective? If your who-dunnit books are right, he'll be a peer's nephew, or if he's dull himself, he'll bring a friend who's a peer, or an Oxford professor, who laughs very loudly and drinks gallons of beer and quotes from Restoration comedies.'

'I expect he'll be quite an ordinary sort of man,' Sir Charles said. 'A bit more acute, I expect, than Treadwell. I do hope you'll be discreet, darling, and remember that what you say in the gallery can be heard at the foot of the stairs.'

'But I *do* hate policemen,' said Bunny. 'It's not a generality. No one naturally sympathetic to me would choose to be a policeman. Charles, if Elizabeth really was poisoned, who do you think did it?'

Sir Charles got up and walked about the room.

'I can't believe she was poisoned, because I can't begin to think who could have done it or what motive there could have been. I don't think Mrs Scampnell liked her: they were like a couple of cats always after hunting, but you don't kill someone because you think you ride better than she does. Elizabeth didn't care for the Roses, but it seemed to me that the more she snubbed them the more they smarmed up to her – Rose is a thoroughgoing snob, you know. If I had the handling of the affair – which, thank God, I haven't – I should be inclined to look into Elizabeth's past life for a motive; not that I should expect to find any murky secrets – a straighter creature never lived – but there might have been something. And that, of course, would make one think of Marvin; he seems a nice quiet fellow, though I wish he'd trim his moustache, I must say; but he's the only one of our lodgers she knew before she came here.'

Bunny ventured, 'Of course Elizabeth could be irritating . . . '

'Irritating?' cried Sir Charles. 'She was outspoken, that's what you mean; but those blunt, downright people are never irritating – you know where you are with them.'

'They're irritating to some people,' argued Bunny. 'Weaker people, perhaps, who know they can be dominated and in consequence are desperately afraid of domination – don't you see?'

Sir Charles didn't. He said, 'That sounds like psychological stuff – what the police will go on will be plain facts and I'm damned if I know of any. Anyhow, it's time we were in bed and asleep.'

Bunny lay awake for some time repeating to herself that the police would go on plain facts, not on psychological stuff suggested by such remarks as 'I could strangle that woman' from an author (unbalanced lot, authors), half French by birth and French again by marriage (an immoral lot, the Frenchies), whom Sir Charles d'Estray had picked up in the South of France (a hot spot, the Riviera) and imprudently and probably unnecessarily married, and 'you beast, you pig, you cow, I'd like to kill you' from an adolescent (a queer time, adolescence), who, besides being three-quarters French and a Roman Catholic, was the child of a tubercular and notoriously difficult father. In the small hours, however, she fell asleep and slept dreamlessly until the grey thought, I made my bed and I must lie on it, formed itself on the translucent emptiness of her mind. Then she heard the chink of china, smelt coffee, remembered her manners and muttered 'Good morning, Beatrice,' realized it was Beatrice with her breakfast and not Nanny with dreadful news for her, realized that Elizabeth was dead and that a detective from Scotland Yard was coming, opened her eyes and sat up in a hurry. Beatrice was setting the tray on the bedside table and Bunny asked her usual question, 'Is it raining?'

'No, my lady. It's a lovely autumn day – nice and crisp,' answered Beatrice, drawing back the curtains.

'Oh God,' groaned Bunny, and reached for the pink

cardigan which served her as a bed-jacket. 'Do you think it would be extravagant if I had the stove on?'

'If you want it on, I should have it on,' said Beatrice, and bent to the switch.

'Any policemen about yet?' asked Bunny.

'Not yet,' said Beatrice. 'I told young Les last night that it was no use 'im coming till ten o'clock at the earliest, but 'e said the case was out of 'is 'ands now, not because of 'is being unable to 'andle it, but on account of the Colonel being a friend of the Family and wanting no unpleasantness, and 'e 'imself 'aving been born and bred in the village. So we're to 'ave a deteck from London and I reckon that'll cause much more unpleasantness than the Colonel and Les and Sergeant Blow and that soft young Constable Smallbone all together. Now get on and eat your breakfast while it's 'ot, if you want a bath, I should 'urry up before them p.gs. take all the water.'

Obediently Bunny poured coffee and milk. 'Beatrice – who do *you* think poisoned Miss Hudson?'

'An outside job,' said Beatrice unexpectedly. 'I don't trust any of them p.gs., but they'd no motive, unless young Marvin 'ad, which is Mr Benson's theory. Of course, m'lady, we don't mention anything to do with the case in the servants' 'all, but we talk it over in the 'ousekeeper's room, which is only natural. Mrs Capes is too upset to form a theory, on account of some remarks Miss 'Udson passed about 'er cooking.'

'I remember them. They were dam' silly remarks,' said Bunny.

'Miss 'Udson,' said Beatrice, 'was all right when you got to know 'er. She was as 'ard as nails, but you knew where you were with 'er. 'Owever, I reckon she was 'ard once too often and this is the vengeance of someone who 'ad a grouse against 'er. Well, I must get on – 'ere's Miss Lisa without any slippers on 'er feet again in spite of what Nanny told 'er.'

Beatrice went out and Lisa came in and Bunny said, 'What did Nanny tell you, Lisa?'

'Only that I'd catch my death,' said Lisa. 'Who do you

think poisoned the Hudson, Bunny? I think the Scampnell did because of being rivals in the hunting-field, or isn't that enough for grown-ups to murder each other over? Sylvia doesn't think it was the Scampnell. She thinks it was Marvin . . . '

Bunny interrupted her. 'Lisa, you shouldn't gossip with the servants.' But she went on, 'Why does Sylvia think it was Marvin?'

'She thinks he was tired of being bossed about by the Hudson. Toast again. Oh, for a croissant!'

'He could have gone away if he didn't like it,' said Bunny.

'Perhaps she had a hold on him,' said Lisa. 'Perhaps he owed her money or was her illegitimate son or was in love with Patricia and the Hudson knew he had a wife in a lunatic asylum and threatened to split on him.'

'All most unlikely,' Bunny said. 'How's Romanée Conti?'

'Well, I haven't seen him yet,' said Lisa. 'Nanny said I wasn't to go to the stables in my pyjamas. She said I'd catch my death of cold and it was indecent. If we're not all arrested by this afternoon I shall pull his mane. I'm going to plait him for the Opening Meet, Patricia or no Patricia.'

Lisa was still chattering about her pony when Sir Charles came in. He was fond of Lisa and, to Bunny's admiration, thought no worse of her because she agreed so badly with Patricia, his daughter and friend. But this morning he told her quite sharply to get out into the fresh air, instead of lolling in bedrooms. Lisa said how queer it was that the English all subconsciously disapproved of bedrooms, but, meeting Bunny's eye, withdrew, and Sir Charles said he wished Bunny would come downstairs to breakfast; hardly a morning passed without trouble over someone's marmalade and this morning it had been definitely uncomfortable. Bunny didn't speak her thought – that if she had been in the habit of coming down to breakfast Elizabeth Hudson might have died sooner; she asked Sir Charles if he had slept well and he replied what a question! he had lain awake all night worrying, and no sooner had he fallen asleep than Beatrice had called him with a telephone message from Detective-

Inspector Price of Scotland Yard to say that he would be at the Park at ten o'clock and expected to find the whole household available. 'And Philip Jardine will be down in the course of the morning, and we'll have to give him lunch – he was Elizabeth's lawyer as well as mine, thank goodness. You'd better put on something dark,' said Sir Charles, who wore a blue suit and a black tie, 'not slacks, for goodness' sake, or espadrilles or bedroom slippers. And look sharp, won't you? It's five-and-twenty to ten already. . . . '

But after he had gone Bunny poured out another cup of coffee and lit another cigarette and thought she must have been mad to exchange her life in the sun, her little pink villa between the pines and the water, France and the light that falls on her and the matchless fruits of her soil, liberty, so dear, so sacred, so necessary to the artist, for this climate, only fine when it was cold, this grand unmanageable mansion, these stiff, proper d'Estrays with their shibboleths, their financial problems, and now their murder. . . .

CHAPTER THREE

DETECTIVE-INSPECTOR RONALD PRICE had slept badly on a sagging bed, of which he made haste to complain to
the manageress next morning. He was perfectly polite. 'The
curved position of the spinal column necessitated by the un-
due resilience of the springs under the weight of the body has
been condemned by the medical profession,' he told fat
Florence Dawes, but she stared at him from brown bovine
eyes, scratched her bird's nest of a head with the nib of her pen
and instead of trying to learn something, stupidly protested,
'We've never 'ad a complaint about the bed in number twelve
before.' 'Well, you've got one now,' said Price and went into
the coffee-room to find a senile waiter, afflicted with bunions,
swotting flies. The tea was weak. 'Don't blame me. Blame
Strachey,' the old man mumbled when Price complained,
and, 'Blame the paper controller,' said the waitress when she
told him that he couldn't buy a newspaper in the hotel, and
'Blame the Government,' said the odd-man when, emerging
from the lavatory, Price tripped over a hole in the linoleum
and angrily exclaimed that it was a death-trap. Exasperated
by this string of Tory lies he drove along deserted and
dangerous lanes and, after losing himself twice, came to a high
park wall and presently to a pair of iron gates between posts,
surmounted by pelicans. A small stone lodge stood within the
gates, so Price sounded his horn and waited, reflecting with
annoyance that there were still Some who, with walls and
gates, delighted to bar Others from their pleasant places, till
his eye happened to light on a notice, which announced that
Aston Park was open to Horsemen, Cyclists, and Pedestrians.
Incensed by the loss of his grievance, he sounded his horn
again and roughly informed the crone who hobbled slowly
from the lodge that his business was urgent. 'So's my
ironing,' replied the widow Toomer, the nonagenarian
mother of the d'Estrays' Nanny: 'but it don't stop me from
keeping a civil tongue in me 'ead.' Past her work . . . should
be in a home for the aged . . . thought Price and, in spite of

notices saying *10 mph, please* and *Beware of Cattle* and *Very Slow*, dashed through the deer park and into the main drive, where he narrowly missed Lisa, bicycling to her lessons in the village. 'You silly bloody fool,' shouted Lisa and then, as he rounded the last bend, there was a lawn, shaded with cedars, and, towering above him, the great house with its six Palladian pillars, its double flight of stone steps, its portico – the size of his kitchen, not counting the dining recess – surmounted by statuary. And there are whole families living in single rooms in tenements ... thought Price, drawing up and switching off his engine, and: supposing I won a football pool . . . he thought, getting out, slamming his car door and noticing, for the first time, the tinny sound of it. The house would be all right; the snag would be the skivvies, he thought, walking briskly up the steps, recalling how, when he had got his promotion and suggested having a woman for the rough, Valerie had protested that it would fidget her. I'm different, of course; I'm used to giving orders; I'd keep them up to the mark, he thought, ringing the bell for the second time in thirty seconds and watching through the glass door the leisurely arrival of Benson. 'Detective-Inspector Price of Scotland Yard,' he snapped. 'Sir Charles d'Estray is expecting me.'

Benson, tall, white-haired, ecclesiastical, looked him over; then, 'This way, please,' he said in a hushed voice, and led him into the hall, which, with its coloured marble walls and fireplace and marble-topped tables, seemed to Price more like a mortuary than a home, though it only needed some of that wicker furniture in pastel shades and a few bright modern rugs to transform it into a tasteful and spacious lounge. From the back of the hall, a fine but, he thought, quite senselessly double staircase led in shallow, unhurried steps to the first floor, and at the foot of the flight, towards which the butler had turned, a large black dog, lying on a shabby Persian rug, raised its sinister head and fixed a pair of yellow eyes on him. 'That dog – is it harmless?' he asked, since the dog was rising and the butler made no effort to control it. 'Definitely,' pronounced the butler, 'unless of course he happened to take a dislike to you.' The brute was sniffing at Price's trousers. 'Go away, dog, go away,' he sharply ordered. The yellow eyes blinked; the shining black body crouched to spring, he thought, and leaped away; but looking back saw that a yawn and a stretch was all that the Labrador had intended. Hurrying after the grossly indifferent butler, he found himself in a broad panelled corridor, which, after turning to the left, led past a green baize door and the foot of an unsupported stone staircase to a door on the opposite side, which the butler was holding open. 'Sir Charles will be with you in a moment,' he said, and Price passed into a larger and considerably less cosy edition of the Chief Constable's 'study'. From one of the two tall windows he looked out and discovered that the house had been built round three sides of a square. He looked across a neglected formal garden to the shrouded windows of the closed east wing: on his left stood the sunny façade of the main building and its imposing entrance with broad steps flanked by stone lions; there was also a garden door in the east wing and, since symmetry seemed a mania with whatever old Johnny had built the place (Price now decided that, having won the football pool, he'd prefer a more artistic rambling kind of house), he deduced that there would be a similar entrance into the west wing, in which he found himself. On the fourth side the garden was bounded by a stone balustrade, ornamented by urns, from which straggled the frost-bitten remains of ivy geraniums, and beyond the wall the ground fell, giving a view of ascending woodlands. Later from an upper window he saw that in this valley a little river lingered – Rushbrook on its way to the county town.

When at last the door of the study opened he somehow expected to see a larger edition of the Chief Constable, but Sir Charles d'Estray was of quite a different type – taller, certainly, but more finely made, with a cameo profile and the bloodless look, Price thought, of the effete aristocracy. As he shook hands and asked if Price was quite comfortable at the Red Lion and had found his way to the Park quite easily and was warm enough in this terribly cold little room

39

with only the log fire and was sure he wouldn't like a whisky or a cup of coffee or tea or a cigar or a cigarette, his manner was gentle, but at the same time distant, and when he had finished what Price afterwards thought of as his kindness to animals Price felt a remarkable and inexplicable loss of his usual self-confidence. He began to doubt if, as he'd always affirmed, a ready-made suit looked as well as one made to measure: saying 'I hope to inconvenience your household as little as possible,' he dropped an aitch, replaced it, and wondered if he would have been wiser to ignore the slip or to have passed it off with a laugh as something that might happen to anybody.

The interview was longer than Price had intended. Sir Charles took charge of it and before Price could frame the first of a series of questions, embarked on a narrative. On Monday evening Elizabeth Hudson had gone to bed at ten o'clock, having risen early that morning for cub-hunting, and for the same reason Mrs Scampnell had quickly followed her. About the same time Patricia had gone out to take a last look at the horses, and Mr Rose, the fourth of the cub-hunting party, had yawned his head off at the bridge-table until nearly eleven, when his wife had gone upstairs with him. Mr Scampnell and his step-daughter, Margot Rattray, had gone up-stairs soon after eleven and then Sir Charles and his wife and son had adjourned, as they usually did, to the study, where drinks were set out for them earlier in the evening by Benson, or Eric, the footman, at least Benson called him the foot-man, but he was really a sort of odd-job boy. As far as Sir Charles remembered, his wife had been the first to leave the study: he and his son had gone up about a quarter of an hour later. 'After locking up, I suppose?' put in Price. 'No, I don't do any locking up,' said Sir Charles. 'Who does?' asked Price. 'Well, I really don't know,' said Sir Charles, 'but I suppose it would be Benson.' 'And upstairs?' asked Price. 'You didn't hear any sounds from the deceased's bedroom?' Sir Charles said, 'Well, we didn't pass her door or anywhere near it. There's a staircase – perhaps you noticed it – a little farther back in this corridor, which serves the west wing,

40

where our rooms are, and from this room it's much shorter to go that way than round by the main staircase. From the drawing-room it would be different. Our lodgers, on the other hand, are all in the main building. The two married couples have rooms facing south over the garden here, my cousin's room looks north over the drive, and young Rose and Flight-Lieutenant Marvin face the same way, but they're on this side of the gallery. Margot Rattray is beyond my cousin's room, at the corner of the house, but there's a bathroom and an empty bedroom between. If my cousin had called out, the Scampnells are most likely to have heard her, but it would have had to be a pretty loud cry. The house is solidly built, you know, and the bedrooms have mahogany doors like this one, and they aren't like modern doors – they fit superbly. I've never listened at one,' said Sir Charles, smiling, 'but even if you stood in the corridor, unless you actually put your ear to the keyhole, I doubt if you would hear low moaning.'

Price said, 'It appears to be impossible at this juncture to estimate with any accuracy the time at which such moaning or cries would have commenced. If the deceased called out it was probably after Mrs Scampnell was in bed and before her husband retired an hour later. A peculiar feature of the case is that the deceased could have rung the bell and summoned the assistance of the domestics. I assume there are bells in the bedrooms?'

'I should think so,' said Sir Charles. 'There's one in mine, anyway. And now I come to think of it, I've heard some chat going on between my wife and Beatrice, the head-housemaid, about Mrs Rose ringing every five minutes. But my cousin was rather a peculiar woman. She prided herself on what I believe your generation would call her toughness. Last winter most of us had a week in bed with gastric flu, but she never missed a day's hunting, and has boasted ever since that owing to her healthy outdoor life et cetera she didn't catch it: actually, during a check my daughter saw her being very ill indeed in a wood, but, knowing what she'd get if she interfered, left her to it. I daresay my cousin mistook the symptoms of poisoning for the same kind of thing and thought she'd keep it dark again.'

'It appears,' said Price, 'as though the murderer were familiar with the lady's character.'

Sir Charles said with reluctance, 'It does rather. But I can't think of anyone in this house who would do such a thing.'

Price smiled but made no comment. He said, 'According to the Superintendent's notes, the tumbler was taken up to the deceased's bedroom when her bed was turned down and her electric stove switched on at approximately eight-thirty. The bottle of whisky was kept permanently in the room on an occasional table, so the poison could have been introduced into it at any time during the morning, afternoon, or evening. In fact, every member of the household, except perhaps the male staff, the cook, and the kitchenmaid, whose duties would not normally take them into that part of the house, would have had equal opportunity. His task was made even more easy by the fact that the bathroom communicating with the deceased's bedroom also opens on the corridor, and – again according to the Superintendent's notes – was only locked by the deceased during her ablutions.'

'As you say nowadays – I wouldn't know,' said Sir Charles, 'but it would certainly have been easy enough to slip into the room – at times the corridors are deserted. I'm just trying to think of any time when someone was absent whom one would have expected to be present, if you know what I mean. Otherwise, it seems hopeless.'

'It's far from hopeless, Sir Charles,' said Price, bridling. 'Why, I've hardly commenced my investigations. There's the whole question of motive. Am I correct in supposing that the deceased was a very wealthy woman?'

'We're none of us wealthy now,' said Sir Charles, with an indifference which Price found vaguely irritating. 'But my cousin was on her own; she hadn't a place to keep up, and a moderate income goes a long way in those circumstances.'

'And who will inherit her fortune?'

42

'It's not a fortune,' protested Sir Charles. 'It could never have been more than a comfortable income for a single woman and today it's probably scarcely worth having. I haven't the least idea who gets it. She may have made small bequests to all or any of us – I've heard her mention some family jewellery which was to come to my daughter – but she had several nearer relatives and one or two pet charities: Homes for Worn-out Horses and that kind of thing. However, you'll be able to get that from her lawyer, Philip Jardine. He'll be here this afternoon.'

'Flight-Lieutenant Marvin now – according to the Superintendent she brought him here. Could he have had a grudge against her?'

'Scarcely,' said Sir Charles. 'She'd been very good to him. She met him during the war and again afterwards, when he was a bit of a problem – like a good many of these Air Force men. The story goes that she rescued him from the clutches of a doting mother, who was destroying what nerves he had left, and got him keen on riding and hunting and a country life – she had an idea he might join my son in farming later on. But actually he's out of your picture. He was in London visiting his mother and he went up with young Rose on Sunday night.'

Price remembered that Marvin was the Superintendent's fancy – wishful thinking, he'd thought contemptuously, so obvious had been the reluctance of that relic of feudalism to consider a suspect in the family under the thumb of which he had been reared. But this story of a young neurotic, 'taken up' by an elderly woman, certainly smelled a little: money was the commonest motive for murder, and if it turned out that the silly old fool had left him a packet and told him so, there was no more to do than to break a probably amateurishly constructed alibi. In the meantime there was little of value, he felt, to be got out of this old dodderer, who couldn't say for certain who locked up his house at night or whether there were bells in the bedrooms. 'Well thank you, Sir Charles,' he said. 'I think that is all for the moment. I would like to see Mr Hugo d'Estray next, please.'

Sir Charles got up, glancing at his wrist-watch. 'I very much doubt if he'll be back yet, Inspector.'

'Where's he gone? When I telephoned this morning I particularly requested that all the members of the household should be available for questioning.'

Sir Charles said, 'He'd been gone long before you telephoned. He's hunting Lord Badgemoor's hounds this season. The others – my daughter, Mr Rose, and Mrs Scampnell – could have stayed behind if the message had come early enough.'

'This,' Price said, 'is a case of murder. It seems extraordinary that these people should have gone off in this irresponsible way fox-hunting. Granted they had left the premises before you received my telephone communication, but they must have anticipated that police investigations would commence immediately.'

'I suppose,' said Sir Charles, 'I should have stopped them. My son, of course, had to go. We're carrying on under great difficulties. The first whipper-in is only a lad – he couldn't possibly hunt hounds and Badgemoor's much too old and doddery.'

This was Greek to Price. Obviously foxhounds hunted foxes, but the hounds were apparently hunted in their turn by Hugo d'Estray, and what in heaven's name was a whipper-in? He had been enjoying his show of authority, but to say more might reveal ignorance. . . . Best leave it. . . . Sir Charles was saying soothingly, 'They should be back at two o'clock at the latest and meanwhile there are the others – Mrs Rose, Scampnell, Margot Rattray, and all the servants,' so Price only said, 'I'll see Lady d'Estray next, please.'

'Very well,' said Sir Charles, and the telephone rang. The instrument stood on the writing-table and he picked up the receiver and said, 'Yes. Oh, it's you, Treadwell. Good morning to you. How are you? Wife all right? And Pam? That's good. Yes, he's here. For you,' he said at last, and handed the receiver to Price and left the room, quietly shutting the door.

Treadwell had had a further report from the analyst: the

oenanthotoxin which had killed Elizabeth Hudson was believed to have been extracted in some rough-and-ready manner from the root of the *Oenanthe crocata*, or water dropwort, a common plant growing in watery places. 'So at least we're spared a trek round the chemists' shops,' said Treadwell, 'though I suppose some knowledge of chemistry is indicated.'

'Or botany, or access to botanical volumes,' said Price, 'or I should imagine that such information might be obtained from some of these old countrywomen.'

'What old countrywomen?' asked Treadwell.

'Well, there are plenty of old witches around,' said Price. 'I saw one at the lodge when I turned into the park this morning – just the kind of old crone who cooks up herbs and berries.'

Treadwell said coldly, 'That must have been Mrs Toomer, my great-aunt. She was lady's maid to Sir Charles's grandmother and she's lived in most of the embassies in Europe. I don't think *she'd* know much about herbs and berries.'

'Perhaps not,' said Price hastily. 'But there's a type,' he insisted; 'the sort of old woman whom the village maidens consult to procure abortion.'

'That only happens in books,' said the Superintendent. 'When our girls get into trouble, their boys marry them. No, I can't help you there, Inspector; but I can tell you that Sir Charles has a fine library and I've no doubt that the paying guests get the run of it.'

'Thank you, Superintendent,' said Price, and hung up as the door opened and Bunny came in. In response to Sir Charles's request that she wear 'something dark', she had put on a little black frock, in which she looked small and *chic* and quite out of place in an English country house in the middle of the morning; and Price 'placed her' at once as an adventuress, who had 'caught' Sir Charles off his guard in the lax atmosphere of the Riviera. Bunny, for her part, saw a sharp-looking young man, obviously cut out for snooping, smug in his private life, neat, law-abiding, close-fisted. . . . A wave of hostility quivered in the air between them.

45

'Good morning,' said Bunny.

'Good morning, madam,' said Price. 'You are Lady d'Estray, I presume. And before your marriage to Sir Charles your name was – ?'

'Barbara Teresa Desirée Sallust,' said Bunny. When she was nervous she had to talk, and she went on, 'My first husband was French, but my father was English – oddly enough, "a Mr Wilkinson, a clergyman".'

The quotation meant nothing to Price. It merely crossed his mind that the Reverend Mr Wilkinson must do a lot of turning in his grave. He said, 'Incumbent of what parish?'

'Audley Combe, Devon. It's only a tiny parish, but he had other work. He was quite well known as a botanist.'

'And is that a subject which interests you?' asked Price sharply.

'Good God, no!' said Bunny.

'Still you must have acquired some knowledge of it.' He had opened his note-book and recorded her names, and now he made another jotting.

'You look like the Recording Angel,' she told him.

He made no answer to a remark he considered frivolous, if not fresh. He said, 'How long have you known Miss Hudson?'

'Only since I've been here,' said Bunny. 'When I persuaded my husband to take paying guests she was one of the first to be suggested. Apparently she had always been fond of the place and they thought she might like to come and live here.'

'Exactly from whom did the suggestion emanate?'

'Oh, I don't remember that. It was ages ago, and we were all suggesting people.'

'And when Miss Hudson came, was she a satisfactory guest? Single ladies can be very trying.'

'Do you think so?' said Bunny. 'I don't. I think marriage brings out the worst in one. Are you married, Inspector?'

'I am; but let us keep to the point, Lady d'Estray. Did you like Miss Hudson?'

'I admired her in some ways. She was terrifically tough,

46

and I'm a terrible sissy. We hadn't very much in common – she didn't care for books or pictures or music and she'd scarcely been out of England, which made her rather narrow-minded.'

Price had never been out of England and he was tempted to enquire of Lady d'Estray why she imagined that visiting inferior countries and communities should have a beneficial effect on the mind. He restrained himself, however, and instead asserted, 'So you didn't care for the deceased?'

'I certainly wouldn't have chosen her for my companion on a desert island,' said Bunny and wished once again she could remember to whom she had said, I should like to murder – or was it strangle? or was it poison? – that woman.

'And have you any idea who can have wished to make away with her?'

'I haven't the slightest idea,' said Bunny.

Price said that was all for the moment and as Mr Hugo d'Estray and Miss Patricia d'Estray were not available, though he had particularly requested that they should be, he would like to see Mr Scampnell, Mrs Rose, and Miss Rattray. Bunny went away and he took the opportunity to add *dislike of deceased* to her name and *knowledge of botany* in his notebook. Then Mr Scampnell came in, and here, thought Price, noting the light tweed suit, the semi-stiff collar, the neat silk tie, the fountain pen and pencil in the waistcoat pocket, the well-shaven neither handsome nor ugly countenance, is an ordinary reasonable specimen of *homo sapiens*, who goes about the world with his eyes open and from whom I may get some sensible information. There was no hostility in the air now. George Henry Scampnell, Company Director, expressed himself willing to assist the police in any way within his power, as behoved a good citizen. Unfortunately, he'd no solid evidence to set before the Detective-Inspector: though the bedroom occupied by himself and his wife was directly across the corridor from that occupied by the deceased lady, neither he, who had gone to bed at eleven, nor his wife, who had preceded him by about an hour, had heard any unusual noises during the night of Monday, nor in the course of the day had they noticed anyone entering the room or loitering in the corridor. No, it was all very vague and the Detective-Inspector must not take what he was going to say too seriously, but in all communities, however peaceful they might appear to a stranger, there were undercurrents and emotions ranging from mild dislike to seething hatred. 'You know what women are, Detective-Inspector. Even between Mrs Scampnell and the deceased there was petty jealousy, such as you'd never get between men, over their exploits out hunting; and poor little Mrs Rose was so constantly snubbed in her efforts to become a county lady that though she took it like a lamb and never answered back, she *must* have disliked Miss Hudson. Discounting Patricia d'Estray, who, I should say, was genuinely fond of her cousin, the only woman here who really hit it off with the deceased was my stepdaughter, Margot Rattray. She doesn't ride – like myself, she prefers a good tramp or a round of golf – so there was no kind of rivalry, and . . . well . . . she comes of Army folk, so the good lady had no excuse for snubbing her.'

'And Lady d'Estray?'

'Quite frankly,' said Scampnell, 'I was hoping to avoid that question. But as you've asked it I can't do less than answer it truthfully. Lady d'Estray hated Miss Hudson – you could feel it in the air even if you shut your ears to the catty remarks they flung at one another. With all her faults, Miss Hudson was a good old-fashioned type: went to church every Sunday morning – Early Service sometimes too, I believe – thoroughly disapproved of the powder and paint and stuff that Lady d'Estray smothers her face with, couldn't abide her scarlet fingernails, and particularly disliked her habit of using cheap French perfumes. She was upset too by the way that "Bunny" as she calls herself – rather ridiculous at her age – turned the house upside down without respect to the memory of the first Lady d'Estray. I never met her, but I believe she was a real lady. "Bunny" of course resented the old girl's advice and still more her very outspoken criticism, and I think she feared Miss Hudson's influence over Sir Charles, which I have reason to believe was considerable. Now, don't get me wrong, Detective-Inspector. I've no reason in the world to suspect Lady d'Estray of this dreadful crime. I'm simply telling you that she hated Miss Hudson.'

Price said, 'I quite understand, Mr Scampnell: no facts, but a situation one should bear in mind if and when facts emerge to strengthen it. Thank you very much.' He rose. 'If anything more occurs to you, I shall be glad to have another talk with you. It's a treat to find someone who knows the difference between facts and impressions, and the value of both.'

'I shall be delighted to help in any way I can,' replied Scampnell. 'You'll be seeing my stepdaughter – she knows no more than I do, but she was really fond of the old woman. I suppose it would be indiscreet to ask if you've traced any purchase of the poison?'

'It wasn't purchased,' said Price. 'It was a home-made concoction. I'm hoping the servants may throw some light on that matter. You and Mrs Scampnell have a private bath-room, I understand, which is shared by Miss Rattray?'

'That is correct,' said Scampnell. 'The Roses' is private too. Miss Hudson would have shared hers with the occupant of the empty room and Marvin and young Rose share another. I've no idea what the family's arrangements are. They "keep themselves to themselves" in the west wing.'

'Thank you,' said Price, and 'Right,' said Scampnell and 'I'll tell my stepdaughter to come in next,' and scarcely had Price written in his note-book, *Motive, none. Means: seems more of a townsman, but possible slight knowledge of chemistry*, and added: *out to help*, than Margot Rattray slipped into the room with a quiet 'Good morning'.

She was almost pretty. Eyes of smoky-blue were set under level eyebrows and a broad forehead, the dark hair, cut in a girlish 'bob', looked, he thought, delightfully natural, and the large well-shaped mouth was innocent of lipstick – a wholesome English girl, he would have said, but for her pasty complexion and the fact that when you'd looked twice you saw that she was a girl no longer. Scampnell's wife must be a good deal older than himself, Price thought: this Margot was in her thirties – he noticed grey hair in the girlish 'bob' – and Scampnell didn't look a day over fifty. Still, she was obviously a sensible sort of young woman, and Price, after jotting down Margaret Elizabeth Rattray, said, 'Now Miss Rattray, I'm expecting a lot from you. Mr Scampnell tells me that you were friendly with the deceased – got along with her better than most people.'

'I think I did,' said Margot, in a low quiet voice – a contrast, he thought, to Lady d'Estray's nervous gabble. 'You see, though I'm fond of animals, I'm not "horsey". I was at school when my mother and father were in India and she did so much riding, and I spent my holidays with an aunt in London, so I didn't have a country childhood, like Mother did – in Ireland. Mother always pities me for that, but I don't pity myself – I think country children are apt to be terrible tomboys. When my father died and Mother came back to England she tried to teach me to ride, but I hated it . . . oh dear, how I hated it! I expect you think this is all off the point, but what I'm trying to explain is that Miss Hudson didn't look on me as a rival – it was that which spoilt her relationship with Mother; they were always vying with one another and it was quite amusing to hear them after they had been hunting and, having tired themselves to death, poor old dears, were in a snappish mood. I'm fond of old people, and I used to listen to Miss Hudson's stories about the huge fences she'd jumped and how much better she'd ridden than anyone else, and I used to humour her, which of course Mother wouldn't do. And I fetched and carried for her – very unobtrusively, of course: old people don't like to think you think they're old. I know she liked me, because she gave me this wee brooch.' Margot indicated a cameo on the lapel of her blue homespun suit. 'I was quite afraid that Patricia would be cross about it, but she never said a word.'

Price asked, 'And did your old friend confide in you at all – any likes or dislikes for those she lived among?'

'She did a bit,' said Margot. 'She loved all the d'Estrays, I'm convinced of that, except of course the present Lady

50

d'Estray, whom she loathed – rather unreasonably, I thought, because Lady d'Estray can't help being Frenchified and looking like mutton dressed as lamb – at least, she can't help being mutton, though I suppose she needn't dress as lamb. Miss Hudson didn't like the Roses; she thought them Jewish and common, but she was very fond of Geoffrey Marvin and of course she was very good to him. She was paying for his riding and hunting here.'

'And did he reciprocate?'

'I beg your pardon?'

'Did he return her affection?'

'Well, I always thought he was inclined to take her kindness for granted. After a day's hunting, for which Patricia d'Estray charged three guineas, he made less fuss than I did over this wee brooch.'

Price said, 'To some natures patronage can be very irritating. Lady Bountiful sees to it that she gets paid and payments can be made in other ways than by coin of the realm. Would you say that the Flight-Lieutenant was bored by having to dance attendance on the deceased, or anything of that kind?'

Margot said, 'Certainly when he spoke of her behind her back he didn't always speak very respectfully. I've heard him allude to her as "the old girl", and even "the old bitch". I think it's a shame to speak like that of old people, don't you?'

'Old people can be very trying,' said Price, thinking of his mother, 'but of course there's no need to speak disrespectfully of them – that only shows you up for what you are. Well, thank you very much, Miss Rattray. Oh – just one more thing. Are any of you good people interested in botany?'

'Botany?' said Margot, opening her eyes wide. 'I don't think so – no. Mr Rose couldn't tell wheat from barley when he came here, but he's very anxious to become a country gentleman and he does know a little more now. But you mean flowers rather than crops, don't you?'

'Well, either,' said Price.

'Howard Rose,' Margot went on, 'is in the same position

as his father – always asking about the crops – but neither of them seems interested in flowers. Mrs Rose gushes over them when they're arranged indoors, but she's a complete towns-person – she'd be much happier living in a flat in London than here. Geoffrey Marvin – well, I've never heard him taking any interest in Nature, though Miss Hudson wanted him to be a farmer. Oh, then there's us. Father's hopeless – he hardly knows a primrose when he sees it. I love flowers and I know all the ordinary ones; I can tell wheat from barley, but I get stumped on cow-parsley and that kind of thing. Mother knows lots more than I do. She knows the names of the wild flowers and all about the crops, and, of course, Patricia does, too. I don't know about Hugo – he's too haughty to talk to anyone, but I shouldn't think he's interested in anything but those hounds. I don't think Lady d'Estray knows much about flowers because Miss Hudson, who *did* know, was always putting her right about them, and Lady d'Estray didn't like being corrected, so then the fur flew. But Lady d'Estray knew something about herbs, I'm sure. We had the weirdest things in the salads – most of us used to pick them out – and when anyone had a cold she made them what she called *tisanes* – infusions that looked like tea, but tasted foul. Most of us emptied them down our wash-basins.'

'That's all very interesting,' said Price, rapidly transposing the names of Barbara Teresa Desirée d'Estray and Flight-Lieutenant Geoffrey Marvin in his mind. 'I suppose you can't tell me where Lady d'Estray cooked up these messes?'

'Oh yes,' said Margot. 'There's a sort of housemaids' closet just at the head of the main staircase, and when the d'Estrays started taking paying guests they had an electric heater put in there so that the housemaid could make the early morning tea for everybody and save carrying trays up and down the stairs. I know that's right because once, when Mother had a cold, Lady d'Estray insisted on making her one of these *tisanes* and when it was ready she called me in there. I took it and pretended to be grateful, but of course I emptied it straight down the drain.'

'Well, Miss Rattray,' said Price, 'I'm *really* grateful to you. What you have said will be of great assistance. Would it be troubling you too much to ask Mrs Rose if I could see her next? She seems to be one of the few people who haven't gone off fox-hunting.'

'She's like me,' said Margot, rising from the armchair, where she had been sitting very quietly with her hands clasped round her knees. 'She doesn't ride. Actually, if I did I shouldn't have gone out today: I think it was rather disrespectful to Miss Hudson and I told Mother so, but she said it was stuffy and middle-class of me. Good morning, Inspector.'

And it *is* a good morning, thought Price, writing *Motive: none. Means: knowledge of botany, nil: knowledge of and access to pantry, yes*, and turning a page and adding under Bunny's name: *thorough knowledge of herbal beverages. Knowledge of and access to pantry, yes plus.* That's substantial progress, that is. . . . I'll see the housemaid after this Mrs Rose. . . . Then Sybella Rose came in, wearing a tan wool dress and several rows of pearls and fluttering her long eyelashes over her fine brown eyes. Except for her eyes, which were unusually large, and her feet, which were unusually small, her appearance was undistinguished. Thousands like her tripped through the better-class shops of Oxford Street every day.

Price felt well disposed towards her. A nice little woman, he thought; makes the most of herself, visits the hairdresser regularly, knows how to coax her husband into buying an expensive bit of nonsense she calls a hat, but no harm in her . . . not like her ladyship. 'Good morning, Mrs Rose,' he said pleasantly. 'Come right in and sit down – that sounds a little like the spider talking to the fly, doesn't it? but I hope you don't think of me as a spider.' The sort of little woman one can talk to, he thought approvingly.

Sybella Rose said, 'Well, of course, it's a bit frightening. I was ever so scared this morning when I heard a detective from Scotland Yard was coming, 'specially as my hubby had gone out huntin', but Bunny – Lady d'Estray – told me you weren't a bit alarming, and, of course, I want to do all I can

53

to help. Miss Hudson didn't think much of poor little me, I'm afraid, but I always felt sorry for her. A woman without a man always seems a bit pathetic to me.'

'A *vee manky*,' said Price.

'Pardon?' said Mrs Rose.

'A *vee manky*, as the French say,' he amplified. 'Now tell me, Mrs Rose: the ladies see and hear far more of what goes on than we mere males – can you tell me of any little thing you've noticed – and kept to yourself perhaps – which might throw some light on our mystery? Don't hold back for fear of incriminating anyone: the innocent never suffer and what appears to *you* to point to one individual may lead *us* to another.' The little woman needed reassuring, he told himself compassionately: sitting bolt upright on the very edge of her chair and fluttering her eyelashes, she looked like a plump and startled hind.

'I wonder what I can tell you,' she said, nervously twisting the fine rings on her little white hands. 'I didn't poison Miss Hudson. Even if I'd wanted to, I shouldn't have dared – she was a most terrifying person. And I know my hubby didn't, and my boy didn't – he was away, you know; and I'm sure the baronet didn't or Patricia or Hugo – they were all so fond of the old lady. I expect people have been telling you that Bunny d'Estray disliked Miss Hudson, but I hope you won't take any notice of that because you can dislike a person without murdering them, and Bunny and I are very close friends, and I should know if she'd done it – I'm sensitive in that sort of way. I know people will suspect Bunny just because she's Frenchy – those Scampnells will – but of course it's ridiculous.'

Price said, 'I can assure you, Mrs Rose, we need a great deal of really solid evidence before we allow ourselves even to suspect anybody, and though crimes of passion – love, revenge, et cetera – are common on the Continent, among English people money is the motive nine times out of ten,' and, with no sense at all of racial shame, he went on, 'As you are such a friend of Lady d'Estray's, I assume that you were aware of the existence of a kind of upstairs pantry, where she sometimes prepared infusions of medicinal herbs?'

'You naughty man, you make the little pantry sound like a witches' kitchen,' laughed Mrs Rose. 'It's really used by Beatrice, the housemaid, for making the early morning teas. It was only when one of us had a cold or 'flu that Lady d'Estray made us French remedies – *tisanes*. They were awfully good and I think it was very kind of her.'

'Has she used the pantry in the last few days, Mrs Rose?'

'Oh no. None of us had colds; besides, she found out that the Scampnells and Miss Hudson didn't even try their drinks but just poured them away down their wash-basins. I think it was horrid of them when a famous author, like she is, had been kind enough to bother over their sniffs.'

'A famous author?' said Price. 'I can't say I've heard of her under any of her names. I've very little time for sedentary relaxation, but my wife's a great reader – always down at the library changing her books.'

'Perhaps,' returned Sybella, 'she prefers a lighter type. Bunny's books aren't heavy, but in a way they're highbrow. I read an article in a paper about them and it said that they would become classics because of their exquisite prose. And she writes as beautifully in French as in English – in fact I think that in France she's better known.'

'I should think that's quite possible,' said Price, who believed that all French books are hot stuff. 'Well, Mrs Rose, I think that's all for the moment.' A nice little woman, he thought again, but too fond of her 'Bunny' to be much use at present. 'Thank you, Mrs Rose,' he said, and Sybella left him and he noted: *Motive – none. Knowledge of Botany – unlikely. Knowledge of and access to Pantry – yes.* He then consulted his wrist-watch, which, differing considerably from the clock on the mantelpiece, announced that the time was a quarter to one. With a mind for lunch – back at the Red Lion, he supposed – he was half-way to the door when it was violently opened and a small fresh-faced boy in a white coat staggered in with a loaded tray. There was a miniature casserole of mushroom soup and, lifting the lid of a silver entrée dish when

55

the boy had gone, Price discovered lobster mayonnaise. A *carafe* of white wine, biscuits, butter and cheese, and a bunch of black hothouse grapes completed the meal. So this is how they live, is it? ... Talk about equal sacrifice, thought Price, and fell to. ...

CHAPTER FOUR

OVER sherry in the library Philip Jardine was asking Sir Charles, 'Do you know how Elizabeth left her money?'

Sir Charles said, 'As I believe they say nowadays, I haven't a clue.'

'Apart from a few small bequests, contained in a codicil – a necklace to your Pat, her horse to her Marvin protegé and so on – the whole boiling – a matter of between thirty and forty thousand pounds – goes straight to Hugo.'

Sir Charles passed his hand wearily across his eyes.

'That will simplify life for Hugo. But at the same time . . .'

'Yes,' said Jardine. 'At the moment it carries a sting in its tail – let us be frank, Charles; we've known each other long enough – a motive for murder. But that will pass; innocent men don't get hanged nowadays; and it'll make all the difference to Hugo. I suppose he hasn't, by any chance, an alibi?'

'I gather,' said Sir Charles, 'that we need all-day alibis for Monday. None of us has them but Marvin and young Rose.'

'I should suspect them instantly,' said Jardine, and as he spoke Bunny came in and said, 'How mean of you to drink without me! How are you, Philip Jardine?'

Jardine, from Winchester and New College, didn't care for the new Lady d'Estray, had thought Charles an ass for marrying so far outside his class and kind and had been further exasperated by discovering later that the Reverend Mr Wilkinson had been also of Winchester and New College. Bunny's method of addressing him seemed to him a literary affectation: why couldn't she behave like other people and call him Philip, as Charles did, or Mr Jardine? Now it occurred to him: one knows very little about her . . . practically a foreigner . . . forty-ish . . . French ideas on sex . . . supposing she had designs on Hugo? . . . Bunny was telling Sir Charles that she had had a sumptuous lunch taken in to the Gestapo, and Sir Charles said that it was hardly fair to call him that – a decent little fellow, who was only doing his duty. Bunny said, 'Well, I think he's a ghastly little man and

57

it's all very well to say that innocent people needn't worry, but Sybella says he's asking about the upstairs pantry and the hot drinks I made for people when they had colds, so I suppose he thinks I brewed up some deadly nightshade or something and put it in Elizabeth's whisky. Philip Jardine, do you think I should refuse to answer any more questions except in your presence?'

'I think it's best to be absolutely frank,' Jardine told her, and added, 'You mustn't worry. The police aren't fools.'

Sir Charles said dryly, 'You needn't be afraid for yourself, Bunny. You had no motive. It's poor old Hugo who's been provided with that. Elizabeth's left him all her money.'

'I knew she had.'

'Good God! how did you know? I've just been telling Philip that I hadn't an inkling.'

Practically a foreigner . . . thought Jardine. They haven't our codes about poking and prying. . . . But Bunny said, 'Elizabeth told me soon after she came here. If you remember, I had a brain-wave about Hugo learning hotel-keeping, and she was very much against it. I'd nearly persuaded Hugo, so she took me apart one evening and told me she was leaving him her money, and, though it takes a thousand a year merely to keep the roof on this house, she made me promise to drop the idea, and I did; I never mentioned it again, but I still think that Hugo should go in for hotel-keeping.'

'Well, we needn't go through all that again now,' said Charles irritably. 'You didn't, I hope, blurt this out to that fellow Price?'

'No, I didn't. He never mentioned Elizabeth's money.'

'He mentioned it to me and I told him I knew nothing about it. He will never believe that you knew and I didn't.'

'Why not? I promised Elizabeth I wouldn't tell any-body.'

Sir Charles said, 'Everyone knows that women can't keep secrets.'

'Oh, Charles, you're marvellous,' said Bunny. 'Well, then, I'm afraid that all I can do is to break Philip Jardine's rule of absolute frankness.'

58

'What about it, Philip?'

Jardine said, 'I think it might be wise, for the moment,' and the gong rang then, and as he followed Bunny into the dining-room he thought: that's it . . . moonlight on the Mediterranean, wine and roses, and so she caught poor silly old Charles for his title and his position, and then found that he was getting on and wasn't much fun, and then the good-looking son appeared and she learned that he was coming in for money. Hugo's a nice boy but guileless – he'd be wax in the hands of an experienced woman. My God, he thought, smiling and bowing as Bunny introduced him to the Scampnells and Sybella, already seated at their respective tables, supposing Charles is next on her list . . . he well may be. I can't let that happen, he thought, sitting down and unfolding with dislike an unstarched checked napkin, I was at school with old Charles. . . . Unless the detective produces some startling theory, I'll give old Charles a hint, if it cost me his friendship. . . . He became aware that Bunny was speaking to him. 'I beg your pardon? . . . '

The long talk that he had later in the afternoon with Price did little to shake his conviction. Immediately Price had finished his lunch he had rung the bell and told the boy who came for his tray that he was ready to see Miss Hudson's lawyer. Eric said, 'What?' and Price asked him where his manners were: 'Mr What died years ago and Mr Pardon took his place – didn't they tell you that at school?' he asked him. 'Sir Charles won't 'ave pardon in the 'ouse,' said Eric. 'I beg your pardon to the upper servants and the gentry and what to hequals and hanimals – that's what we 'aves 'ere.' 'That's quite enough of your cheek, my boy,' said Price. 'And, as you don't seem too bright in the head, send the butler to me.' 'Mr Benson is at present occupied in serving the dining-room luncheon, but I will endeavour to communicate with him,' said Eric, now speaking in tones of exaggerated refinement, and before Price's surprise had turned to annoyance he was out of the room. In a few moments Benson, looking harassed, opened the door.

'That boy of yours,' said Price; 'is he normal? One minute

he plays the village idiot, and the next he talks with an Oxford accent – la-di-dah.'

'He's quite a clever boy,' said Benson. 'A couple of years ago he won a scholarship to Harborough Grammar, but his father wouldn't let him take it up – doesn't hold with education.'

'Good heavens! can such people exist? One can hardly credit it. But that's by the way. What I was trying to get into the boy's head was that I should like to see Miss Hudson's lawyer. I understand he was arriving in time for the midday meal.'

'Mr Jardine is here, but I've only just served the third course. Then there'll be the coffee.'

Price said, 'I shouldn't like to hurry them for a mere matter of murder. While I await their pleasure I'll see the old nurse and the housemaid.' His sarcasm seemed to be lost on Benson, who, murmuring that he would send a message to Miss Blythe and Miss Toomer, hastened from the room.

Beatrice Blythe, stiff and stocky, could add little to what she had told the Superintendent: to Price's questions on the subject of the upstairs pantry she replied that in the last few days she had noticed no sign of the electric ring having been used by anyone but herself, and that on the comparatively rare occasions when her ladyship had made hot drinks for the guests or the family she had left the place in a state of confusion – 'not,' put in Beatrice, 'that I minded.' Nanny, fresh from destroying the collections of wild flowers which the young d'Estrays had made under the influence of their cousin – Bunny, who had gone up to the nursery for a franker gossip than she suspected Charles would countenance, had told her that the detective had asked about botany – uttered, through compressed lips, a string of negatives, but on leaving volunteered that Miss Hudson had been a hard woman and generally disliked for years before she had come to Aston, and that Price, instead of hindering those with more to do than they had time for, should look elsewhere.

Jardine in the meantime had had a talk with Hugo, whom a telephone message to the Kennels had brought home shortly

after Patricia, Cecily Scampnell, and Sidney Rose. Hugo
d'Estray was as dark as his sister was fair, and his appearance
was such that the sight of him was apt to draw mutters of
'gigolo', 'Rudolf Valentino', and 'tailor's dummy' from less
well-favoured men. Lately a sardonic look had clouded but
added character to his perfect features, but his trouble wasn't,
like Geoffrey Marvin's nervous exhaustion, prolonged by dis-
inclination to adjust himself to civilian life: Hugo had nerves
of iron. What irked him was that he had discovered his
vocation and it was impossible: learning of it, people said
don't be silly, Hugo, and: is that really all you want to do
with your life, Hugo? and: you know, Hugo, one day you'll
want to get married. For, since the squirearchy was done for
and he couldn't be an amateur huntsman, Hugo wanted to be
a professional huntsman: he didn't care in the least if, as he
was warned, he never owned a car, a wife, a dress-suit, if he
lost his friends, his comforts, his gentility: he had had the in-
estimable good fortune to come at the age of twenty-five to
the end of his pursuit of happiness; but so far from envying
him, those around him prepared to pinch and scrape and
sacrifice themselves to teach him hotel-keeping, start him in
market-gardening or buy him a dairy herd. Philip Jardine
had been kindness itself, consulting and even getting offers of
jobs from influential clients until Hugo's lack of interest had
discouraged him and he had dismissed poor Charles's heir
as a ne'er-do-well and then remembered his war record.
When Price said to him, 'And what does that young gentleman do to earn his living?' and smiled contemptuously at
the answer, 'He's looking round,' Jardine went on, 'You
mustn't get the idea that he's a waster. He did extra-
ordinarily well in the war in North Africa.' 'So did plenty
of others,' said Price: 'but it doesn't follow that they do
well in the peace in England – in fact the reverse is frequently
the case.' Jardine loved the King's English enough to
wince visibly, and Price, mistaking the cause of his pain,
added, 'That sounds ungrateful, perhaps, but in our job
it's essential to avoid sentimentality.' 'Oh, quite,' said
Jardine. 'One must look facts in the face, but at least the

boy didn't have a commando training.' Price said, 'In any case this has the appearance of a woman's crime,' and, back in the library, Jardine repeated that, with the double purpose of reassuring Hugo and observing Bunny. Hugo, who had received the news of his good fortune without apparent emotion, merely remarking that it was sweet of Cousin Elizabeth and he wished she had been out to-day to see how excellently Rambler was shaping, said, 'I'm inclined to agree with him, if, as rumour has it, the poison was something cooked up in Beatrice's pantry. I've never cooked anything without hearing afterwards about the number of saucepans I've used and the mess I've made.' He went off to his interview, and Bunny said she needed fresh air and would take a message that she was next on the list to Patricia, who was cleaning tack in the stable.

Jardine said, 'Before I catch my train, Charles, there's something I want to say to you. There's only one member of your household who has an obvious straightforward motive for this murder, and that's Hugo, and I'm perfectly certain he didn't do it. He's a curious character; at one time, I admit, I thought him work-shy; but now I'm beginning to think that his lack of interest in anything we've tried to arrange for him is due to the strange fact that he's got no use for money. As far as I know – correct me if I'm wrong – he's perfectly content to spend all day and every day at the kennels.'

'That's perfectly true,' said Charles. 'He drinks and smokes very moderately, he loathes motor cars, and even Pat can't get him to London.'

'We'll rule out Hugo then, and that means we're looking for someone with a motive we can't even guess at. It leaves us damnably in the dark, Charles. I do want you to realize that any or all of you may be in grave danger. For all we know this may be the work of a homicidal maniac or of someone with a grudge against the whole family, or of someone . . . well, you take my advice, Charles, and don't trust even your nearest and dearest. Price believes this to be the work of a woman – well, some women get queer in their forties,' said Jardine with relish, for his wife, saying that he was a stuffed shirt, had left him in nineteen-twenty, and it pleased him to think that she now had her difficulties.

Sir Charles said, 'Hmm,' and then Benson at the door announced Mr Jardine's taxi and Jardine hurried away, congratulating himself on his tactful timing. Until tea was brought in and with it came Bunny, followed by Hugo and Patricia, inclined to giggle and imitate Price as they compared their respective interviews, Sir Charles sat thinking of what Jardine had said to him: 'Certainly not Hugo . . . don't trust your nearest and dearest . . . a woman's crime . . . women get queer in their forties . . . ' He meant Bunny, of course. It had been obvious from the first that he didn't cotton to her . . . naturally he wouldn't; she wasn't his type; he didn't like outstanding women, queer women, clever women, exotic women: his type was the ordinary, straightforward, quietly dressed, quietly mannered, upper-class Englishwoman, the kind of woman Hermione had been and Patricia would be . . . my type, too, thought Sir Charles, except when I'm in the mood in which I married Bunny. The thought shook him: it was the first time he had thought like that of his marriage and he realized that was how others must have thought of it – his children, his friends, his servants – the outcome of a mad mood, induced by the sun and the wine of the Mediterranean, a holiday indiscretion. And they were right, he thought, getting up, lighting another cigarette and walking restlessly to the window; they were right . . . he'd been a ridiculous old man and, God bless them, it was marvellous that they'd kept straight faces: like some silly impulsive youth he, old enough to be a grandfather, had married a woman of whom even now he knew nothing. It had been her gaiety, the sharpness of her mind, what the Victorians would have called her sauciness, which had bewitched him, and then there had been the pink villa, the charming meals on the diminutive terrace, the romantic backcloth of the medieval village and the blue mountains and the sea; and there had been her friends, so casual and so distinguished, and the picturesque little daughter to remind you that life wasn't all beer and skittles to a woman who must face it alone. Half amused, half protective, he had married her, and presently, with the sudden eruption of the long-quiescent volcano of his financial difficulties, he had found, in place of his amusing poppet, a creature of inflexible will, unshakeable self-confidence, and merciless industry. In France he had dipped into her books and, since they were about children and gardens and Siamese cats, he had thought them delightfully feminine, and had shut them up and returned to the life of the Duke of Wellington: he'd never guessed at the sweat and the toil of the forge from which had issued that prose of finest steel. When Bunny had suggested the guest house, he had said, 'It'll mean so much work for you, darling. Surely with your knack it would be less trouble to dash off a best-seller,' and had defined as mulish the stricken look on her face. Patricia and Hugo . . . he knew them as he believed he had known his Hermione, through and through, but even before this wretched business he had realized that he was at sea with Bunny . . . how, now, could he be sure of her? She said, 'Pat, darling, you pour out,' and her diffidence exasperated him: she should take her place even if it had been Hermione's and, for a short time, Patricia's. 'It's your job, Barbara,' he said sharply.

Bunny made no move from the sofa, into which she had sunk in an attitude which showed her shapely legs to the knees, robbing her black dress of any suggestion of mourning. 'You must all prepare to take on my jobs,' she said. 'I'm sure I'm Suspect Number One. Since the 'tec finished with Pat, he's been prowling about the upstairs pantry. I shall be surprised if I'm not in gaol by nightfall. Actually, Mrs Capes is quite capable of doing the housekeeping, and if someone will drive Nanny into Harborough once or twice a week she could do the odd bits of shopping. Charles, you'll have to do the accounts – Lisa will help you if it comes to long division.' 'I'm quite capable of doing long division,' said Sir Charles, 'but I wish you wouldn't talk like that – you know I dislike flippant talk on serious subjects.' 'Oh, my feet!' said Bunny, kicking off her shoes. 'I shall pass out, Charles, if you don't let me soon change into espadrilles.' 'Why aren't you wearing espadrilles?' asked Hugo. 'Your father didn't think them suitable for to-day,' said Bunny. Patricia, trim in three-guinea 'Coolies', said, 'The more you wear sloppy shoes the more you have to.' 'I don't see why Bunny shouldn't wear what she likes on her own feet,' said Hugo. Sir Charles said, 'Don't be impertinent, Hugo,' and Hugo had opened his mouth to reply when a diversion was created by the entrance of Lisa with Babette and Captain at her heels.

Lisa said, 'Do you know what? I've been detecting down in the Low Meadow. There's marks of heels and you can see where someone's been puddling about round the water drop-wort. I did hope there'd be a handkerchief with a laundry mark on it or a hairpin but all I found was a cigarette-end, and everyone in the house smokes except me and Nannie and Sylvia – even Eric does sometimes – and it hasn't got any lipstick on it. If we could find out who knew that dropwort grows in the Low Meadow . . . '

Sir Charles checked her. 'Just a minute, Lisa. How did you know what I didn't know myself – that water dropwort was the poison?'

'Everyone knows that,' said Lisa impatiently. 'The detective asked Benson if there was any on the property and Benson didn't know. He told Beatrice about it and Sylvia overheard him and told Eric and he told me.'

'Associating with the boot-boy again,' sighed Patricia.

'Leave that at the moment, Pat,' said her father. 'Lisa, you've never shown any interest in botany – how did you know where the dropwort grows?'

'Cousin Elizabeth told me ages ago. Bunny wanted me to do the flowers and it was autumn and there weren't any, and Cousin Elizabeth said surely I wasn't blind to the beauty of the autumnal tints and made me go all the way down to the knoll with her to get some beastly beech leaves, which had dropped off their sticks anyway by the time we got home. All the time she was pointing out botanical facts – it was fright-fully boring – and she pointed out the dropwort and said that once in a village where she had lived a carter had pulled some up and eaten the root in mistake for parsnips, and he had given some to his horse and both of them had died. She said that Mother Nature . . . '

This time it was Bunny who interrupted her. 'Elizabeth must have told that to someone else too – someone she went strolling round the place with, or to whom she talked about horses . . . '

'I've heard her say thank goodness we've no yew hedges,' said Patricia, 'but I've never heard her mention dropwort, not even when we've talked about turning out the horses and you know how she fussed over Brutus.'

'If the dropwort was eaten in mistake for parsnips it must have been the root that was eaten, not the leaves,' said Lisa. 'Horses don't go digging up roots. In Cousin Elizabeth's anecdote the man pulled the plant up like you'd pull up a parsnip. I daresay the leaves aren't poisonous.'

'If one part of a plant is poisonous, the rest of it must be,' said Patricia. 'Are you sure it was Cousin Elizabeth who told you about it, Lisa?' She turned the direct gaze of her steady blue eyes on the child.

'Of course I am,' said Lisa, looking on the ground.

'You see, it doesn't make sense that Cousin Elizabeth should have told you, when she never told me. Are you quite sure that it wasn't someone else, Lisa?'

'What are you trying to get at, Patricia?' asked Bunny, straightening up and dragging on her shoes. 'Whatever it is, I'm sure you won't get at it by talking to Lisa like a prefect.'

Patricia flushed angrily. 'When you're dealing with people whom you happen to know are liars . . . '

'Do you mean me?' asked Lisa.

'Be quiet, Lisa. Listen, Pat,' said Sir Charles. 'You're going too fast; you're rushing your fences. Let's think this out logically – sit down and get on with your tea, Lisa. Now, Pat: Elizabeth, as we all know, was well up in botany and was quite the most likely person to have told Lisa about this plant. Lisa, did you tell anybody?'

'Of course not,' said Lisa, through a mouthful of cake. 'Why should I? Going about disseminating botanical facts

66

is not in my line. But Cousin Elizabeth's conversation, when it wasn't just squashing people, was mostly anecdotes; and the man and the horse eating the dropwort was an anecdote quite apart from being botany. She might have told it to anyone.'

'You mean it might have emerged as (*a*) a botanical fact, (*b*) a horsey fact, or (*c*) an anecdote. How nice and clearly you think, Lisa!' said Bunny.

'I don't see that it gets us any farther,' said Patricia.

'Oh, but surely it does,' said Bunny. 'To whom did Elizabeth talk horse, to whom botany, and to whom did she tell anecdotes? No, you're right, Pat. It's useless. She was an Ancient Mariner and she didn't give a damn for her victim's interests – she just talked on.'

Patricia said, 'I don't think it's very good form to make clever remarks at the expense of people who are dead.'

'Play the game, mater,' said Lisa, with a giggle.

'You'd better go to the nursery, Lisa,' said Patricia.

'Don't be an ass, Pat,' said Hugo. 'Lisa's the only one of us who's discovered anything so far. Actually, I think we'd much better leave things to the detective. It's obvious that Cousin Elizabeth was poisoned by one of the lodgers and I don't care which – as far as I can see they're all equally bloody.' He rose. 'If anyone wants me I shall be over at the kennels. Dreamer's cut himself open on some wire and I don't trust the kennelman.'

'I must go and see to Romanée Conti,' said Lisa. 'I got late detecting.'

'You shouldn't keep him waiting,' said Patricia. 'You shouldn't have a pony if you can't look after him properly. I didn't feed him because I know how *that* would end.'

'I don't want you to feed him,' said Lisa. 'I don't want you to touch him, thank you,' and Bunny said, 'I'll come with you, Lisa,' and hurried her daughter from the room. Alone with her father, Patricia, collecting tea-cups, switching on lights, said, 'Lisa's a queer child and at that age they're all terrible little liars – that's why I thought someone other than Elizabeth might have told her about the dropwort. And I'm not sure that I wasn't right. Did you notice that she couldn't look me in the face when she denied it?'

Sir Charles said, 'I still don't see what you're driving at. Lisa thinks she's detecting – surely she'd have been only too pleased to tell us the name of her informant?'

'Not,' said Patricia, 'if it was someone she liked and wanted to shield.'

'Well, who *does* she like?' mused Sir Charles. 'I feel I'm only tolerated; I don't think she's exactly devoted to you, Pat; Hugo doesn't seem to notice her much; I've never heard her say a good word of any of the lodgers.'

'The people she really gets on well with,' said Patricia, 'are the servants. But with kids of that age you never know – they have tremendous secret pashes, as we used to call them at school, for the most unlikely people.'

'I shouldn't think,' said Sir Charles, 'that Lisa has much affection to spare from her mother.'

There was silence then in the library. Patricia had sat down and was smoking; like all the d'Estrays, she could sit still and say nothing, whereas Bunny and Lisa, unless they were reading, when they were apparently and often irritatingly unconscious of what was going on around them, talked, fidgeted, poked the fire, took off their shoes. Lamplight, the quietness of the room, only occasionally broken by the shifting of the log fire, the companionable silence of his flesh and blood, induced in Charles d'Estray's troubled mind a confidential mood – so had he and Hermione sat in the autumn twilights of the good years long ago. Patricia was like her mother, especially in profile, and it was in profile that Sir Charles saw her now. He said, 'Pat, we've always been good friends. I wish you'd be frank with me.'

Patricia said, 'I wish I could be. But there are things one can't say. . . . It's not as if I really know anything. I've only suspicions.'

'Then you'd better speak out,' Sir Charles said. 'Suspicions won't hang anybody but they're poison in the mind. You're thinking of Bunny and Lisa . . . ' He was glad that, after all, he had been able to say it in perfectly normal tones.

Patricia gave a gasp of relief because it had been said. 'I feel so awful, Daddy. It seems so terribly disloyal to you. But I've felt like bursting, and the only other person I could talk to is Hugo, and he just doesn't seem to be interested – he only says to stop bothering, it was one of the lodgers, and I'd like to think so too, but I can't, because it's just wishful thinking: none of them had the slightest motive as far as I can see. Lisa had, of course: as you say, she's devoted to her mother and she might have thought that Bunny would be happier with Cousin Elizabeth out of the way. Or she might have done it in a rage: she's a queer child – goodness knows what they would have thought of her at St Olaf's – and once or twice when she was in a temper she said that she would like to kill Cousin Elizabeth. I was wondering about her father – he was T.B., wasn't he? She may have inherited something . . . '

'I shouldn't think so,' said Sir Charles. 'He was T.B. certainly, and, I imagine, one of those disgruntled near-geniuses, but that's no reason that he should transmit homicidal tendencies. They say young girls are unpredictable, but you weren't, Pat. You were always very steady.'

'I wasn't half French and I didn't spend my childhood being dragged about foreign countries, like poor Lisa. Anyhow, what corners I had were duly knocked off at St Olaf's.' She smiled, evidently recalling humorous incidents connected with the loss of her individuality.

Sir Charles said, 'I see now what you were getting at. You think that Bunny, not Elizabeth, might have told her about the dropwort. That being so, either Bunny or Lisa could have taken advantage of the knowledge.'

'It's awful even to think such things. You must hate me, Daddy.'

'That's nonsense, Pat, old thing. You can't help your thoughts – Jardine's got the same idea, I think; he warned me very solemnly not to trust my nearest and dearest and I don't fancy he meant you or Hugo. We must face facts: Bunny – and Lisa – had a motive: hatred of Elizabeth; and there's Bunny's knowledge of herbs into the bargain. Instead of shutting our eyes to all that, let's try to prove to ourselves, and everyone else if we can, that they are innocent. I don't know where Lisa keeps her possessions – in the schoolroom, perhaps . . . oh, I know it goes against the grain to snoop and spy, but anything's better than that we should nurse these intolerable suspicions.' His voice had lost the forced cheerfulness with which he had been speaking; Patricia caught the note of anguish and her cool heart bled for him.

'I will look round,' she said, 'but I bet a hundred to one that I don't find anything. Somehow, now we've talked about it I feel much less suspicious. But then . . . oh, dear, that's how it goes, round and round in one's head; the only time I've forgotten it was during the run we had this morning, and in the middle of that I thought of Cousin Elizabeth. It must be even worse for you, Daddy.'

'It's certainly not pleasant,' said Sir Charles grimly. 'But our talk has done me good too, Pat. I gather you don't suspect me and I certainly don't suspect you, so I suggest we form an alliance, agreeing to be perfectly open with each other and to pool all our thoughts and fears and discoveries.'

'However awful?'

'However awful,' said Sir Charles, with a faint smile. 'You know, Pat, in the end blood's thicker than water . . . '

Their talk was ended by the arrival of Benson to remove the tea-tray. 'Is the Inspector still about?' Sir Charles asked him, and Benson said, 'No, Sir Charles. After spending a long time upstairs, especially in Miss Hudson's bedroom, he's motored back to Harborough to confer, I gather, with Colonel Rivett-Bankes and young Treadwell.'

'And how did you gather that?' asked Sir Charles. 'Did he tell you?'

'Oh no, Sir Charles. He's not the kind with whom one can get into conversation. But one of the younger servants happened to be passing the study door when he was telephoning. He mentioned – to the Colonel I think – that he had made up his mind as to the guilty party but was stuck for evidence.'

'It's all very well for you to sound pleased, Ben,' said Patricia, getting up with a sigh, 'but nothing, however awful, could be worse than never knowing who was the murderer. It would poison all our relationships.'

She left the room, and Benson, standing for a moment before he lifted the tray, said to Sir Charles, 'Miss Pat's young enough to want the truth out. When you get to my age you know that it's best left in its grave.' 'You amaze me, Benson,' said Sir Charles, shocked. 'Surely that's a very unusual view.' 'I'm ten years older than what you are, Sir Charles,' said Benson, 'and, one way and another, we see more of life than the gentry do.' He lifted the tray and carried it out and for a moment or two Sir Charles wondered if the old chap were right – if man were so vile a thing that, in his interests, truth had best lie low. But he had been taught early and thoroughly the habit of loyalty: 'the best school of all' . . . 'Well rowed, Oxford' . . . 'England, my England' . . . and he was a man, and, of course, there were exceptions, but men were decent fellows on the whole. . . .

And Benson was one of the best of them, a splendid old chap, who thought things out for himself instead of getting his opinions, as most of the lower classes did, from *The News of the World*; but he was quite on the wrong lines when he pictured truth in its grave and best left there: probably owing to poor feeding in childhood, he lacked moral courage, thought Sir Charles. . . .

When Lisa had brought hay and water to her pony and she and Bunny had stood for a long while leaning on the door of the loose box, which Patricia said was wasted on him, and ignorantly admiring him, they strolled on down the row of boxes and visited Iona's hot little chestnut, Champagne; Simon's stolid efficient Brandy; Patricia's handsome grey Huntsman, whom no one but herself might ride; big dark bay Sir Roger, who alone would take his fences with Sidney Rose unsteadily anchored to his ever-hardening mouth; Quiver, the temperamental dark-brown thoroughbred mare, generally hunted by Cecily Scampnell; star-gazing chestnut Sonia, forever afidget under the heavy hands of Howard Rose; and the commoners, plain roan Redskin, chosen under the influence of Elizabeth Hudson for the beginner, Marvin, and Safety First, a heavy hairy black cob, deputy of the often unsound Sonia. Dusk in the stable yard, the smell of hay and horse-flesh, the sounds of munching and the rustle of straw, the gentle welcome of the horses, were soothing to Bunny's vexed spirit: listening to Lisa recounting their virtues and failings, she forgot that, too worldly-wise to believe that the innocent don't suffer, she expected, as she had lightly put it, to be in gaol by nightfall, until Lisa said, '...And Brutus...' and there was the big brown horse, that had been so dear to Elizabeth Hudson. 'He always seemed fond of his missis, but he doesn't seem to pine for her,' said Lisa. 'Horses don't pine, like dogs, do they?' Bunny said. 'Did you know he's been left to Geoffrey Marvin?' 'Gosh,' said Lisa, 'then he *had* got a motive.' 'Grown-up people don't risk hanging for horses,' said Bunny. 'A very horsey person might,' said Lisa. 'After all, people risk it for husbands. All the same I believe he was only bossed into being horsey. I shan't be a bit surprised if he gives up riding.' Bunny said, 'You don't think he's in love with Pat, do you?' 'Good lord, no,' said Lisa. 'He hates Pat. He thinks she puts on side, which actually she doesn't do, and anyhow he's in love with that awful Suzanne at the local.' 'What extraordinary things you know!' said Bunny. 'I don't think that's extraordinary,' said Lisa. 'He's awfully brave and a pilot and all that, but really he's of the people, and Suzanne must have been a rest to him after the strain of living up to Cousin Elizabeth. He'd be able to relax with Suzanne and use the words he learned at his mother's knee – perspiration and serviette and excuse me and pardon.' 'I wonder if there's a motive there,' mused Bunny as, calling Babette, she turned towards the house. 'He's got an alibi, of course, but it might be a faked one. Supposing Elizabeth had found out about Suzanne ... But I can't see that it would have mattered. ... It's not as though she had left him her money ...'

Indoors, it seemed to Bunny that the great house was very quiet at a time when it was usually filled with voices. The drawing-room and the morning-room were empty, everyone preferring, she imagined, to be in the company of the one or two he could trust – husbands with wives . . . 'I wonder where the Great White Chief is?' she said to Lisa. 'Still in the library, I expect,' said Lisa. But he wasn't, and Lisa, who, according to d'Estray custom, ate supper in the schoolroom at seven, sat down with a book while Bunny went upstairs to change for dinner. A long soak in a deep hot bath . . . she planned, and the pink corduroy housecoat . . . Charles will be as solemn as an owl and Pat like an iceberg. Lisa would have helped me . . . She opened the door of her room and there was Charles, starting away from the corner cupboard, where, since she shared the west-wing bathroom with her husband and Hugo and Patricia, she kept her toilet things and a few common remedies.

Bunny thought, Poor thing! . . . so embarrassed . . . the embarrassed baronet met the harassed novelist. Sir Charles gave a feeble laugh and said, 'You startled me, creeping in like that on those rope soles. I've a headache. I was looking for an aspirin.'

Bunny knew what she should say. She should say, 'I'll find you them,' or 'I haven't any but I'll try Nanny.' Thus Hermione, only no one would have suspected Hermione. But Bunny wasn't made like that, so she said 'Liar!' and Sir Charles said, 'Really, Barbara,' and Bunny said, ' "Really Barbara!" Well, of all the damned hypocrites! You were no more looking for aspirin than the man in the moon is. You were looking for traces of hemlock or dropwort or whatever it's called. If you suspect me of poisoning Elizabeth, why the hell don't you say so, instead of waiting till my back's turned and then snooping about my bedroom, you sordid spy?'

Sir Charles made a face and a sound which indicated teeth on edge, and said, 'Spare me a vulgar scene, Barbara.'

'Spare you a vulgar scene indeed!' cried Bunny. 'Spare me your squalid suspicions!'

'You don't understand,' said Sir Charles. 'You don't begin to understand, Barbara. I've no reason to suspect

73

anyone, but in the case of one's nearest and dearest one's naturally eager to make sure . . . '

'Not "in the case of", please, Charles,' said Bunny, and with that anger left her and she said, 'Poor Charles!'

'What d'you mean?' said Sir Charles sharply.

Bunny couldn't say what she meant, how pathetic, how old, how denuded he'd looked, shorn of his dignity when, like a child found out, he had jumped away from her cupboard: she couldn't say how pathetic he seemed now, trying to lie himself out of a situation impossible to his portrait of himself, though evidently not to him. It wasn't his fault that he believed he could do no wrong. . . . Poor wretch! he'd a code, a code he'd accepted practically in infancy: he knew it, but he didn't know himself; he had thought and felt and spoken and acted according to his code too long. She could never again respect him, but, faintly amused, she could humour him, just as for pity's sake she had humoured the invalid Raoul. Slipping off her coat, sitting down at her dressing-table, picking up a comb and passing it through her tangled curls, she said, 'Poor Charles because of all this worry and because you've a wife you just picked up on the Riviera.' 'I didn't pick you up,' said Sir Charles, affronted. 'We were properly introduced at the Howlands' party. But, Bunny, don't you see – as much for your sake as for mine I wanted to make sure.' Bunny wanted to say: And are you sure now? and then she didn't want to make the poor thing lie again, so she said, 'Yes, I see, Charles. Now buzz off. I want a long, hot bath.'

'I hope the water's hot for you,' said Sir Charles kindly. 'I suppose the hunting party bathed earlier, so I daresay it will be. Don't be too long; come down into the library and we'll have a drink before dinner. I'll tell Hugo and Pat to come too.' And he left the room with the face of a schoolboy surprised and relieved to have escaped with a pi-jaw.

CHAPTER FIVE

The Chief Constable said, 'It's not to-morrow that worries me – obviously we shall get an open verdict; but from then on I simply don't see what line we can follow. Of course, the fact that the ticket-girl can swear that Marvin left with Rose on Sunday evening doesn't let him out; he may well have come back, as Treadwell suggests, by car. However, we shall hear from your chaps to-morrow whether his alibi is as water-tight in London as it seems to be here. Your suspect is another matter. I can't see you getting more than you've got on Lady d'Estray unless someone's actually holding out on you, someone who saw her rooting up the dropwort or stewing it or pouring it into the bottle . . . '

Price took him up. 'One of which actions I think it is more than probable someone did see. The mansion has a great many windows, which overlook the fields by the river where I imagine this water-loving plant would be located; they are also overlooked by the terrace. I anticipate questioning the outside staff to-morrow' – 'You won't get much out of old Perry' put in Treadwell – 'and there are several junior members of the indoor staff, whom I have not yet interviewed. Young people, being more alert mentally than older ones, are more apt to look about them while they work. Furthermore, as a result of the superior education now provided, they are quicker to perceive the relevancy of what they observe.'

'Oh, that's what education does for them, is it? I always wondered,' said the Chief Constable innocently. 'Well, good luck to you, Price; but I don't think it was Lady d'Estray. I don't think the motive's strong enough.'

Price said, 'The only individual with a stronger motive is Mr Hugo d'Estray, and the lawyer, Mr Jardine, assured me that he could have had no prior knowledge of the will. At the time it was drawn up the deceased expressed her opinion that the prospect of inheriting money is detrimental to a young man's character and she was determined that Mr Hugo should remain in ignorance of her intentions.''

'Well, Hugo was never my bet,' said the Colonel. 'My money's on one of those dam' paying guests. Old Hudson had a tongue like a knife and I think she snubbed one of them once too often. Not much of a motive, perhaps, but the chap – or the lady – may have had homicidal tendencies anyway. What do we know about any of them?'

'They seem perfectly on the level,' said Price defensively. 'Mr Scampnell is connected with a well-known firm of manufacturers. Mr Rose, of course, is of the Jewish persuasion, but his firm – Rosenbaum and Steingletscher, the hatters – have been established for many years: they have spacious premises in the vicinity of Ludgate Hill. If his son were unreliable it is unlikely that he would be retained in the capacity of business manager, and in any case Mr Rose assures me that his conduct has never caused his parents a moment's anxiety.'

Treadwell said, 'Then that only leaves us Marvin.'

'And we shall hear about him to-morrow,' said the Chief Constable, pushing back his chair, 'so we might as well get home to our nosebags. Are you tolerably comfortable at the Red Lion, Inspector? I'm told that the bath-water's hot, which is the main thing.'

'It was certainly unnecessarily hot this morning,' Price told him. 'I've no doubt that later in the year the management will be complaining that their allocation of fuel is insufficient for their requirements. I suppose these old-fashioned places are difficult to run, but surely some effort could be made to furnish them tastefully and introduce a few of the ordinary amenities of modern life. I slept badly. Sagging springs and a lumpy mattress are hardly conducive to restful slumber.'

'I have the advantage of you there,' said the Colonel cheerily. 'I can sleep on anything – got used to that in the trenches during the Old War. Eat anything too – even what my wife cooks, ha-ha-ha. . . . '

And that's a strange way for a man to speak of his wife, thought Price, who, to sustain his portrait of himself, must believe that Valerie was the best cook as well as the cleverest

76

manager and the smartest little woman in Finchley. In point of fact Valerie, like most women in love with cleanliness, was an atrocious cook, and excess of starch and lack of grease in her husband's diet were manifest in the mirror-fronted Bluebeard's cupboard of aperients, which, with a cork-seated receptacle for soiled linen, furnished their tin-tiled bathroom.

The Chief Constable and the Superintendent left the police station together and Price drove back to the Red Lion and ate tinned soup, a potato pie of sausage meat, and a stale slice of plain cake, over which had been poured strawberry jam made of marrows, and custard made of dehydrated milk and custard powder: he did not criticize the meal, for so, at a time and in a state that he intensely admired, are the fruits of earth represented, but he was exasperated by the slowness of the service: it was nearly bedtime when he settled down in the dismally deserted lounge to smoke one of his rare cigarettes and ponder his note-book. He wasn't an obstinate man and he was able to bring a fresh mind to his problem, but at the end of an hour's thought he summed up again: *her ladyship*, and as he turned and twisted through the night he found some comfort in the supposition that on the box mattress of the French marquetry bed in the frivolous pink room, which he had wasted half an hour in searching, Lady d'Estray was tossing in an anguish worse than that, or than pins and needles, or the cramp, which several times seized, alarmingly distorted, and transfixed his big toe.

He erred. He forgot that Lady d'Estray was Barbara Sallust. Harassed, betrayed, and perhaps in danger of hanging, Bunny's reaction was to express herself, and the toil and the joy of finding and stringing the words into lines good enough to send the authentic shiver down her back drove all personal anxiety from her mind. It's the best thing I've ever written, she thought, laying down the chewed pencil and the crumpled envelope, punching her pillows, turning off the light; and she slept soundly and dreamlessly until Beatrice brought in her breakfast at eight o'clock.

Then it was raining. Gusts of wind blew the rain against

77

the windows and shabby leaves were flying from the oak trees in the park. Sir Charles came in and, apparently as unaware that his wife could no longer respect him as he was ignorant that immortal lines, inspired by his perfidy, lay on the bedside table, said that the inquest was at noon and that it would be best to wear something darkish. Bunny said that the black dress she had worn yesterday would do, wouldn't it? and Sir Charles said she needn't necessarily wear black – he really meant something longish. Bunny said she couldn't start letting hems down now and Sir Charles said he hadn't asked her to let down hems: he simply meant that a Coroner's Court wasn't a *place* on the Riviera. 'Worse luck,' said Bunny, suddenly gripped by nostalgia for the pink villa, the great blue mountains, the idle little port, the shiny sea. Breakfast on the terrace . . . coffee and peaches . . . Jean-Paul Bartoli splashing saffron paint on the oars of his emerald green fishing boat . . . Justin, wet as a seal, coming back over the red rocks from bathing . . . Marie-Louise Arnotin singing as she mopped the terrace of the Poisson d'Or . . . what's your secret, France, for all that is so very little and often the sun shines in England and there are peaches and there's coffee, though, however you make it, it never tastes the same? It was the Reformation, thought Bunny, and she said, 'Charles – the Reformation – that's when England went wrong.'

Sir Charles at one time had been amused by her flights of fancy, but now he said, 'What on earth are you talking about? We can't start discussing history at this time in the morning with an inquest coming off at twelve. You've been sub-poenaed, so you'll be questioned, Barbara. You don't want to hesitate and contradict yourself. You'd better consider carefully what you mean to say.'

Bunny said, 'Do I usually hesitate and contradict myself? What's eating you, Charles?' She looked him in the eye, and he turned away. 'Oh, well, if you won't be advised . . . ' he said, and left the room.

The Reformation . . . thought Bunny.

Sir Charles drove the family car into Harborough, and with him went Bunny, Patricia, Nanny, and Beatrice;

78

behind them went what Patricia disdainfully described as 'a carload of rubber necks' – Sidney Rose, driving his wife and the Scampnells. Bunny, looking more than a little odd in a dark grey coat and skirt and a felt hat borrowed from Sybella, felt talkative, but Patricia said that she had had enough of the Reformation at St Olaf's, and Nanny and Beatrice, whether out of respect for the dead or apprehension of the ordeal before them, confined themselves to whispered monosyllables and short forced laughs. Sir Charles drove in silence. On enquiring where on earth Bunny's rig-out had come from, he had seemed both surprised and annoyed that it was borrowed. 'One just doesn't do these things,' he had angrily muttered and he hadn't spoken to her again.

He came into the court-room looking very pale and severe after identifying the body, and though Bunny made room for him beside her, he sat down by Patricia, and Jardine came over and whispered to them, and Bunny thought that at such moments one knows where one gets off and knew that to the common man and woman, though they bought her books and begged for her autograph and pretended to be a friend of hers when they had really only met her in a fish queue or in the train, she was and would always be exiled from their intimacy, being an oddity, a conjuror of something out of nothing, a creator, presumptuous and strange. With treachery you could conform to their standards; with infinite pains you could imitate their behaviour; you could bottle fruit, watch cricket, and hunt the fox; but they'd smell you out, as of old they smelt out witches, and then they'd put on a face for you, and behind the face was a wariness, never the open silly hearts that they showed to their own kind.

Sir Charles's voice affirming that his cousin was sixty-eight years of age, had no financial trouble, no enemies that he knew of; that she had retired to bed apparently in her usual excellent state of health and spirits on the night of Monday, October the twelfth, woke Bunny from her irrelevant daydream. The Coroner, a precise grey little man, whom you'd have summed up as 'type of all that's dullest in the British' if you hadn't heard of the prodigies of valour performed by

him during the brief unreasonable and devastating Harborough blitz, had little more to ask Sir Charles, and he was
replaced by Beatrice, tight-faced and trembling. Her story
was dragged from her, question by question. Nanny, in her
turn, was more voluble: with a person lying dead on the bed
you didn't bother your head about whisky bottles and tum-
blers; no, she hadn't suspected foul play: there was no one
you could suspect at the Park, but before Miss Hudson came
there to live she had had nearly seventy years in which to
make enemies. Then Bunny was called. On the morning of
Tuesday the thirteenth she had been wakened by the last
witness, who told her that Miss Hudson was dead. She went
with her to Miss Hudson's room and found her – er – dead.
No, she hadn't noticed if there was a tumbler on the bedside
table, but, as Miss Hudson always drank a nightcap of
whisky and water, it must have been there. 'I agreed with
Nanny – Miss Toomer – that Miss Hudson was – er – dead,'
said Bunny, 'and then I went to call my husband and he got
up and telephoned Dr Hope-Johnstone. . . . No, I never
heard that she had an enemy but I haven't known her long
or intimately . . . Well, my own relationship with her was
quite ordinary. We hadn't much in common but I took her as
I found her – she was my husband's cousin and one of our
paying guests.'

Dr Hope-Johnstone was the next witness. Death had been
due to poisoning by oenanthotoxin, obtained by some rough-
and-ready method from the root of the *Oenanthe crocata* or
water dropwort. Death from this poison had been known to
take place in such varying times as five minutes and eleven
days. In his opinion Miss Hudson had passed away between
one and two o'clock on the Tuesday morning. Yes, he had
been a little surprised that nothing had been heard by the
other members of the household during the night – among the
symptoms of oenanthotoxin poisoning was delirium and
gastroenteric disturbance – but he had noticed that the bedroom doors at the Park were of solid mahogany and he
understood that Miss Hudson was a lady of determined
character and not likely to call or ring for help. No, the taste of

the whisky would not be bitter: the root of the *Oenanthe crocata* had been eaten in mistake for parsnip; there would be a taste, but the deceased might have gulped down the whisky or possibly she had just brushed her teeth; they were her own and he had noticed that she used a strong germicide.

The Coroner summed up the evidence and delivered himself of the verdict of murder by a person or persons unknown. The proceedings had taken less than an hour. 'That doesn't seem to have got us any forrader,' said Bunny, as the car waited at the traffic lights where the highroad crossed the undistinguished market square. 'It wasn't meant to,' said Sir Charles irritably. 'Before the coroners' powers were curtailed, inquests were a bugbear to the police – under an officious man all sorts of evidence came out before they were ready for it.' 'But,' said Bunny, 'wasn't that more English – more "playing the game"?' The light turned green; Sir Charles ground his gears horribly and the car stalled and refused to start till the light was against them again. 'That was your fault, Barbara,' said Sir Charles through his teeth, because of the servants. 'Dam' silly thing to say. You want to see justice done, don't you?' 'If I knew it was justice . . .' 'That sort of half-baked high-brow talk,' said Sir Charles between his teeth still, 'annoys me.'

They drove home in silence. Price's small blue car had passed them at the traffic lights and was considerately parked under the windows of the dining-room. Bunny sighed, 'I suppose we must give him lunch again. It's already a moot point whether those three old boiling hens will go round.' 'Of course we must give him lunch,' said Sir Charles, always inclined to suspect his half-French wife of cheese-paring. But Price, discovered in the walled garden where he was attempting to interrogate Perry's deaf-and-dumb assistant, Clarence Reed, replied that he would lunch in Harborough – he wouldn't be troubling them at the Park, he said, that afternoon. 'I bet he's going to have a conference with his chief before arresting someone,' said Bunny, whose spirits, dashed by Sir Charles's admonishments, had been revived by the spectacle of the self-confident Price helpless in the face of rustic inanity. 'Only, of course, he would call it "prior to concluding the case".' 'How do you know what he'd call it?' said Sir Charles, still apparently in a state of nervous irritability. 'We poor bloody authors know that kind of thing,' said Bunny. 'No need to tell us the story of your lives or to make a face for us; one look, and we know just what nasty little boys you were at your prep schools and how you felt the first time you tipped a butler and what in your heart of hearts you really think of your wives.' 'It's easy to make a claim like that,' Sir Charles snubbed her, 'but all the time you're probably quite wrong.'

Bunny was right, however, in so far that during the afternoon Price reported progress to his chief, but he was not yet ready to speak of 'concluding the case,' and was further discouraged by a summing up very similar to that which he had impatiently heard last night from the Chief Constable: *not much to go upon. . . . Unless some new evidence turns up and why should it? . . . Difficult to see what line to follow. . . .* Later in the evening, in a characterless flat at Earl's Court, he interviewed Geoffrey Marvin, blue-eyed, golden-haired, and perfectly candid. His alibi in London had been checked and found satisfactory and Price only asked for any light he could throw on the situation. Marvin told his story. He had met the deceased in Ireland. They were staying at the same hotel and they got into conversation and . . . well, she was a queer old girl and no picture, but she had seemed to understand how bloody civilian life was after the Service. She had persuaded him to take up riding; there was a thrill to be got out of hunting, she promised him, though he hadn't found it; and she had kept in touch with him, and when she had settled down at Aston Park she had invited him there to get some cub-hunting and at the same time to try out country life with a view to farming. 'Like a lot of these old girls, she was a bit on the domineering side,' said Marvin chattily. 'She'd made up her mind that I should join up with Hugo d'Estray, but I'd no intention of doing so. He's a stick, that character, and anyhow I'd decided against farming – too slow.' 'Had you communicated your decision to the deceased?' Price asked him, and Marvin said no; it was dull down at Aston but it was comfortable, the food was wizard, and the old girl liked having him: he had intended to stop there until he found a job he fancied, but now . . . Price asked if Miss Hudson's death hadn't cleared the way for him: hadn't he anticipated unpleasantness ensuing from his decision to dissociate himself with the plans she had made? Marvin said good lord no; she'd no claim on him, and Price asked if he had anticipated any legacy and Marvin said good lord no; he was a comparatively new acquaintance and there were all the d'Estrays without a cent between them. Price told him that Miss Hudson had left her horse to him and Marvin said good lord! and oh well, he must talk to Pat – perhaps she'd buy the brute from him. Then Price asked if Marvin had noticed any antipathies between any members of the d'Estrays' household, and Marvin said it was common talk that there was no love lost between Miss Hudson and Lady d'Estray and that he had heard a row going on between Miss Hudson and the kid, Lisa; Hugo, Sir Charles, and Patricia were, he felt sure, devoted to their cousin, and with the exception of Mrs Scampnell, her rival in the hunting-field, the paying guests put up with her rudeness for snobbish reasons and let off steam by laughing at her behind her back.

Price said, 'Well, that confirms all I've heard,' and was about to take his leave when Marvin's mother came in and, on being introduced to Detective-Inspector Price, surmised that he had come about Geoffrey's horrid old Miss Hudson. Stout and smart, with grey hair tightly curled, rings on her fingers and snowy frills cascading down the lapels of her neat black suit, she was almost Price's ideal of an elderly lady; motherly, but no dowd; a little foolish and on deep or difficult subjects glad of a man's opinion, but capable of coping with the mechanics of life and of following her own interests – bridge, matinees, an occasional dress-show – suitable interests for her age and sex.

Price asked Joan Marvin if she had been with her son when he met Miss Hudson in Ireland, and she said no, and told Geoffrey to go and mix them all a little drink, and when

he had gone she said no again; if she had been with Geoffrey, Miss Hudson would never have got hold of him. 'Horse-faced old thing,' she said angrily, and Price, who, believing that every mother idolized her son, had sustained throughout his married life a fiction that his mother was insanely jealous of Valerie, began to wonder whether he hadn't stumbled on a motive stronger than any he had found at Aston Park. He was not to be influenced by a pink, plump face, forget-me-not-blue eyes, and tiny hands; it was Joan Marvin's 'normalcy' that he found in her favour and he would have been amazed to hear that there were people – Bunny d'Estray among them – who would sum up as sheer madness her life of walking round shops when she'd nothing to buy, wearing shoes that pinched and a corselet that suffocated her, wracking her brains at card-tables, doing, thinking, saying nothing that was not as well undone, unthought, unsaid. All the same, mother-love was a strong and quite un-reasonable emotion and it would be as well to make sure . . .
'Now, Mrs Marvin, just a few routine questions: your son tells me that he spent Sunday evening with friends of yours at Surbiton.'

'That's right – with the Taylors – very nice people. I had accepted an invitation, and I had simply to drag Geoffrey. There are some nice girls there too, and they made a great fuss of him, and I'm sure he must have enjoyed himself, though he pretended he didn't.'

'And Monday?'

'Well, on Monday we were both rather late getting up. I let Geoffrey lie till twelve o'clock and then we went up west and had lunch at the Troc and went on to a matinee of *Bless the Bride*. Ever so pretty it was, at least I thought so, but Geoffrey wasn't struck on it. We had tea in the theatre – don't they charge for it? – and some supper when we got home and I invited the couple from the flat above to come in for coffee and a rubber of bridge – nice people retired from India, but Geoffrey didn't care for them much.' She stopped suddenly and stared. 'You're not . . . you don't . . . you're not asking me all this because you suspect Geoffrey of anything?'

Price said, 'We suspect everyone who ever came into contact with the deceased, Mrs Marvin, but, with the exception of young Mr Rose, your son is the only member of the Aston Park household who can supply us with an alibi, and I called here to-day because I hoped he might have been taken into the confidence of the deceased, particularly with reference to any enemies she might have possessed. What is hindering us is lack of adequate motive,' he went on as Marvin, bearing a small tray of very small cocktails, came back into the room. 'Many people disliked Miss Hudson, but as a motive for murder dislike can hardly be said to meet the case.'

'Who has she left her money to?' asked Joan Marvin. 'Or is it very naughty of me to ask you that?'

'Except for her horse and saddlery, which go to the Flight-Lieutenant, everything has been left to Mr Hugo d'Estray.'

Joan Marvin said, 'I should suspect him then. But whatever will you do with a horse, Geoffrey? They're such awkward things to keep.'

Price set down his glass. 'I'll leave you to discuss that knotty problem.' He rose. 'I suppose you'll be staying in London, Flight-Lieutenant?'

'That's right,' said Joan Marvin.

'I shall have to go down to Aston, Mother,' said Geoffrey. 'I've left most of my gear there, and then there's this horse business, and I suppose I ought to show up at the funeral, whenever it is.' 'It will take place to-morrow afternoon,' Price told him. 'I'll go down to-morrow morning then,' Marvin decided. 'And I daresay I'll stay over the week-end.' 'Oh, Geoffrey, surely now Miss Hudson's gone . . . ' protested his mother. 'Well, Mother, I've got to fix things up, haven't I?' said Geoffrey irritably, and then, 'Will you be there, Inspector?' but Price couldn't tell him. This interview had got him nowhere; the Marvins were both beyond suspicion; it was a million to one against picking up anything if he turned the only stone he'd left unturned and went gossiping round Hugo d'Estray's dog-kennels and in the village. But there *was* that chance and, 'Yes, I shall have to get back there,' he told Valerie as they sat in the dining-recess eating a substitute for macaroni, covered with a sauce made from dehydrated milk and faintly flavoured with cheese fit for mousetraps, and he sighed, 'Nothing to look at but cows and cabbages, nothing to hear but the rain dripping off the trees – it's all very well to spend a day in the country, but you've no idea how stopping there gets you down. . . . '

CHAPTER SIX

On Friday October the sixteenth Elizabeth Hudson was buried in the churchyard at Aston. With her will she had left a sheet of paper directing, '*My funeral to be very simple – no hearse or mutes – only garden flowers – a farm wagon if possible,*' and the d'Estrays carried out her wishes: she went to her rest in a yellow wagon piled with Michaelmas daisies and drawn by two shire horses, and behind the wagon Patricia led Brutus with an empty saddle. Hugo brought his hounds to the gate of the churchyard and blew the 'gone away' when the service was over, and though Ronald Price wasn't a Christian, he thought it all very shocking. The villagers, however, didn't agree with him; they said it was nice to see the 'ounds and things done as they used to be; they said that the d'Estrays were good people and it was a shame they should be done away with; they reckoned that Miss Hudson had been poisoned by one of them paying guests from London. They spoke with reserve, knowing who Price was, but being puzzled by his manner; because they were country folks – to him a cross between a cow and cabbage – on addressing them he raised his light voice to its loudest, grinned like a Cheshire cat, gripped their hands ferociously, beat his leg with a stick, asked how 'the crops' did, opined that rain was needed. At the kennels, hounds, breathing fish, leaped up at him, soiled his suit, clawed his tie, knocked his nose and set it bleeding; the kennelman was affability itself, even showing him the most disgusting sight he'd ever seen – the skinning-shed. For his pains he learned that Hugo d'Estray was a grand sportsman, a real gentleman, and the finest amateur huntsman in the land.

At the Park the rest of the day passed quietly. The family retired into the west wing, leaving the guests free to discuss the funeral. Cecily Scampnell, with tears in her eyes, said that it had been topping and hoped that her husband or Margot would give her just such a send-off when her time came to gallop on. Henry Scampnell said that it wasn't every parson who would allow it; the d'Estrays, of course, had the Rector in their pocket. Margot thought that the blowing of the horn was just a little irreverent. Sidney Rose agreed absolutely with Mrs Scampnell, but Mrs Rose thought that garden flowers, though a nice idea, looked poor. Geoffrey Marvin angrily said, what the hell! plenty of blokes had had to do without funerals during the war, whereat Sybella Rose said she couldn't agree more, only if you did have a ceremony, you didn't want people to think that you'd grudged money, and if you used your own farm wagon it did look as though you were saving money on a motor hearse. Sidney Rose retorted that he had read quite lately about a Duke or an Earl whose coffin had been taken to the church on a farm cart, and Margot said she thought it was just a little theatrical, and her mother said what rot, Margot, if people liked simple country things and had spent their lives among them, the least you could do was to see that they jolly well had them at the end. She left the room abruptly, and her husband excused her. 'She's taking this hard, you know. I expect that you, like Margot and myself, were often amused by the rivalry between our two Dianas, but I honestly believe that in a queer way of their own they were fond of one another.'

'I can quite believe that,' said Sidney Rose, looking up from his newspaper. 'There's a lot more in huntin' than killin' a fox, you know. One of its greatest joys is the sense of companionship. Hackin' home after a good day, you're a band of brothers.' He thought of his dropped 'gs': at last they're beginning to come quite naturally.

Scampnell said, 'Then you'd hardly consider it possible that Miss Hudson was poisoned by a member of the hunting fraternity?'

Sybella didn't give her husband time to answer. She said, 'I don't consider it possible that she was poisoned by a member of this household. I think it was a groom or someone like that, whom she'd dismissed, or had sent to prison, and he nursed a grudge against her, and when he came out of prison he found out where she lived and somehow managed to creep into the house and up to her bedroom. Perhaps he managed to get friendly with one of the maids and she let him into the house and now she daren't own up to it.'

'Sybella, what tripe have you been readin'?' asked Sidney Rose.

'I think it's quite a feasible explanation,' said Henry Scampnell, showing his well-kept false teeth as he smiled reassuringly at Sybella. 'I'm sure we'd all prefer it to turn out that way, anyhow. What I think the Inspector has in mind, besides being very distressing, would mean the end of our pleasant life here – at least, I suppose so.'

'I'm sure it would,' said Sidney Rose. 'She really runs the whole show – I believe it was her idea to start with. The rest of the family would simply have drifted. By the way, I suppose we're talkin' about the same person?'

Scampnell said, 'Well, in my case the questions the Inspector asked showed quite plainly whom he suspected. Then I believe that he was particularly interested in the upstairs pantry and the hot drinks that were made for us up there last winter.'

'He asked me about them,' said Sybella. 'But I just told him that I *knew* it wasn't Bunny. He . . .'

Her husband interrupted her. 'Now, Sybella – no names, no pack drill.'

'I can't see that it's any worse to mention names than to hint, as you've been doing. Anyhow, I'm saying that it *wasn't* Bunny. She's outspoken, sometimes she's even rude, but people who poison people are sly people – I've always been thought a good judge of character.'

'By whom?' asked her husband.

'Lots of people.'

'Give us the names of some of them.'

'If you don't mind my saying so, Mrs Rose,' said Scampnell, 'your championship of Lady d'Estray, admirable though it is, misses the point, because neither your husband nor I intimated in the least that we suspected her. We were referring to the Inspector's suspicions.'

Then Margot Rattray, who had been quietly knitting,

intervened. 'Scamp!' This was her name for him. 'Don't you think it's a wee bit silly to discuss poor Miss Hudson's death? The detective's working on it – time will show – we're all such good friends now – it would be a tremendous pity . . .'

Her stepfather said, 'Upon my word, the wise little woman's right. I suggest we make the subject taboo among us. One can't help thinking, of course, and in the still watches of the night I find myself planning – for instance, should the case be shelved, will one feel like staying on here? I doubt if one would find better food anywhere in England; in that respect either Lady d'Estray or her cook is a genius, and my wife tells me that she's perfectly satisfied with the way Miss d'Estray runs the hunting side of the business. By the way, Margot and I thought of going to the meet to-morrow, and we can squash three into the back seat if any of you would like to come along. But it means early rising . . .'

And Cecily Scampnell, some twenty hours later, thought really it's hard lines . . . one child and I nearly died of her, and she comes to a meet in a car, whines about the cold, and refuses cherry brandy because it might make her feel 'funny'. *Fair girls . . . who never went wide of a fence or a kiss* – that's the kind of daughter I should have had, and I got Margot – dumpy frumpy Margot, always indoors with her knitting. When I was her age I'd been married ten years . . . the finest horsewoman in British India, according to H.H., the biggest flirt, so Jack said, that night at Simla. If only I'd gone away with him – or even with 'Copper' Carruthers – instead of waiting till Basil died and there was no one but Henry – twirpy chirpy Henry, fussing over his ingrowing toenail and whether or not to change into his winter pants, namby-pamby Henry, who doesn't know one end of a gee from the other . . . neither he nor dumpy, frumpy Margot are company for a dare-devil like me. Consciously now, she was missing Elizabeth Hudson: Patricia kept with young friends; Sidney Rose hung back; young Marvin, though he'd said he was coming and had let Patricia get his horse ready for him, had stayed in bed; all along he'd merely been bossed into riding. Elizabeth had been irritating; she had bored one stiff with her obstinate championship of such old-fashioned notions as the backward seat, nagging, the dumb jockey; but she had been company in a first flight, otherwise composed of indifferent young people. There was a group of them now, coffee-housing quietly enough at the corner of the beechwood; Cecily herself had turned fidgety Quiver into a broad ride, carpeted with fallen leaves of orange-brown, spanned by the pewter-grey branches of the beeches, through which fell pale shafts of sunshine from the October sky of mild Cerulean blue. If Elizabeth Hudson hadn't been dead she would have been here on Brutus standing like a statue; Quiver would have stood instead of jigging about, throwing her head up, pawing the leaves, running backwards; and Elizabeth wouldn't have been jabbering about dances and Swiss holidays and the New Look: she would have been listening . . .

A hound spoke. Both Quiver and her rider stiffened, but it was nothing – a babbling young hound, perhaps, after a squirrel. With a horse's inexplicable change of mood, Quiver now elected to stand still, and Cecily thought of her sandwiches – the wafer-thin ham sandwiches which Bunny somehow contrived to provide for the fox-hunters. This was no time to open a sandwich case, but it was Cecily's habit, when she filled her case from the pile conveniently set on the sideboard at breakfast on hunting mornings, to place a couple in an envelope, which she then carried in her pocket. She ate these now, and before she moved on down the ride uncorked her flask and took a drink of the claret about which she had so often argued with the whisky-loving Elizabeth. She had barely replaced the stopper when another hound spoke. 'Rambler,' she said aloud, and no voice irritatingly but companionably argued that it wasn't Rambler, but Ranger. That Rambler never lied was reaffirmed by a burst of hound music. Cecily gathered up her reins, and it scarcely needed the light pressure of her calves to send the eager mare off at a canter.

The ride petered out among the rhododendrons where hounds had found their fox, and beyond the rhododendrons was a road, and across the road a wood of mixed trees and tangled undergrowth, through which hounds were hunting slowly. Cecily checked the mare, looked behind her and found that she was alone; she guessed that the rest of the Field, having preferred to the beechwood the tempting pasture which lay to windward of it, were now endeavouring to extract themselves from a birdcage of electric fencing, which she had met with before and had had the sense to memorize. Silly fools! she thought, but her pleasure in her superior wits was dimmed by a sudden and surprising nausea. They're running, she thought, hearing Hugo blow them away, and I'm going to be sick. . . . I shall miss it. Quiver had heard the horn too; she threw her head up, found it free and set off at a gallop. Cecily Scampnell, wheeling darkness before her eyes, swayed this way and that until she slipped from the saddle.

*

Hugo d'Estray heard a horse galloping behind him and looked round to curse the bloody fool who in a couple of seconds would be over-riding his hounds. He saw Quiver riderless, thought, the old girl's taken a toss, and on the other side of a stake-and-bound fence was relieved to find that the mare hadn't followed him. Three minutes later Patricia jumped Huntsman over a hurdle into the field and shouted to a friend, 'Oh hell, loose horse, and one of mine too.' Quiver, stirrups flying, reins trailing, galloped towards the other horses and Patricia complaining, 'That's the end of my hunt – damn paying guests,' pulled up, while the mare trotted to her stable companion. Sidney Rose, hanging on Sir Roger's mouth in nervous anticipation of the stake-and-bound, shouted, 'I hope Mrs Scampnell's all right,' as he went by, and then Patricia was alone in the field except for a young man on a magnificent thoroughbred, which was steadily refusing the jump. 'Can't get the brute over,' he said with a forced laugh, and Patricia said, 'You didn't happen to see where the woman, who was riding this mare, came off, did you?' The young man said, 'I'm afraid not. What do you think is the matter with this brute?' and Patricia said,

'Nothing, I should think. I should think it's the way you're riding him. She's an elderly woman in a coloured tie, yellow with red spots. I can't for the life of me remember when I last saw her.' 'I expect she'll be along,' said the young man disinterestedly. 'Couldn't you tie her horse up somewhere? I'm sure if you gave me a lead this brute would go over.' Patricia said, 'No, I can't. For all I know she may have broken her neck. I shall have to go back and look for her.' Leading Quiver, she cantered back across the field and jumped both horses neatly over the hurdles.

She retraced then the way the Field had taken and came to the road which Cecily Scampnell had crossed between the beechwood and the wood where she was lying. From the road Patricia could look across the 'birdcage'; surely if Cecily had been with the Field there she would have had something to say which would have made one aware of her presence. And if she hadn't been with the Field, Patricia reasoned, she would have been as near as she could get to Hugo and hounds: Hugo had often complained that while she and Elizabeth never overstepped the mark, it was irritating to see them always being clever. Cecily must have come through the beechwood, Patricia thought on, and she must have waited in the ride while Hugo drew the rhododendrons; and on the thought she turned her horses up the road and almost immediately came upon a set of hoof-prints smaller, she thought, than those of Hugo's big Sportsman. The same prints continued into the farther wood, but for all one knew the mare might already have been riderless when she crossed the road, and it would save time, Patricia decided, if she searched the beechwood. Calling cheerfully, for she had seen dozens of tosses, of which no harm had come, she skirted the rhododendrons and cantered up the ride, where she found, as well as Quiver's hoof-prints, larger ones, obviously Sportman's. But there was no sign of the disgruntled figure ploughing along among the leaves which her mind's eye gave her; no voice answered her calling; and presently she rode out of the wood into the sunny stubble where the Field had waited. Oh well, it was a fifty-fifty chance, she told herself, and turned back; the Scampnell will be livid if she's hoping to see any more of hounds this morning, but I've had it too – silly old bitch, she's spoilt my hunt . . . but I suppose she thinks that's what I'm paid for. Patricia swung round the rhododendrons, clattered across the road and pulled up to follow the hoof-prints less easily here among the brambles and bracken. 'Mrs Scampnell!' she called now and then, and was almost through the wood when she saw the body stretched out motionless on the brown fern. 'Hell!' she said, and dismounted, and with the reins over her arm would have run forward, but the horses thought otherwise. They jibbed, threw up their heads and snorted, and there was nothing that Patricia could do but take off her gloves, unbuckle the reins and tie the horses to a tree, where you could be practically certain they would tangle their legs in the reins and break their bridles.

Patricia was young, unimaginative, and optimistic. She spoke to the dead woman, lifted the lolling head, loosened the red and yellow hunting tie and took off her own coat and laid it across the knees, before the thought of death stopped her heart for a suffocating second and sent it racing on. Then she felt for the pulse and found none, but perhaps she was feeling the wrong place, so, lacking a mirror, she took out her silver cigarette case, held it to the purplish lips, withdrew it unclouded and knew that Cecily Scampnell was dead. Oh well, she was old, thought Patricia; in a few years she would have died of cancer or a stroke or something; and with her heart beating normally she walked to the edge of the wood and there was no one and no house in sight; but now she realized where she was, and knew that under the line of elms bordering the field beyond the stake-and-bound fence a lane led from the highroad to one of Lord Badgemoor's farms. She went back into the wood for the horses and had barely freed their forelegs from the expected tangle of reins when she heard the short note of Hugo's horn calling his hounds to him. Leading the horses, who had heard the horn too and danced behind her, she hurried out of the wood again and there was Hugo, the first whipper-in and hounds coming through a gate over on her left, and the chattering Field behind them.

Patricia was discreet enough not to shout her news. She waited till her brother was near and then, 'There's been an accident,' she told him. 'It's Mrs Scampnell, and she's dead. Where's Hope-Johnstone?' Hugo turned in his saddle and scanned the Field. 'There he is. Doctor! Here, a moment.' The group of riders parted and Hope-Johnstone rode forward on his big grey heavyweight hunter. 'Pat's got a corpse for you,' said Hugo and dismounted. 'Here, somebody, hold these horses.'

Patricia led the way into the wood. 'There she is! The bracken's so trampled it looks as though Quiver came down,' she said to her brother as the doctor bent over the body. 'Is she really dead?' asked Hugo. 'Yes, she's dead all right – been dead for half an hour or so,' said Hope-Johnstone. Hugo said, 'This *would* happen when the Master's in bed with lumbago. I suppose I'd better take hounds home – I was on my way back to the rhododendrons. I'll go and tell the Field that we're packing up – no use keeping the silly fools standing there.' Like most huntsmen, Hugo loathed his Field, and seldom alluded to it save in terms of opprobrium.

Hope-Johnstone said, 'Yes, for God's sake get rid of them. There's no need to tell them about this – if you go home, they will; but if they ask, tell them there's been a slight accident. But send me someone reliable – we must find a telephone and get the police here before we move her. I don't like it. It's dam' queer, Hugo.'

'You don't mean to say that it's poison again?' asked Hugo, and Patricia gasped, 'Oh, *no*.'

'It looks to me like it,' said the doctor. 'Anyhow, don't breathe a word of that. I may be wrong. Let's see, who is there?'

'Colonel Rivett-Bankes was about earlier,' said Patricia, and the doctor said, 'Of course, I saw him just now. Send him along, Hugo, but do it unobtrusively.' Hugo set off and Patricia asked, 'Is it the same poison?' but only got, 'My dear child, with all my talents I can't see inside people,' and

95

then the doctor hummed and remarked on the beauty of the autumn colouring until Colonel Rivett-Bankes came crashing into the wood on his brown dock-tailed cob. He said, 'Good God! Broken her neck, has she?' and the doctor said, 'Patricia, you'll want to get your horses home, but mind, you're not to say anything about this to anyone but Sir Charles or Lady d'Estray.' Patricia, though she felt aggrieved – for it was she, wasn't it? who had found the body – offered, 'Shall I take Justice too?' and the doctor said, 'Thanks very much, Pat. If you'll take him back to your place I'll collect him later.' Patricia walked out of the wood. Hugo, the hunt servants and hounds were gone, but some of the Field stayed chattering and wondering while they ate their sandwiches, and though Patricia walked briskly to the spot where somebody's groom was holding Quiver and Huntsman and the doctor's Justice, acquaintances hurried after her to ask, 'Who is it?' 'Is it serious?' and offer, 'I was a V.A.D. . . . ' and Patricia was obliged to answer sourly, 'I don't know how bad it is. The doctor's there and everything's under control.' Patricia was not popular in the county: though she wasn't disdainful, she looked it, and she had yet to discard the snubbing manner of St Olaf's; so the acquaintances fell back, disliking her more than ever, and she was able to mount in silence and ride away. And after an eight-miles hack home with a murder to think about and three quarrelling horses to manage, she felt not at all averse to snubbing Lisa, who, with the exception of the dull-witted stable-boy, Jimmy Funge, was by fortunate chance the only member of the household whom she encountered when at long last she rode into the stableyard. 'Hullo, have you killed the Scampnell?' asked Lisa gaily. 'Instead of standing there and asking dam' silly questions, why don't you come and take one of these dam' fools of horses?' Patricia said.

Despite his raincoat, Ronald Price had shivered in the wood; he had sneezed twice in the police car on the way to the mortuary; his socks were torn by brambles; burrs clung to the legs of his trousers; his cuff was stained green where it had been slobbered on by the Chief Constable's hunter; and, sitting now with damp feet, risking pneumonia, he was in no mood to consider the sensibilities of Sir Charles d'Estray's drawling daughter. 'Now, Miss d'Estray,' he snapped, 'the motive for this second murder sticks out a mile. What knowledge did Mrs Scampnell possess which made her dangerous to Miss Hudson's murderer?'

'I haven't a clue,' said Patricia.

'You were expecting something to happen to her,' said Price, 'or why else did you go in search of the body?'

'If you're hunting,' said Patricia as though to a half-wit, 'and you find a riderless horse careering about, you catch it and naturally you return it to its rider. If he or she is not about, you wonder what's happened to him or her, and you try to find out, because sometimes there are accidents. I wasn't exactly responsible for Mrs Scampnell because she's ridden all her life and she would have been furious if I had fussed after her – Mr Rose is a novice and I'm teaching him, so that's different. All the same, Mrs Scampnell lives here and she was riding one of my horses, so if she had taken a toss I was the obvious person to look after her.'

Price said, 'Well, that's as it may be, Miss d'Estray, but there can be no doubt now that these murders have been committed by a member of this household – no outsider can have had the opportunity to tamper with the contents of Mrs Scampnell's flask. When she was going hunting, it was her habit to leave it overnight in the butler's pantry: he filled it in the morning and placed it beside the sandwiches on the sideboard in the dining-room. No doubt you would all be immensely relieved if these crimes could be traced to a servant, but in the case of the butler the absence of motive is strengthened by the fact that no individual of average mental development would formulate a plan so likely to bring himself under suspicion.'

Patricia said indignantly, 'I can't imagine why you think we want to pin it on the servants. They've all been here for years – Benny and Nanny and Beatrice and Mrs Capes – and they're part of the family. If it must be someone inside the house, we'd rather it was the paying guests than the servants.'

'That's an unusual point of view,' said Price sneeringly. 'The lower classes, as you call them, are generally blamed for everything.' Ignoring Patricia's protests of 'I don't' and 'What rot!' he continued, 'I have ascertained that this morning the deceased and Mr Rose encountered one another in the gallery upstairs and came down into the dining-room together. Mr Scampnell and his step-daughter were going to the meet in their car, so they also partook of the early breakfast, but, as a car affords a more speedy mode of locomotion than a horse, they did not hurry down, and Mr Scampnell arrived as his wife left the table, taking her flask and sandwiches, and Miss Rattray a few moments later. The remainder of the guests breakfasted at nine as usual, with the exception of Flight-Lieutenant Marvin, who came down at ten. Now, Miss d'Estray, which members of your family came downstairs prior to the arrival of the deceased?'

'I did, for one,' said Patricia readily. 'I have to get up early on hunting mornings. I asked the kitchenmaid, who's up first, to bang on my door at half past six, and I came in to the house again at half past seven and I yelled for Benny and he brought me my breakfast on a tray into the dining-room.'

'And were the sandwiches and the flasks already on the sideboard?'

'No, they weren't. I rushed in and got mine before we started for the meet. Only mine were left then.'

'While you were having breakfast did anyone else enter the dining-room?'

'Only Eric on his lawful occasions. He was laying places and bringing in sugar and salt and that kind of thing.'

'When you "yelled for Benson", Miss d'Estray, where were you? Did you make your way towards the pantry in search of him?' While the police ambulance had taken Cecily Scampnell's body to the mortuary in Harborough, Price had called on the public analyst with her flask, in which the same poison that had killed Elizabeth Hudson had been duly discovered, but the bottle from which Benson had poured out her claret had yet to be analysed. Benson, however, declared that he had filled Mr Rose's flask from the same bottle, so that, if the man could be believed, it must have been the flask which had been tampered with. Price need have concerned himself only with those members of the household who had entered the dining-room after the flasks and sandwiches had been placed there and before the departure of the riders, had it not been for the fact that the flasks had spent the night in the pantry, having been placed there, as the custom was, by their owners at various times during the previous evening. Against that, Benson most firmly stated that he never filled a flask without first swilling it out and standing it upside down on the draining-board.

Patricia said, 'No. I stood at the dining-room door and yelled that I was ready.'

'Would it not have been more usual to ring the bell in the dining-room?'

'Oh well,' said Patricia, 'we're not great bell-ringers. It means the servants have to come and ask what you want and then go back again, so it saves their legs if you yell. Of course the lodgers are always bell-ringing.'

'To return to the point,' said Price, surprised and not altogether pleased to find among the effete aristocracy such consideration for those misguided enough to serve them, 'can you tell me in what order the riders proceeded to the stable?'

'Mrs Scampnell came first – she's . . . she was always punctual. She was mounted by the time that Mr Rose came, but of course that doesn't mean that they left the dining-room in the same order – Mr Rose may not have come straight out; he may have gone to get his hat or to the bath-room.'

'That possibility does not escape me. And Lady d'Estray – did she come to see the party off?'

'Oh no. She has breakfast in her room, like the French, and generally Lisa has it with her. Is that all, Inspector, because I'm in an awful hurry? I've three sets of tack to clean before dinner.'

When he had let her go and was alone, sitting at Sir

Charles's desk and staring in front of him, Price came as near as he ever was to swearing. He had interviewed Benson, Eric, Beatrice, Sidney Rose, the bereaved Henry Scampnell, and his tearful step-daughter: between them they had established beyond doubt that Mrs Scampnell and Mr Rose had gone into the dining-room to breakfast together; that Henry Scampnell had come in as his wife was leaving the table, taking her sandwiches and flask with her, and Miss Rattray had appeared a few moments later. Unless Benson was lying, the poison had been introduced into the flask while it stood 'for a few moments', he said, on the sideboard before Mrs Scampnell's arrival. Patricia, by her own account and Benson's, had come and gone before the flask was filled, and Beatrice, supported by Nanny, had an alibi for Hugo. He had had no breakfast beyond the cup of tea and a couple of gingerbreads, which Beatrice had taken to his room at seven: approximately ten minutes later he had shouted to Nanny to sew on a button and both women had heard him thunder downstairs and slam the door on his way to the garage and the kennels. The evidence, which Price felt was being withheld from him, was evidence that Lady d'Estray had been seen near the dining-room. He had cajoled young Eric: 'Now, my boy, think carefully. There are people you see as you go about the house that you hardly notice – Lady d'Estray, for instance – didn't you catch a glimpse of her as you went in and out with the dishes?' 'No, I didn't,' said Eric, 'and I should have noticed 'er in particklar – couldn't 'ave been off it on account of 'er never coming down for breakfast.' Price said peevishly, 'I should have expected her to come down to see that her guests had all their requirements.' 'Cor,' said Eric, 'what's Mr Benson and me for? We shouldn't be much good of if we couldn't see to a few breakfasts . . . '

The two long windows of Sir Charles's study were growing dark now: true to his type, Price disliked to sit in uncurtained rooms at night; he rose and drew together the folds of frayed and faded damask – shabby things, he thought, comparing them with the orange-and-brown 'home-weave' at his own windows. Drawing the second pair, he peered out on the terrace; there was no light in the east wing; from a window above him a beam fell on the silent fountain; with dusk, melancholy gathered and clung about the walls of the great outmoded mansion – enough to give you the pip, Price put it. But it wasn't, and he knew it wasn't, the atmosphere of the place which was causing an unease, seldom experienced, at the pit of his stomach: it was the nagging consciousness that while, practically under his nose, a second murder had been committed, he, the astute and successful Ron Price, had advanced no farther and saw no prospect of advancing any farther in his investigation of either of the crimes. He had no doubt that Bunny d'Estray was the poisoner, that, hating Elizabeth Hudson for her domestic tyranny and for her influence over the d'Estrays – motives insufficient to a man, perhaps, but typical of the smaller-minded female – she had dug her roots, brewed them in some secret hour – and who knew better than she the employments of the household? – and poured her potion at a time convenient to her into the bottle of whisky standing so conveniently in her victim's room. She had hoped, of course, that the poison would be undetected: Miss Hudson was elderly and, where doctors were concerned, had a bee in her bonnet, and murder was the last thing that a toady like that doctor would look for in the family he smarmed over; it was a miracle that he hadn't certified a death from gastritis. To do away with Mrs Scampnell had been much more risky, but she knew or suspected too much and the risks had to be taken. To meet such a contingency some of the poison had been kept and – for he had searched Lady d'Estray's rooms – very cunningly hidden. Knowing the routine of the hunting-flasks, she had crept down the west-wing staircase, from the foot of which she would obtain a clear view along the passage to the door of the dining-room. It was true that the boy Eric had been going to and from the dining-room with the breakfast dishes, but his eyes would have been fixed on his trays; he wouldn't have turned his head to look down the passage, and the creak of the moth-eaten green baize door which led from the kitchens and pantries would have warned the murderess of his approach. That's how it was, said Price to himself, and he rang the bell, and when Benson came at last, told him that he wished to see Lady d'Estray.

Benson said that her ladyship would be dressing for dinner, and Price snapped, 'I can't help that, man. Look sharp and fetch her.' With a pained expression Benson went out and presently Bunny came, looking pale and, he thought, anxious, in her pink corduroy housecoat. Before he could speak, she said, 'Oh, Mr Price – I mean, Detective-Inspector – I do hope you've found out something. We really can't go on like this – everyone's getting jittery.'

'Only one individual need get jittery, Lady d'Estray, and that's the murderer.'

'You mean you know who it is? Oh, good,' said Bunny.

She spoke so naturally that he had to reassure himself, a consummate actress . . . she thinks I'm on the wrong tack. . . . I'll play it that way. He said, 'No doubt you've a theory of your own, Lady d'Estray. I'd be interested to know if you suspect the same party?' but instead of the hints, that were the least he had expected, he got, 'I haven't a theory. I'm completely flummoxed. Elizabeth was a disagreeable old thing, but everyone liked Mrs Scampnell. The only explanation is that she knew too much, but if that was so why didn't she tell someone?'

'She may have underestimated the value of her information. It may have been quite a trivial thing, or something that to her untrained mind seemed to have no connexion. That often happens. You yourself, Lady d'Estray, haven't told me whom you saw when you came downstairs this morning.'

Bunny looked puzzled. 'Well, but I saw everybody – except those who had gone out hunting. I met Nanny in the corridor, and she said there was a button off my blouse and I'd better take it off and let her have it, and then I went to the kitchen and saw Mrs Capes about the menu, and then to the drawing-room to see if there were any dead flowers, and Mrs Rose was there reading the paper . . . '

Price checked her with a gesture. 'My reference was not to the time when you finally came down, Lady d'Estray. I have reason to believe that you came out of your bedroom before the serving of the first breakfast.'

'I don't know what reason you can have for believing that because I didn't,' said Bunny. 'I was tired last night and I never batted an eyelid until Beatrice brought in my breakfast. She'll bear me out. And I know the hunting people had gone by then, because I asked her if they had got off all right, and she said yes.'

'One can get up and retire again,' Price said.

'Well, I didn't. Who says I did?' asked Bunny.

Price took refuge in 'I'm not here to answer questions, but to ask them. Did you hear Mr Hugo d'Estray come down?'

'No, I didn't. He must have been before the others anyway.'

'Yet it's strange that you didn't hear him, Lady d'Estray. He slammed the door after "thundering downstairs".'

'But in this kind of house one doesn't hear that kind of thing,' said Bunny. 'It's stone-built and the doors are solid. I don't suppose my husband heard him either.'

'Very well,' said Price, 'we'll leave that for the moment. Perhaps you can help me on another point, Lady d'Estray. What were Mrs Scampnell's views on the death of Miss Hudson?'

'She was more upset than any of the other p.gs. There was a lot of rivalry between her and Miss Hudson, but also, I suppose, a kind of comradeship.'

'A relationship which seldom exists between members of the female sex,' said Price censoriously. 'However, they were both elderly ladies, so it may have been possible. Whom did Mrs Scampnell suspect, Lady d'Estray?'

'I don't remember discussing the murder with her. Her husband might know, or Miss Rattray. When there's an unidentified murderer about, one naturally opens one's mouth to the people one's sure of.'

'And who are you sure of, Lady d'Estray?'

'My husband . . . my stepson and my stepdaughter . . . my own daughter . . . the servants.'

'I suppose it's natural, though it can hardly be termed logical, to trust one's own. The idea had not escaped me. I've already spoken to Mr Scampnell and Miss Rattray. They tell me that the matter was discussed at length between them, but that Mrs Scampnell suspected no one in particular; she did, however, mention the hostility which existed between yourself and Miss Hudson.'

'Hostility's too strong a word,' said Bunny, growing paler. 'We had nothing in common; we disagreed on many subjects, but . . .'

'Exactly,' Price interrupted her. 'You had nothing in common; you disagreed on many subjects; Miss Hudson thought you unworthy of your position as mistress of her cousin's house, and you feared her influence over your husband. You had row after row – I've proof of that, Lady d'Estray – and as time went on you decided that her presence in the house was intolerable, yet, owing to the affection felt for her by Sir Charles and his family, you could not legitimately terminate it.'

Bunny stubbed out her cigarette – how I dislike, Price thought, nicotine-stained fingers in a woman – and got to her feet and looked down on him.

'Are you accusing me of the murders?'

'I have made no accusation,' said Price coldly. 'It is you who are fitting the cap, Lady d'Estray.'

'What nonsense! You've just said that I couldn't "legitimately terminate" – by which I suppose you mean "lawfully end" – Miss Hudson's stay here, and what could that mean except that you think I poisoned her? Just because I disliked the woman – if I murdered everyone I disliked there'd be no end to it. Anyhow, what about Mrs Scampnell? I never quarrelled with her; I thought her about the nicest of our lodgers.'

Price leant back at his ease in Sir Charles's chair, and his cold grey eyes met Bunny's warm brown ones. 'Pursuing, as they did, a similar hobby, Miss Hudson and Mrs Scampnell often had a long ride home after hunting, and it is not unreasonable to suppose that a lonely unmarried lady like Miss Hudson would, under such circumstances, confide in her friend. Miss Rattray thinks it more probable that Mrs Scampnell was killed on account of information so obtained than because she saw or heard anything of the actual murder. In the latter event one would have expected her to confide in her husband or daughter; if not, as was of course her duty, in the police: in the former case, however, she may have felt bound by some promise of secrecy, or may not have realized the importance of what she knew. Now, Lady d'Estray, what was that information?'

'Non-existent, I should imagine. You know, you've got quite a wrong picture of Elizabeth. She wasn't the lonely pathetic figure that men like to visualize when they think of an unmarried woman: she was self-satisfied, self-reliant, completely at home in the world. If there had been a skeleton in her cupboard she would have dealt with it herself – she certainly wouldn't have gone snivelling to Cecily Scampnell, whom she despised.'

'I'm afraid your estimate of her character is at fault there, Lady d'Estray. Miss Hudson may have concealed her loneliness and frustration behind a mannish exterior and a domineering manner, but they were there. I have reason to believe that she confided considerably in little Miss Rattray and even presented her with a trinket as a mark of their friendship.'

'That was last Christmas. And she presented us all with "trinkets", even me. Actually I think she did get on quite well with Margot Rattray – they went for a walk together last Sunday – but that's understandable: Margot's a yes-woman, if there ever was one.'

'If Miss Hudson confided in Miss Rattray, it's logical to assume that she confided in Miss Rattray's mother, a woman much nearer her own age. She must have done so, Lady d'Estray, unless after Miss Hudson's death Mrs Scampnell came into possession of some clue to the murder. In either event Mrs Scampnell must have told someone of her discovery or suspicion – not necessarily the murderer, for her confidant may have repeated it. I can well imagine the tittle-tattle that goes on. As I previously indicated, the unfortunate woman's knowledge may not have been very important or well-substantiated: fear sets the nerves on edge, Lady d'Estray,' said Price, with a significant glance at Bunny's restless hands. 'Perhaps she only mentioned that there was something she wanted to tell me and, as murderers will, the murderer panicked and her death warrant was signed.'

'Well, I daresay you're right,' said Bunny, too fatigued to argue further, and Price thought, she's tiring. . . . I'm wearing her down. This neurotic type . . . he thought; with American police methods, it wouldn't be long before she broke. Take her back over it all again? he asked himself, or surprise her? 'Can I go now?' said Bunny childishly into the silence, and her defeated look encouraged him. 'Would it surprise you, Lady d'Estray, if I told you you had been seen in the vicinity of the plant concerned – water dropwort?'

For an instant, as if collecting her wits, she hesitated. Then, 'Not in the least,' she said. 'I don't know where it grows, so for all I know I may often have been near it.' But Bunny, though she lied often in this cause and that, was not a good liar, and the embarrassment in her voice did not escape him. He said harshly, 'With your knowledge of herbs that seems unbelievable.'

'But I've no knowledge of herbs. I just know the few that in France every housewife uses for cooking – the *tisanes* I made for the paying guests when they had colds were simply infusions of the dried leaves of the lime-tree.'

'A little rash, wasn't it, for such an ignoramus to embark on dosing sick people?'

'Scarcely "dosing". In France . . '

'We're not in France now, Lady d'Estray. In England such outlandish remedies are unheard of, and it seems to me very curious that you should have messed about with them, especially as you've a houseful of servants at your beck and call.'

Bunny protested, 'But we haven't. We're miserably under-staffed,' but he went on, 'I put it to you that you've made a study of herbal concoctions and that when your position here was threatened you used your knowledge to eliminate the threat.'

'But my position here hasn't been threatened . . .'

'Not by Miss Hudson? Socially she looked down on you: rightly or wrongly she thought you had trapped her cousin into marriage, and she had, I believe, a tremendous influence over Sir Charles.'

Bunny said, 'What a squalid little story you've made up, haven't you? If you believe it, why don't you arrest me?'

'Squalid or not, it's possible. Come now, Lady d'Estray, you're a writer. As a plot for a tale it's not improbable?'

'It is – because you've got the wrong characters,' Bunny said thoughtfully. 'Serious writers don't trap people into marriage. Men of Sir Charles's experience aren't trapped. Women as well-born as Miss Hudson don't "look down" on their social inferiors.'

'I venture to differ. However, Lady d'Estray, as in your own case you admit nothing and yet are unable to make the smallest suggestion as to the author of these crimes, though you should – and I expect you do – know the ins and outs of this household better than anyone, I won't waste my time in putting any further questions to you. Would you tell Sir Charles that I should like to speak to him?'

Bunny said, 'I will, but he may be a minute or two – I expect he's dressing for dinner,' and that'll give me time, she thought, to warn him not to admit that Lisa knew about the dropwort. She glanced at her wrist watch, surmised that the ever-punctual Charles was already dressed and taking his sherry, hurried along the corridor to the hall and found him, as she had guessed, in the library. He had his glass in his hand: he looked up and down again.

Bunny sank into the armchair opposite his and said, 'Oh dear.'

He shot her a brief cold glance. 'Well, Barbara?' and then

it was impossible to ask him to support the lie she'd told: he was against her; only she and Lisa were together. With luck and by the mercy of Lisa's saints, Price might omit the question of the dropwort. She said, 'The 'tec wants you now, Charles. Shall I tell them to put back dinner?'

And that was a bad sign, thought Sir Charles, saying, 'No, no. Just tell them to keep something hot for me'; to bother about dinner when two murders had been committed in the house showed a lack of proportion – a warped mind: murderers didn't realize the enormity of their crimes. That was the trouble – it wasn't wickedness; it was amorality; and he had known from the first, but somehow down there in the South he hadn't minded, that, though she herself was living a perfectly respectable life, her friends were a raffish lot, adulterers and fornicators, poor as church mice, spongers, drunkards, idlers, content, while others ran the world, to dream and daub and scribble. Down there he had admired her tolerance; he had taken it for granted that it sprang from kindliness and in one instance – those dreadful fellows from the Villa Mimosa – from comparative innocence. But he knew now that her tolerance was the result of a deep and, in his opinion, dangerous conviction that in comparison with the sins of the spirit, the sins of the flesh are unimportant, just a pity, like a raucous voice or a damp handclasp. As he dressed for dinner he had struggled briefly with an uneasy conscience; during his interview with the detective he had told the truth, nothing but the truth, but not all the truth; he hadn't mentioned the hostility between his wife and his cousin, or that Lisa – a strange precocious passionate child – had not only screamed that Elizabeth should be painlessly destroyed, but had known how to come by the poison which had destroyed her. Now there had been another murder and in so desperate a situation even love and loyalty must be jettisoned: the moment had come when there was virtue in truth alone. Because you had loved a woman and married her, it didn't prove that she wasn't a murderess; because a child was your stepdaughter, it didn't follow that she wasn't a juvenile delinquent. . . . One must get rid of one's fixed idea that such things don't happen to oneself, thought Sir Charles, as he opened the study door.

Price rose as he entered, but sat down again when it became obvious that Sir Charles meant to stand on the hearth-rug with his back to the fire: it was difficult to dominate a conversation when the other man towered above you, Price had always found. He began, 'This is a terrible tragedy, Sir Charles – a second murder, and I feel that it might have been prevented if certain people had been more open with me. I don't say they've lied to me, but in the case of Miss Hudson certain animosities have been glossed over, and now it's ridiculous to pretend that Mrs Scampnell confided her suspicions to no one but the murderer: if she had been sure of his identity she would have spoken to myself or to her husband – vague suspicions would have been voiced during general conversation – the fair sex are given to indulgence in tittle-tattle over a cup of tea. As I was informing Lady d'Estray just now, a guilty conscience sets the nerves on edge, and the murderer may have jumped to the conclusion that the deceased knew more than she did.'

'You haven't spoken to Mrs Rose yet?' Sir Charles asked him. 'She's a sharp little woman – if anything had been said over the teacups, she'd know.'

Price complained, 'She was not outstandingly helpful when I spoke to her about Miss Hudson. Her heart rules her head, I'm afraid. She would not even admit that Lady d'Estray disliked Miss Hudson.'

'That was very silly of her,' said Sir Charles evenly, but turning away as he spoke and fixing his gaze on the fire. 'It must have been plain to everyone that my wife and Miss Hudson had very little in common. I am sure Lady d'Estray would have admitted it if you had questioned her.'

'Oh, she admitted it,' said Price, leaning back in his chair and thrusting a hand into his pocket, 'but at the same time she contrived to give me the impression that their differences were on general subjects, as it might be politics or religion. It was from others I learned of the cat-and-dog life they lived together.'

'Now that,' said Sir Charles, able to look Price in the face, 'is an exaggeration. There was never a scene, not even what I believe is called "words", between them. It was sometimes apparent that my wife was irritated by Miss Hudson's criticism of this and that, but she controlled herself admirably.'

'Supposing,' said Price, 'that it had come to a show-down between them, a point where it was evident that they could no longer continue as members of the same household – would your wife have remained here, Sir Charles, or Miss Hudson?'

'My wife – naturally.'

'I wonder if she was aware of that,' Price pondered.

'I am sure of it. She knows my character.' Then Sir Charles remembered Bunny saying, 'Well, if I don't fit in, you'll be free to call it off at any time,' and his shocked rejoinder, 'I don't regard marriage as a thing you can call off,' and her 'Wait until you see the mess I make of being a nob.' Perhaps, after being married to a foreigner and then knocking about with Tom, Dick, and Harry on the Riviera, she had forgotten what she must have known once, Wilkinson having been Winchester and New College – that men like himself existed. Should he qualify his statement? . . . but already Price had gone on to ' – a difficult question, but it's my duty to put it to you: could there be anything in Lady d'Estray's past, which Miss Hudson could have got hold of and held against her?'

This time Sir Charles took care to think before speaking. He said, 'I am not aware of anything,' and then, 'Had it been so, it is quite impossible for me to believe that my cousin would have threatened my wife: she would have kept silent, or come straight to me, if she had thought it necessary. She was the straightest of women.'

Price lifted his eyebrows and lines showed on his waxy forehead.

'You know, Sir Charles, it's almost incredible. Two murders have been committed in this house, yet no one has observed the smallest cogent detail, and, according to your good self, every member of the household is an angel.'

'Well, not quite,' said Sir Charles, 'though they seem to me to be all very nice people. But I see your point: I am – I must be – mistaken in someone.' Now or never, he thought. 'There was one small detail mentioned – I think it was yesterday. My step-daughter told us she had known – for some time, I gather – where the dropwort grows and that it was poisonous. She doesn't remember having told anyone about it, but she's only a child – goodness knows whom she may have chattered to.'

Price clicked his tongue. 'I wish I'd known of this before – it may be very important. Of course I should have questioned her, but unless circumstances necessitate such a procedure, I avoid obtaining information from kiddies – it seems un-English.'

Thinking how decent was the average lower-middle-class Englishman, Sir Charles said, 'Lisa is by no means an ordinary child.'

'Oh dear,' said Price in a sympathetic voice. 'I'm sorry for that, Sir Charles, very sorry.'

'Oh, I don't mean there's anything wrong with her,' said Sir Charles hastily. 'What I mean is that she's an only child and she's lived with grown-ups and on the Continent, so that she's too forward for her age, if anything. And, of course, she's a Catholic.'

'But I suppose she'd know right from wrong?' asked Price, who, while he merely despised the Church of England, loathed fanatically, and perhaps fearfully, the Church of Rome.

'Of course, of course; she's been well brought up,' said Sir Charles indignantly.

'Naturally,' agreed Price, 'but in a pathological case the best upbringing in the world is no deterrent.' He hoped it wasn't the child. He believed that he loved children, and longed for a couple of boys of his own, who would look up to him, yet to whom he'd be a real pal – he couldn't understand why so few fathers seemed able to understand such a relationship with their sons . . .

Sir Charles was thinking: if it's Lisa there'd be no hanging

... it would be an illness, perhaps curable ... some hereditary taint in that French chap's family . . . not even Bunny need be ashamed. Poor little Lisa's charming . . . but loonies often are. . . . He volunteered, 'This would be a good time if you want to question her. Her mother's at dinner – well, I mean, we know what mothers are, especially the mothers of "only" children.'

'Quite,' said Price; 'but I would like you to be present. I don't want it said afterwards that there was any bullying or intimidation.'

'I'll certainly stay if you think I'll be of help to you.' Sir Charles rang the bell. 'I'm afraid we shall be unpopular, ringing bells in the middle of dinner . . .'

The boy, Eric, certainly looked aggrieved when he came in, and he expressed the obviously obstructive opinion that Miss Lisa would be in the bath. When Lisa appeared, however, she was dressed in dungarees: there were straws in her hair and with her came a faint aroma of the stable. Price wouldn't have liked, he thought, to see a kid of his in such a pickle, but Sir Charles made no comment. 'The Detective-Inspector wants to ask you a few questions, Lisa,' was all he said.

Lisa turned her amber eyes on Price. Curious colour, he thought . . . foreign . . . untrustworthy. 'They're quite simple questions,' he said in a reassuring tone of voice, 'and I'm sure that a clever little girl like you will be able to answer them. You mustn't be afraid; you've only got to tell the truth. I suppose you know what the truth is?'

'No,' said Lisa, 'I don't. Nobody does. "*What is truth?* asked jesting Pilate." Keats said it was Beauty. Plato said we shan't find it until we have lost our ears and eyes. Aristotle – '

Sir Charles said, 'Come down to earth, Lisa. The Inspector means – well, he means he wants facts, whatever you and Plato may think of them. Now, Inspector – '

'Did you,' asked Price hurriedly, 'dislike Miss Hudson?'

'Not exactly,' said Lisa. 'I did not find her *simpatica* or she me. I thought her a dictator and she thought me queer.'

'And did you resent the way she treated your Mummy?'

'Not particularly. My mother and I can answer back. It was much worse when she was rude to Mrs Rose.'

'And did you dislike Mrs Scampnell?'

'No. I rather liked her. She was old-fashioned, and her hunting anecdotes were rather boring, but she was always polite.'

'Are you interested in botany?'

'No,' said Lisa. 'I'm interested in art, literature, and horses. Actually now I'm getting interested in criminal psychology.'

'That's not a very nice study for a little girl,' said Price disapprovingly. 'But even though you're not interested in botany, you know about plants – you knew, didn't you, where the dropwort grows?'

'Oh yes. Cousin Elizabeth showed it to me ages ago. It's down by the river, in the corner of Low Meadow. She told me about a man who ate it in mistake for a parsnip and gave a bit to his horse – the silly idiot – and they both died. I suppose you've looked at the place and noted the heelmarks?'

Price said, 'It's only to-night, from you, that I've ascertained the location of the dropwort. Surely you're old enough to know that you should have informed some responsible person?'

'I did tell the family.' Lisa addressed Sir Charles. 'Didn't I?' She turned back to Price. 'But I really haven't seen you to speak to – in fact, I've only seen you once, and that was when you came hurtling round the corner of the drive in your car and nearly killed me.'

'You mustn't exaggerate,' said Price.

'Well, it was a dam' near thing,' said Lisa.

'These heelmarks . . .' said Price.

'They're not much use,' Lisa told him. 'The ground's too squoggy to tell whether they're male or female.'

'Grown-up people can tell lots of things that little girls can't,' said Price snubbingly. 'Now, Lisa, think carefully. Before Miss Hudson died did you tell anyone about the poisonous dropwort?'

'I didn't. I'm not interested in beastly botany. But I

expect Cousin Elizabeth did, only you can eliminate my mother and Patricia, because I've already asked them and they say she didn't. Actually I've been thinking that it was probably someone she went for walks with, because you don't suddenly start off about plants, especially weeds, in the middle of dinner – you talk about them when you're out for a walk and you see them. Cousin Elizabeth talked to Mrs Scampnell a lot, but they didn't go out for walks – Mrs Scampnell hated walking. The people who went for walks with Cousin Elizabeth were Margot Rattray and Geoffrey Marvin – he *had* to.'

Sir Charles said, 'Lisa, my dear, it's facts the Inspector wants, not your deductions,' and Price said, 'You're only a little girl, you know. You don't need to dwell on these sad things – just answer my questions. Have you ever helped your mother make beverages from herbs for sick people?'

'No, I haven't,' said Lisa. 'I hate sick people.'

'You shouldn't do that,' said Price. 'You should be sorry for them and try to help them. But I expect you've often boiled up leaves or roots in make-belief for tea for your dollies?'

'No fear,' said Lisa. 'Cooking's an art, and when I cook I cook something decent, like *sole mornay* or *soufflé surprise*.'

'That's very clever of you,' said Price ingratiatingly. 'But then I'm sure you're a very clever little girl. I'm sure if anyone – even a grown-up person – annoyed you, you'd get the better of them.'

Lisa looked puzzled. 'I'm not the least clever. I've never got the better of anyone. Actually if someone annoys me I answer back, but I generally get the worst of it.'

'And then do you brood over it and think out your revenge?'

'Good gracious no! I'm not a character out of *Wuthering Heights*,' said Lisa, laughing merrily.

'Well,' said Price, 'I think that's all I have to ask you at present. I hope you've told me the truth – it's a very serious offence to tell fibs to the police, you know, Lisa. Think over what you've said, and if there's anything you missed out or haven't been quite truthful about you must be sure and tell me. Even though you've been brought up abroad, you're half English, and English children are always truthful....'

'Mother of God!' said Lisa.

'Lisa!' said Sir Charles.

'Sorry, I meant gosh,' said Lisa. 'But really – '

'We don't want any argument,' said Sir Charles hastily. 'If the Detective-Inspector has finished with you, run along.'

'Good night, Detective-Inspector Price,' said Lisa, raising her amber eyes to his, looking far too demure to be straightforward, looking fragile and foreign, the antithesis of the jolly rosy schoolgirl that Price felt his daughter would be, if he had one. 'Good night, Beaupère,' she said to Sir Charles, and Sir Charles said, 'Good night, dear. Get off to bed now and don't bother your head about this miserable business,' and when the door had shut behind her he said to Price, 'I'm really rather sorry we worried her – she obviously knows nothing more than she's told us. Don't you think so?'

Price mused. 'Well, she is a strange type . . . unchildlike . . . some maladjustment . . . well, we'll see. Now I mustn't keep you from your dinner any longer.' He didn't care a pin about Sir Charles's dinner, but there was no sense to be got from this old ditherer and he wanted his own. . . .

As Lisa shut the study door behind her, the baize door farther along the passage opened and Eric's freckled face peered out and breathed, 'Oi! Miss Lisa!'

Lisa beckoned, pointed to the west-wing staircase and led on. Eric followed on tiptoe. At the turn of the stair she waited for him. 'Well, my dear Watson?'

Eric jerked his thumb towards the study. 'Third degree, was it?'

'Oh no,' said Lisa. 'A slimy sort of cunning. He tries to put you off your guard with dear-little-kiddy tactics.'

'He didn't,' said Eric, 'try any kiddy stuff with me. 'Ere, Miss Lisa, I've gotta clue.'

'Mother of God!' said Lisa. 'Spit it out, for mercy's sake, boy.'

'It come into my mind when I was getting their trays ready
– the bereaved 'usband's and young Margot's. Them flasks,
I 'as the cleaning of 'em. I knows 'em like the palm of me 'and
– dints, 'inges and so on. Old Cecily 'ad two, both 'ad 'er
initials on top, sometimes one come down and sometimes
t'other: but one of the lids was dinted.'

'So what?'

'Use your loaf, gal. If the murderer 'ad a flask ready doped,
that nobody couldn't tell from the one Mr Benson 'ad filled up
in the pantry, 'e didn't need to be left alone in the dining-
room while 'e poured out some of the booze and poured in the
poison; 'e could 'ave changed the flasks easy as pie in a split
second. The old girl, she didn't used to come down to breakfast in 'er coat and bowler 'at; she used to go back upstairs to
put 'em on before she went over to the stables. Them flasks
could've been switched while she was picking 'er false teeth or
fixing 'er 'air-net. 'Im in there, 'e's trying to puzzle out
who was near the dining-room, but what 'e should be arsking
is: who knew that she 'as *two* flasks? and that was me, so I'm
not all that keen on telling 'im.'

'Still, other people besides you must have known it.
Margot, for one. I'd know how many flasks my mother had, if
she had any. "Scamp" may not have known – men never
notice anything, but I bet Cousin Elizabeth knew, only she's
dead so it doesn't matter, and Patricia may have. Probably
Marvin knew and Mr Rose – you're apt to talk about things
like that when you're riding home for miles and you're not
very intelligent. Beastly though he is, I think we ought to
tell Price, Eric. I don't think it will put you in an invidious
position.'

'If by that you mean a spot, I'm not so sure, gal. Any'ow,
'e's knocking off now . . . there 'e goes . . . thin on top, ain't
'e?' When Price had disappeared round the corner of the
corridor, 'Reckon I'll sleep on it,' he added.

'If there's another murder in the night you'll be sorry,'
warned Lisa. 'I think we'd better tell some grown-up. Shall
I tell Bunny and swear her to secrecy?'

'She's all right, but she'll split to 'er old man, won't she?'

'How Victorian you are, Eric. Modern wives have hundreds of secrets from their husbands.'

'O.K., then. I must shift off to bed now or Mr Benson will be after me. Be seeing you, Miss Lisa.'

Eric ran downstairs, and Lisa went up and along the corridor to her mother's sitting-room. Bunny, huddled over a dying fire, said, 'I've been looking for you. I must talk to someone, and your stepfather thinks I'm the murderer. *Who is on my side, who?*'

'Well, I am,' said Lisa, sitting down at her feet. 'And so are Babette and Romanée Conti. Anyhow I don't think the 'tec believes you did it. He asked *me* some very searching questions.'

'You? When did he see you?' asked Bunny, startled.

'Just now in the study. Beaupère sent for me and stayed there in case the kiddy should be frightened of the great big policeman, I suppose. I think the 'tec thought I might be a problem child.'

'The idiot. If he wants an oddity, why doesn't he try Patricia – still a school prefect at twenty-three? What did he ask you, Lisa?'

'Oh, mostly about the dropwort and where to find it.'

Bunny groaned. 'That wretched man must have told him you knew. Lisa, when this is over let's go back to the villa.'

'All right, let's. But we shall have to take Romanée Conti, or Patricia will send him to the kennels.'

'Oh, we'll take him. He'll look sweet under Père Bonnard's olives. *O to be lying under the olives . . .*'

'Eating peaches.'

'Looking at the mountains.'

'In the sunshine.'

'In France.'

'Away from Patricia.'

'Away from all the d'Estrays . . . But in the meantime,' said Bunny, 'how to avoid being hanged?'

'Oh, look, Eric's got a new clue, so it's a good thing,' said Lisa, 'that I did "associate with the boot-boy". He wouldn't tell Price tonight – he thinks it's incriminating, but he said I could tell you if you promised not to tell anybody.'

'All right, I promise.'

Lisa got up, tiptoed across the room and flung the door open. 'Excuse melodrama,' she said, closing it softly, 'but the Scampnell may have died for less. Look, according to Eric she had two flasks.' Sitting down again at Bunny's feet she told the boy's story, adding, 'Eric seems to think it's frightfully important, but I can't see that it helps us much.'

Bunny thought aloud. 'It widens the field and then narrows it. Now the possibles are not only the people who were down to the early breakfast, or those who could have crept down knowing that it wouldn't cause much excitement if they *were* seen: it's everybody again until you remember that it must have been someone who knew that Mrs Scampnell had two flasks. I didn't: you didn't. But we can't prove it. The people who knew were Eric, Margot Rattray, Mr Scampnell, and probably Beatrice and Sylvia, who would have seen them when they did the room.'

'I told Eric that I thought all the hunting people probably knew. I thought they might have talked about their sandwich cases and flasks when they used them, or on the way home. *What a nice flask! Mrs Scampnell. It is, is it not? My dear first husband gave me a pair of them.* I thought Mr Scampnell was doubtful – husbands don't notice much, do they? But Margot must have known.'

'The other flask . . . ' cried Bunny, sitting up suddenly – 'the flask that Eric cleaned and Benson filled . . . no, that's no use,' she said dejectedly. 'The murderer had all day in which to wash it and put it back where it – or rather the poisoned one – belonged.'

'Where does it belong?' asked Lisa. 'There must have been a time when both flasks were missing. If they sit, or even one of them sits on a shelf and we found out when they, or it, were missing, we'd narrow down the time again.'

'Beatrice would know. She'd know where they were kept, though if they were on a shelf or a chest-of-drawers I don't suppose she'd notice if they were missing, except when she dusted at intervals of twenty-four hours, which isn't very narrow. D'you think she's in bed yet, Lisa?'

'If she is, we couldn't ask her. It's Eric's clue, and we promised.'

'Oh damn, so we did.' What, Bunny wondered, were the ethics? A promise made to a silly child, was it binding? You mustn't do evil that good might come of it . . . but the boy was only fourteen and practically half-witted, and Lisa was an absurd little Quixote . . . impossible to let her know that you'd even considered it. She said, 'Well, I suppose we must wait till the morning and hope that Eric will feel moved to confide in the detective – if not, we'll have to try to persuade him. Go to bed, Lisa, and lock your door; there's an angel. On second thoughts, I'll come up and look under the bed before you get into it.'

Lisa's room was on the second floor of the west wing, near the nurseries. It had belonged to Patricia, and although she had long since moved into a more imposing room on the first floor, she had been quite put out when Bunny had had the walls stripped of a drab and faded paper and distempered yellow; even now she alluded to it as 'my old bedroom'. While Lisa splashed in the nursery bathroom, Bunny inspected the large built-in cupboard and, feeling a little foolish, peered beneath the bed, on which she had already installed the delighted Boxer; and she stayed in the room until Lisa was ready to lock the door, and heard the key turn before she went downstairs. And that's all very well, she worried, but to-morrow will be another day, and Cecily Scampnell was killed because she knew too much, and now Lisa knows about these flasks, and though it doesn't seem a very important piece of information, it may lead somewhere. If I talked to Margot and mentioned the original flask she might volunteer that there was a second, and that wouldn't give Eric away in the least – few people realize what tiny details a child does notice. Passing her bedroom door, Bunny crossed the gallery, but stopped outside the little pantry, from which came the faint sound of bubbling water. Her heart stood still. Then she told herself, idiot . . .

it's far too early for anyone to be cooking up poison, and she opened the door.

Beatrice was standing beside the electric ring, on which a kettle was steaming. She started and dropped the rubber hot-water bottle, which she had been holding against her chest. 'Oh my lady,' she said reproachfully. 'How you did make me jump!'

'I'm terribly sorry,' said Bunny. 'I've just got Lisa into bed and I was going along to ask if I could do anything for the Scampnells. It's embarrassing, but I don't want to seem callous.'

'This bottle's for Mr Scampnell,' said Beatrice. 'I moved his things into the little green room as you suggested, and I've 'ad a bottle in the bed all evening, but it still feels a bit damp to me: in fact I'm in two minds about moving 'im back again. When it first came up 'e didn't seem to care either way.'

'I expect he feels too miserable to care, but I'm sure he'll be better in the green room. It would be awful for him to wake up in the morning and see all her things around him.'

Pouring the hot water into the bottle and thrusting it into its case of green chintz, Beatrice said, 'They wasn't all that loving.'

'I daresay not,' agreed Bunny. 'It was a second marriage, probably for companionship, and not very romantic, but I always thought they got on very well considering how their tastes differed.'

'At times,' said Beatrice, 'with the best will in the world we can't 'elp 'earing what we're not meant to. I've 'eard 'im call 'er an 'orrible name – the Unspeakable.'

'That's a joke. *The Unspeakable in pursuit of the Uneatable.* Oscar Wilde. He meant hunting people chasing foxes.'

'Well, I shouldn't want it,' said Beatrice. 'Nor for my stepdaughter to call me Scamp, if I were a man. Miss 'Udson, she agreed with me about that, though she did take up with Miss Margot. Well, this won't do. I wish you'd come and feel that mattress, my lady.'

Bunny followed her into the small and charming green room between Margot Rattray's room and the room that had been

Elizabeth Hudson's, and Beatrice, seeing her in the brighter light, exclaimed, 'Oh, my lady, you do look tired! Why don't you get off to bed now?' 'That's perfectly dry,' pronounced Bunny, feeling the mattress. 'I'll go to bed as soon as I've seen the Scampnells, but it's awful in bed when you can't sleep, and really, after two murders . . . ' 'I thought I should never drop off the night after Miss 'Udson died,' said Beatrice, 'but I made myself a nice cup of Ovaltine and I took two Aspros and never knew no more till young Sylvia brought in my tea in the morning. That's what I shall 'ave to-night, and while I'm making it I might just as well make a cup for you -- it won't be no trouble.'

'Oh, don't bother, Beatrice; you're as tired as I am.'

'It won't be no bother. I'll put it in your room, so don't stop too long with them Scampnells. Good night, my lady.'

'Sleep well, Beatrice,' said Bunny, and knocked on the door of Margot's room.

Through the thick mahogany panels a faint 'Come in' reached her and she entered. Before a blazing log fire, which presumably the kind Beatrice had substituted for the less comforting electric stove, Henry Scampnell was sitting in a little chintz-covered early Victorian armchair; Margot sat on the hearthrug at his feet. *Bereaved*, by the Hon. John Collier, thought Bunny and chid herself. She noticed, however, with relief that they were both dry-eyed.

She said, 'Oh don't move, please. I haven't come to worry you; I just came to ask if you've got everything you want – if there's anything . . . ?' 'Thank you very much, Lady d'Estray,' said Margot, rising. 'It's good of you to come, but we've got everything. Beatrice has been most kind: she insisted on lighting the fire for us, and the dinner-tray was a kind thought – I expect we owe that to you, don't we?'

'Well, I thought perhaps you'd sooner be by yourselves,' said Bunny. 'Apart from everything else, it was all so sudden, and the shock must have been considerable. Have you anything to take to make you sleep – bromide or anything?'

'I don't think we like the idea of drugs, do we, Scamp?' said Margot.

Scampnell, compromising by jerking himself into a more upright position, said, 'I certainly don't. Even if I lie awake all night, my memories of *her* are not the sort one needs to run away from.'

'I'm sure of that,' said Bunny, abashed. 'We all thought you were wonderful. Very few men have the generosity to allow their wives to enjoy a sport in which they've no interest – at the best they're martyrs. Mrs Scampnell was a very lucky woman.'

'That's my one consolation – nothing to reproach myself with,' said Scampnell. 'And Margot was just saying, too, that her mother wouldn't have liked to grow old. It would have been a terrible wrench for her to give up hunting.'

'Yes, indeed,' said Bunny absently, for she was wondering how on earth she could turn the conversation to the subject of flasks without mentioning Eric. Then, 'By the way,' she said, 'I've been thinking, and I'm sure you can help me. We've assumed that because the flasks were supposed to be put in the pantry the night before hunting, there could be no deviation from the routine, but that's ridiculous – people often forget a little job like that, and if one did I suppose one would dash downstairs with one's flask in the morning. I just wondered if we were right in taking it for granted that Mrs Scampnell's flask did spend the night in the pantry.'

Margot looked at her stepfather. He said, 'I can put you right about that, Lady d'Estray. As I told the detective, my wife took her flask with her when we went down to dinner. As a matter of fact, it's a point of no importance: according to your butler, he swills the flasks out under the tap before filling them, so it's only from that point that they become interesting. Price has merely to concentrate on the movement of everybody from that moment to the time my wife got up from the table and collected her flask and sandwiches – quite a short time, and though there are a good many people in the house, quite a number have very definite alibis.'

'I see. It was just a silly little idea of mine,' said Bunny with unwonted humility, but: 'I suppose Mrs Scampnell had only the one flask?' she added.

'Naturally,' said Scampnell. 'There's a leather case for it, which straps on the saddle. I suppose a "two-bottle man" might carry two flasks,' he went on with a faint smile, 'but I've never heard of it.'

'Mummy's flask dated from her Indian days,' put in Margot. 'I've always known it. It was sacrosanct – so was all her tack, for that matter.'

Scampnell said, 'Margot, go and get the photograph of your mother on the Rajah's Arab. She's riding side-saddle there and I believe the flask shows up clearly.' Bunny said, 'I'd love to see it, but you're tired; don't bother now. I must go to bed myself, or I shall get into trouble with Beatrice. She's become quite a tyrant lately. If I don't drink my Ovaltine while it's hot I shall get a smack, I gather.' Margot, already at the door, said, 'I won't take a minute. I know where it is,' and when she had gone Scampnell explained, 'It won't do the poor kid any harm to tire herself physically – she'll sleep better. In her quiet way she was devoted to her mother: there was just the two of them together, you know, for several years – her impressionable years – before I came on the scene, and naturally they were very close to one another. Well, I needn't enlarge on that, of course; you've had the same experience.'

'Yes, of course,' said Bunny, asking herself: are they lying, or has Eric done some wishful thinking and imagined his dint? Husbands have poisoned their wives before, apparently devoted husbands, but Elizabeth was the first victim, and what could Henry Scampnell have had against Elizabeth? there was absolutely no connexion between them. Margot and Elizabeth got on well together . . . again there was no relationship to breed a motive . . . no, my poor Lisa, it's a mare's nest that you've uncovered . . . the boy has kidded himself, or maybe you . . . no wonder he wasn't keen on telling the detective. 'Yes . . . ', she said, 'yes . . . ' for Scampnell was talking on, telling the story of Cecily and the Rajah – the clinic he'd opposed, Cecily's insistence, his ultimate gratitude and offers of jewels worth a king's ransom and Cecily speaking out, asking instead for one of his Arab stallions. Bunny had heard the story before from Cecily: everyone had heard it; Elizabeth had always said that Cecily couldn't have ridden a stallion, she hadn't the hands for it; so that Bunny was able to say, 'yes . . . yes . . .' without listening and, at the end, 'That was just like her,' and, 'I'm sure the horse gave her more pleasure than she would have got from the rubies.' 'And here's Margot with the photograph,' said Scampnell, and Margot came in and showed a large mounted photograph of Cecily, young and pretty, mounted on a decorative grey horse and attended by a bearded and turbanned *syce* – 'absolutely,' said Bunny, 'Kipling.' 'She loved Kipling,' said Margot, but Scampnell pointed out the flask, laid the photograph down and sighed heavily, so Bunny only added, 'It's a beautiful photograph. Thank you for showing it to me,' and took her leave and went out into the deserted corridor. I'm tired; I'm fit to drop, she realized. Damn that boy and his silly story! All this time I could have been soaking in my bath instead of worrying those poor people. As she crossed the gallery she heard footsteps in the hall. . . . Charles . . . but I can't cope with him now. . . . Should I say good night, or cut him? . . . What rules are there for dealing with a husband who suspects one of murder? Between the bathroom and her bedroom she took pains to avoid him, scouting round the door before emerging, waiting, when she fancied she heard the door of her bedroom open and close, till the wastepipe in his bedroom reassured her with a gurgle. If he had looked for her, she thought as, ready for bed, she locked the door and slipped the key under her pillow, what in heaven's name had he intended to say to her? Again and again she and the impossible Sallust had patched and repatched their marriage, and, tattered and tarnished though it was, it had held to the end. But then, she thought, slipping out of her dressing-gown and kicking off her slippers, though they hadn't respected or trusted or even liked one another, they had been young and in love when they had married, and all through the disillusionment there had persisted a thread of that remembered gold. Now Charles, she thought, getting into bed, stretching out a hand for kind Beatrice's cup of

Ovaltine, Charles and I were by no means blinded by passion. I liked and respected him; he admired my talents and found me amusing: I slept on his proposal and accepted it in the sober light of next morning, not as I accepted Raoul's, on a balcony in the Dauphiné, with a dam' fortuitous peasant strumming a zither in the street beneath us, and across the valley the Meije, with his head among the stars. That was a stupid marriage, but it didn't end till death parted us: this was a sensible one, but already it's over, annulled. What has poor dear Charles done that that wretch Raoul didn't? she asked herself, stirring the Ovaltine; Charles suspects me of breaking the sixth commandment, but time and again, when he was in the mood, Raoul accused me of breaking the seventh. Oh, well, she thought, *le cœur a ses raisons* . . . and she looked at the Ovaltine she was mechanically stirring and realized that it was cold and that skin was afloat on it and that she couldn't drink it either to please Beatrice or to insure that she slept. She decided, I'll empty it down the basin before Beatrice comes in with my breakfast, but after a few moments of uneasy self-deception had to admit to herself that she seldom, if ever, woke until Beatrice called her, and presently, muttering, 'Damn all kind people,' she forced herself to rise, scurried to the basin, emptied the cup and replaced it on the bedside table. Then it was bliss to be warm again . . . nothing else mattered . . . neither marriage nor murder . . . and Barbara d'Estray slept.

CHAPTER SEVEN

CHARLES D'ESTRAY was back at New College. In a few minutes' time he was to speak at the Union, seconding a motion that in the opinion of this House the unsatisfactory state of this country is due to the Reformation. In a frantic endeavour to compose a speech, he had sported his oak, but rowing toughs were banging on it. . . . 'Clear off, you cads,' muttered Sir Charles through toothless gums, and wakened and knew it was day . . . another day of miserable uncertainty. 'Come in,' he called, since Benson had apparently gone mad, and a muffled voice told him that the door was locked, and then he remembered that he had locked it. 'Just a minute,' he called, and hurried into his sober dark blue dressing-gown and slippers to match. ' 'Morning, Benson. I thought it wise to tell everyone to lock their doors,' he said, and then he noticed that Benson was in shirt-sleeves and a green baize apron and had brought no tray of early morning tea. 'What's the matter, Benson – not another?'

Benson's always pale face was grey. His hands shook.

'It's a note, Sir Charles. We dursn't touch it. It's in her ladyship's typewriter in her sitting-room.'

'I'll come,' said Sir Charles. 'My specs . . . just a moment.' Collecting his reading-glasses, he took the opportunity to slip his teeth in.

Benson led the way along the corridor. Realizing that the curtains were drawn and the lights burning, Sir Charles glanced at his wrist watch: the time was a quarter past seven. At the door of Bunny's sitting-room, Sylvia, the under-house-maid, was standing; with her blue eyes bulging and her lower lip held between teeth, she looked like a frightened hare. Sir Charles went straight to the battered little typewriter, uncovered, as Bunny always left it, on the writing-table. To catch the eye, a page had been wound almost from the rollers. Sir Charles put on his glasses and read:

To Everyone who it may concern
The game is up, the detective knows, so I am taking the easiest way out. I

poisoned Elizabeth because I hated her and I knew Charles would never get rid of her. In the case of Mrs Scampnell I poisoned her because she knew too much. Now I have taken some of the poison to avoid being hung – forgive me if you can. Barbara.

Sir Charles straightened up and took off his glasses.

'Have you read it, Benson?'

'I glanced through it, Sir Charles, when Sylvia fetched me up and pointed it out to me. It caught her eye when she came to do the grate, and she read it, because her ladyship has left messages in the machine on previous occasions – not to light the fire, or to let the dog out. Can I get you anything, Sir Charles – a little brandy?' Without waiting for an answer, he hurried away.

Sir Charles, who was, in fact, feeling a little faint, turned away from the table and sat down in the armchair by the dead fire. God! he'd made a fool of himself, falling for her, marrying her, bringing her back to Aston as his children's stepmother . . . it was his fault, his foolish, senile fault, that Elizabeth and poor Scampnell's wife had died. Well, it was over – at least she'd had the decency to spare him the anguish of a trial and a conviction. . . . There would be a certain amount of publicity, of course; for some time it would be embarrassing to meet his friends; he would feel humbled before his children; for the rest of his life remorse would strike him when he remembered, or was reminded of Elizabeth. But he was conscious of a certain relief: he had to face things now, he hadn't to fear them . . . with courage and dignity he'd get through . . .

'Bunny didn't write this,' a voice at his elbow repeated.

Startled, he turned. Lisa, barefooted, in yellow pyjamas and a tweed riding-coat, stood frowning at the typewriter.

'My poor child! you shouldn't be here,' said Sir Charles gently, and Benson, coming in with a glass of brandy on a silver salver, said, 'Oh, Miss Lisa, I told Sylvia to keep you upstairs.'

'What *is* this rot? Bunny didn't write it,' said Lisa.

'Lisa, my dear, you must try to understand,' said Sir Charles and swallowed his brandy. 'People are not always responsible for what they do – I don't mean they're mad, but they're ill mentally; a mind can be sick as well as a body, you know. My poor child! this is a terrible shock to you. I know how you loved your mother. You must try to be brave.' He looked into the cold and scornful little face and said, 'I'm no use, I'm afraid. Benson, take her to Nanny.'

Lisa said, 'I don't want to be taken to Nanny. How can you be so idiotic as to think that Bunny wrote *who* where it should be *whom*, or put a comma between two unrelated statements, or used *in the case of*, or *hung* where it should be *hanged*?'

'Come along, Miss Lisa,' said Benson.

'Where is she, anyhow?' asked Lisa.

'Don't you understand?' asked Sir Charles pitifully. 'Your poor mother's gone. That note says she's taken poison. Later on, my dear, it will help us to remember that in the end she did the gallant thing. It was like her, wasn't it, Lisa?'

'But she didn't write the note; somebody else wrote it. Oh,' cried Lisa, 'do you think they've poisoned her?' She dashed to the door, but Benson caught her arm and held her. 'Let me go, let me go,' she shrieked. 'If we're quick we might save her.'

'Lisa, be quiet! You'll wake the whole house,' said Sir Charles in a voice calculated to bring her to her senses. 'I'm going to telephone to the police now, and I'll send Miss Patricia along to help you, Benson.' With Lisa wriggling like an eel, kicking his shins and butting him in the stomach, all that Benson could manage was an unintelligible mono-syllable.

Sir Charles was barely at Patricia's door when it opened and she emerged, fair, fresh, and unruffled, so like her mother that Sir Charles exclaimed, 'Hermione!' and corrected himself, 'I mean Pat – a shocking thing's happened. Bar-bara's committed suicide and left a confession. . . . Lisa's being quite hysterical in the sitting-room and only Benson's with her. I've got to telephone . . . '

'Right. I'll cope,' said Patricia, bless her, and Sir Charles went on down the west-wing staircase to his study and picked up the telephone receiver, thinking how breeding showed in moments of emergency. He called the Harborough police station; the Sergeant on duty would start for Aston immediately, picking up Superintendent Treadwell and Inspector Price on the way.

Sir Charles replaced the receiver and with a lighter heart passed through the baize door into the service quarters. Benson, now in his coat, came from the pantry. 'The police should be here in twenty minutes or so,' Sir Charles told him. 'Did you manage to calm Miss Lisa?' Benson said, 'Miss Pat and Nanny got her upstairs between them, and I took the precaution of locking the sitting-room door. Here's the key, Sir Charles, and should Beatrice carry on as usual with the early morning teas?' 'Yes, I think so,' said Sir Charles. 'We don't want the p.gs. coming out into the passages and investigating. It's Sunday, so she could be a few minutes behind time without arousing any comment. I'd like Mr Hugo to be called now, though. Perhaps you'd call him yourself, Benson, and break the news. I'll dress and be ready when the police come. Get them in quietly, Benson – as quietly as you can.'

Sir Charles was unused to dressing hurriedly; it did not occur to him to depart from his custom of donning a suit on Sundays, and it was fully three-quarters of an hour before he came down the main staircase into the hall. The guests had been called, but the main corridor was quiet still; there was no slamming of doors or running of bath-water. Before Hugo had dressed, he had come into his father's room and avoiding his eyes, had said, 'Bad show, this. I'm sorry.' 'Thanks, old man,' replied Sir Charles. 'I'm sorry too, and particularly sorry I let you and Patricia in for all this through my own stupidity.' 'Oh, that's rot,' said Hugo. 'You can't see into the future any more than the rest of us. Better get dressed now . . . ' and away he'd gone. What was happening on the nursery floor, wasn't, Sir Charles thought, his business: leave the child to the women. . . . As he reached the hall, Benson appeared from the dining-room and said, 'I'll bring a breakfast tray to the study while you're waiting, Sir Charles,' but as he spoke, both men saw, through the glass doors of the vestibule, the first of the two police cars. Benson hurried to the door. Price and Treadwell, followed by a sergeant and two constables, came up the steps side by side.

'There's been another death, then,' said Price, brushing past Benson and hurrying up to Sir Charles. 'I understand that you omitted to inform the sergeant as to the identity of the deceased?'

'It's my wife,' said Sir Charles. 'But it was suicide. She left a note which explains everything.' His voice was expressionless.

Price said, 'That's what I have suspected from the commencement of the case. Where is the body?'

'We all locked our bedroom doors last night; I advised it,' Sir Charles told him. 'The under-housemaid found the note in my wife's typewriter in her sitting-room. When I had read it and pulled myself together, I telephoned to the police station. We haven't attempted to enter her bedroom.'

Price said, 'That's very satisfactory to us. We'll go up at once, Treadwell.' He turned back to Sir Charles. 'Have you a master key, or, if she happens to have taken the key out, would it be possible to unlock the door with a key from any of the other bedrooms?'

'I've never heard of our having a master key. I don't know about the others, do you, Benson?'

'It's possible, Sir Charles. The keys all look alike. There's also a bunch of unidentified keys, which I keep with those of the east wing, in the pantry.'

'Get them,' snapped Price, and started up the stairs with Treadwell, who, as he passed Sir Charles, muttered something about his deepest sympathy.

Reluctant to enter that room, to look, even now that she was dead, on the woman who had made a fool of him, Sir Charles waited for Benson, and when the butler came with a bunch of old-fashioned keys in his hand, they went upstairs together. Benson said, 'It'll be a shock to you, Sir Charles. Wouldn't it be better to let us carry on without you?' but Sir Charles said, 'No, no. It's my responsibility,' and added,

131

'You're a good old friend to us, Benson.' They turned into the west wing and found that Treadwell and Price had opened the door; following Price into the room, Treadwell looked back to say in a low voice, 'The key from the next door did the job all right.'

Bracing his shoulders, compressing his lips, Sir Charles went in behind Treadwell. The light of the wet autumn morning was seeping through the pink-and-white curtains; instinctively Treadwell moved towards the windows, but Price switched on the light and revealed the room which the second Lady d'Estray had herself described as *en gout de cocotte*. That, unlike her victims, she had died peacefully was immediately apparent to all four men. The grey silk eiderdown had slipped sideways, but the pink blankets were as smooth as though the bed had recently been made, and all that could be seen of Lady d'Estray, between the neat turnover of the sheet and a luxurious pile of pillows, was the back of a childish-looking mop of blonde curls. 'A narcotic of some description,' Price thought aloud, and walked round the bed, and turned down the coverings, and started back, crying, 'Great Scott!' as Bunny opened her eyes and blinked at him; and 'Good God!' said Sir Charles, and 'Christ!' said Benson, and 'Strewth!' said Treadwell, as she raised her head, sat up and looked about her.

'What *are* you doing here? What's happened? Not Lisa . . . '

Benson was the first to reassure her. 'No, no, my lady. Miss Lisa's safe and sound. It was your ladyship we feared for . . . '

Price cut in. 'Leave it to me, please. I shall have some questions to ask you, Lady d'Estray. Would you dress as quickly as possible and come down to the study?'

'But I haven't had breakfast yet,' objected Bunny.

Benson said, 'I'll have your breakfast sent up at once, my lady. And Miss Lisa should be told, Sir Charles – shall I see to it?'

'Yes . . . ' said Sir Charles vaguely. 'Yes, Benson, yes.' He couldn't concentrate. It was so horribly embarrassing . . .

these men . . . the pink bed . . . those bare shoulders . . . that transparent black nightgown. . . . Just when everything had seemed clear – grievously clear, but clear – back came the awful uncertainty. If she hadn't poisoned herself, what was the meaning of the note? . . . What had happened?

Bunny, too, was asking 'What's happened?'

'That's what we all want to know,' said Treadwell. 'If we knew that, we should be well away. There's bin some monkeying somewhere.' He looked hopefully at Price, who was at the bedside table.

'This cup and saucer, Lady d'Estray – I presume it contained some beverage, which you drank on retiring? Had an attempt on your life been perpetrated – which I anticipate will be your explanation – how do you account for the failure of the same?'

Bunny looked puzzled.

'I'm sorry. Say that again, will you?'

'The Detective-Inspector means that if the drink was poisoned, why is your ladyship alive this morning?' Treadwell explained.

'But I'm sure it wasn't poisoned – Beatrice made it,' said Bunny. 'Actually, I didn't drink it. She told me not to let it get cold, and of course I did, while I was having my bath, and it got skin on it. I didn't like the look of it, so I poured it down the wash-basin so as not to hurt her feelings.'

'When your ladyship was in the bath, was the door locked?' asked Treadwell.

'No,' said Bunny. 'It was when I got into bed that I locked it.'

Treadwell sighed, 'Ahh. I'm glad to hear that, my lady. It was beginning to look bad for my auntie.'

'Your auntie?'

'Beatrice Blythe, my lady.'

'As if anyone would suspect Beatrice! Besides, we don't know yet if there *was* poison in the cup. It'll have to be analysed,' said Bunny. 'And, furthermore,' she added, 'when I'd finished my bath, as I didn't want to meet . . . well, as I didn't want to meet anyone, I opened the door a crack and listened in case there was anybody in the corridor, and I heard my bedroom door open and shut again – I thought it was you, Charles, come to say good night or something, but of course, if it had been and you were on your way to bed, you would have come on down the corridor.'

'Looks as if whoever-it-was must have gone the other way – towards the east wing,' said Treadwell.

'Or down the main staircase,' said Bunny.

Price had remained silent because he was thinking. Treadwell, he thought, was all too ready to assume from this new turn of events that Lady d'Estray was innocent. But the woman was clever . . . and clever was cunning . . . and it was possible that she had engineered the whole business in the hope of diverting suspicion. Had an attempted murder been staged, he would have felt sure of that; as things were, there was an obvious risk that the police might accept the attempted suicide as genuine . . . it was more than a risk . . . she had never given the impression that she rated his intelligence so highly. She's in the clear, he thought, unless the note tells us something . . . and he turned to Sir Charles and said, 'I'd like to see this note you spoke of. Perhaps, Super, you'd take care of the cup and saucer, and while Lady d'Estray has her breakfast it would be as well – for her protection – to post a constable in the passage. . . . '

Treadwell assented, and Sir Charles led the way to the sitting-room, unlocked the door and stood aside while Price went in. 'Will you be needing me?' he asked. 'If not, I'd like to get a little breakfast inside me.' 'Just a moment,' said Price without mercy, and read the note through. 'Just one question, Sir Charles: is there anything in this note which suggests to you that it was, or was not, written by Lady d'Estray?'

'I read it through quickly and swallowed it whole,' said Sir Charles, coming across to the table. 'But my stepdaughter appeared on the scene, and she picked holes in it – said there were grammatical errors that her mother couldn't have made, and insisted that someone else had written it. I must confess that I pooh-poohed the idea, but now . . . I'm completely confused, but perhaps there was something in it?'

'What were these errors?'

'*Who it may concern* . . . that, of course, should be *whom*. Then, *in the case of Mrs Scampnell* . . . my wife had a definite aversion to *in the case of* . . . almost a mania.'

'I don't see anything wrong with it myself,' said Price. 'It's very usual.'

'Well, it shouldn't be,' said Sir Charles. 'It's what they call jargon. Then somewhere there's a comma where there should be a semi-colon or a colon, and at the end there's *hung* where it should be *hanged*.'

'I see that. But it's a very common mistake.'

'Possibly. But the point is that my wife didn't make common mistakes. She's a writer, and not only a writer but a stylist; she's particularly keen on good English and correct punctuation – a little too fussy, it's always seemed to me. As I say, I was shocked and upset and I didn't, at the time, attach much importance to what the child was saying; then she made a scene and I sent her upstairs to the nursery. But in view of what's happened since, I'm convinced she was right – this was never written by Barbara Sallust.'

'The fact that it's not signed points that way too,' Price said. 'It suggests that the writer was afraid to attempt a forgery of Lady d'Estray's signature. I cannot deny, Sir Charles, that, at any rate in the case of Miss Hudson, the evidence against your wife was stronger than against any other individual – motive particularly. Now we must look elsewhere. That housemaid – she prepared the Ovaltine; but had she any knowledge of typewriting? It is obvious that this note was not typed by a person without prior knowledge of a machine.'

'I can't believe that Beatrice ever learnt typewriting. She came here at fourteen. Admittedly, she prepared the Ovaltine, but there was that door which my wife heard open and close. I didn't go to her room. We had – er – said good night earlier. It must have been the murderer.'

Price said, 'To return to the typewriting: Mr Rose and Mr Scampnell, as business-men, would be conversant with the machine, and probably Flight-Lieutenant Marvin; most young fellows can type after a fashion. Mrs Rose – what was she before she married – a secretary, perhaps? Miss Rattray? Apparently she doesn't have to earn her living. You won't take it amiss if I ask you whether you can type, Sir Charles?'

'I type with two fingers, but quite adequately, well enough to have done this,' said Sir Charles.

'Your son?'

'About the same. Patricia's hopeless. She tried to type a circular about the riding stables, but my wife had to do it in the end.'

'The butler?'

'Not that I've heard.'

'That boy?'

'Eric? No. He came straight here from school.'

'He doesn't attend night school or classes of any kind in his spare time?'

'I'm sure he doesn't. Most of his spare time is spent with my stepdaughter. She's teaching him to ride.'

'Well,' said Price, squaring his narrow shoulders, 'I shall have this machine gone over for finger-prints; up to date we've had no luck with them, but we may be fortunate; it's not easy to typewrite in gloves, and a person handling the machine and the paper might possibly forget afterwards exactly where he had placed his hands. But I anticipate more useful results from a talk with Lady d'Estray: she must have some idea of why an attack was made on her, unless, of course, we are dealing with a maniac.'

'I think that's what we *are* doing,' said Sir Charles.

'Most unlikely,' said Price. 'A homicidal maniac might kill with his hands or with some instrument, but not by poison. I'll lock this room up again, and while I'm waiting to see Lady d'Estray, I wonder if a little something could be provided to pacify the inner man?'

'You mean breakfast? Yes, of course. We'll go down to the dining-room. On Sundays it's served from nine onwards, but Benson will find us something. How about Treadwell?'

Treadwell, Benson told them, had already been provided

136

with a snack and had driven away with the cup from Lady d'Estray's bedroom: and Beatrice, he told them, would like to see the Detective-Inspector as soon as convenient: she was upset, naturally, it being she who had prepared the Ovaltine. Price said he would see her as soon as he had finished breakfast, but as he was masticating his last mouthful of toast Bunny, wearing corduroy slacks and a canary-coloured polo-necked jersey, came in. Sir Charles got up, but after one glance, averted his eyes from her. He had been wondering whether it would be best to apologize for his suspicions at the first opportunity, or to ignore all that and try to get back to their old terms in the excitement of following up new clues, but here she was again in a sweater and slacks and sandals on a Sunday. . . . Now nothing would induce him to apologize, he thought; he'd had every reason to suspect her, and, even though the detective seemed to have eliminated her, one couldn't be sure . . . she was very clever.

'Any coffee left? I could do with another cup,' said Bunny.

Price glanced at Sir Charles. 'With your permission, Sir Charles, I think it would be best if we went to the study – your guests may be down soon, and the less they know the better.' Bunny said, 'Okay. Anyhow it will soon be time for elevenses.' Sir Charles said, as he had said before, 'If you ate a normal breakfast, you wouldn't need to feed again at eleven.' Bunny shrugged. Sir Charles could have slapped her.

In the study, from which Sylvia, carrying a housemaid's box, fled at their approach, Sir Charles said to Price, 'Shall I leave you?' but Price said, 'Not unless you wish to,' so he stayed and sat down in the armchair, while Price sat at the table and Bunny perched on the club fender. Price began, 'Now, Lady d'Estray, can you tell me anything about the note, which was found in your typewriter?'

'I'd never heard of it until now when Beatrice brought in my breakfast. She told me Sylvia had found it. When Lisa and I left my sitting-room last night there was nothing in the typewriter. I haven't done any work – I haven't been able to – since Elizabeth was poisoned.'

137

'Now, Lady d'Estray, I want you to think very carefully: this attack on you may have been made merely to divert suspicion from the murderer; or it may have been made because, as in the case of Mrs Scampnell, you were in possession of some vital piece of information, in which case the suicide note was written in order to kill two birds with one stone, i.e. to prevent you passing on what information you possessed *and* to preclude any further investigation. The former I think unlikely – as far as I am aware I have divulged no suspicions.'

'If you treated the others as you treated me . . .' said Bunny.

Price blushed, or, rather, two reddish spots appeared on his cheek-bones. Sir Charles looked intently at his Sunday shoes.

'Lady d'Estray, this is a very intricate case, and the lack of evidence, the absence of motive . . . well . . . it was unfortunate for all parties that only in your case was there evidence both of motive and opportunity. I hope you will forget that now.'

'Of course. Homer nods,' said Bunny pleasantly.

'Pardon?'

'We all make mistakes. Actually last night I did learn something – very little – I can't see how it fits in. Anyhow, I promised not to tell anyone.'

'Don't be ridiculous, Barbara,' and, 'Lady d'Estray, this is a murder case,' said Sir Charles and Price simultaneously.

'Would you mind if I spoke to Lisa?'

'If you made a promise to Lisa, it's ridiculous to bother about it,' said Sir Charles irritably. 'You're her mother; she's only a child, and there are lives at stake – really, Barbara, do behave sensibly.'

Bunny had stretched out a hand to the bell-push beside the fireplace, and the silence that followed was broken by the entrance of Benson. 'Benson, will you send Lisa here at once, please? I expect she's in the stables.' 'Just a moment – I believe she's in the boot-room, my lady.' 'Helping Eric clean the shoes, I suppose. Nice company and an elegant occupation for a young lady on a Sunday morning,' said Sir

138

Charles disapprovingly. 'The better the day, the better the deed,' said Bunny at random.

Lisa came in. She wore dungarees. She smiled at her mother, but her face was still swollen and her eyes red with crying. A smear of shoe-polish across her cheek confirmed her stepfather's supposition.

'What *have* you been doing to yourself?' asked Bunny.

'At an unearthly hour this morning I was involved in a difference of opinion with some half-wits. I hope they're sorry now,' said Lisa, with a baleful glance at Sir Charles.

'Well, we'll skip that,' said Bunny hastily. 'Have you heard what's happened?'

'I read the note. I knew you hadn't written it. I knew that someone had tried to poison you, but the beasts made me stay upstairs until the police came, and then Benson told me. I've bitten that beast, Patricia . . .'

'Well, you shouldn't have. But never mind that now; it's over. What I want to know is how you-know-who is feeling about you-know-what this morning? I heard more about it last night in another way and it might be important.'

'Oh, when he heard about you he decided to tell at the first opportunity. He says that there are always being miscarriages of justice, but he'd swing for you gladly. Shall I fetch him?'

'Please, Lisa.'

'What,' asked Sir Charles, 'is all this nonsense? We're wasting time.'

'It's Eric, the boy who helps Benson,' said Bunny to Price. 'He knows something connected with Mrs Scampnell's murder. On the other hand – well, here he is. I'll tell you the rest later.'

Eric's hands were clenched at his sides. His face was pale and determined.

'Well,' said Price, 'so you know something? Whatever it is, why did you keep it to yourself? – that's what's called suppressing evidence.'

Eric said, 'It never come into my 'ead till yesterday, when they were talking it over in the 'all, and I'd 'ardly figured it out when off you went, so I told Miss Lisa, and she asked to tell 'er Mum, but they wasn't to tell anyone else till I'd seen the meanin' on it. It's about them flasks . . . '

He told his story. 'Yes . . . yes . . . ' said Price and at the end he said, 'Yes, that's useful; but it would have been more useful last night – this morning we've other clues to think of, unless, of course, it's this matter which Lady d'Estray intends to amplify?'

'It is,' said Bunny.

'All right, boy, you can cut along now; but don't go far: we may want you again. And the same applies to you,' he added, spying Lisa, who had slipped back into the room and was effacing herself beside a bookcase.

The children went out, and Bunny began, 'After I'd seen Lisa into bed last night and left Babette with her and heard her lock her door, it occurred to me that if I had a talk with Margot Rattray I might possibly hear more about the flasks without breaking the promise I'd made to Lisa and Eric. I'd got a good excuse to go to her room – where, as you probably know, she and her stepfather had had dinner – because it was really only decent to ask if she was all right, or if there was anything I could do – I ought to have gone before. On my way I found Beatrice filling hot-water-bottles in the upstairs pantry and that was when she promised me the Ovaltine and told me not to let it get cold. The Scampnells were both in Margot's bedroom, sitting and grieving over the fire, and I managed to linger a bit, and at last I got the conversation – rather clumsily, I'm afraid – round to the flask. They said that there was only one, dating from her days in India, and I must say I believed them; in fact I remember thinking, damn Eric and his silly story, as I went back along the corridor. I expect you think so, too; I expect there's nothing in it really. If Eric was right and they were lying, it would mean . . . well, husbands do poison their wives, of course, but Elizabeth was poisoned too.'

'It's only the boy's word against theirs,' said Sir Charles. 'He probably sees himself as Dick Barton, wants to take a hand in solving the mystery and has invented the whole affair.'

'That's what I thought last night,' said Bunny, 'but now there's been this attack on me, and really the only reason for it that I can think of is the question I asked the Scampnells about the flasks. Beatrice or Sylvia might be able to help us. They may have seen the two flasks when they did the room.'

'I'm inclined to agree with Sir Charles that the boy is romancing,' Price said with less than his usual confidence. 'Husbands have poisoned their wives, as you say, Lady d'Estray, but that doesn't account for Miss Hudson's murder. Further, has there ever been the slightest suggestion that the Scampnells' marriage was an unhappy one?'

'I always thought that they got on very well,' admitted Bunny, 'but I had a gossip with Beatrice while she was filling the hot-water-bottles, and she didn't agree. She said she'd heard things.'

'Servants' gossip,' scornfully exclaimed Sir Charles.

'All the same, it would be advisable to hear it,' Price told him. 'Also I would very much like to ascertain the truth about those flasks. We'll have the head housemaid in and question her, if Lady d'Estray would be so good as to press the bell.'

Beatrice, standing stiffly in her blue print dress and old-fashioned starched white apron, said, 'I wanted to see you, Inspector; I wanted to tell you that it was me that prepared the Ovaltine, but I didn't put nothing in it, and I wouldn't of, either, seeing as I took to Lady d'Estray the first time I set eyes on her and stood up for 'er when the others said she wasn't what they was used to and no better than a foreigner, which they did – if you'll excuse me, my lady – until they got to know your ladyship better and took back their words.' Beatrice paused to draw breath, but before anyone else could speak, she continued, 'Miss Lisa's always been a favourite with me, too; I like that little thing, and I think Miss Patricia and Nanny treated 'er abominable this morning, keeping 'er in the nursery when all she wanted was to set 'er mind at rest about 'er Mum.'

'Listen, Beatrice,' said Bunny. 'Nobody thinks for one moment that you put anything – even if there *was* anything –

in the Ovaltine. As for Patricia, she was only doing what her father told her, and I understand that Lisa bit her, which wasn't very nice. What the Detective-Inspector wants to know is about Mrs Scampnell's flasks . . . '

'You looked after her bedroom, I believe,' Price said quickly. 'You must have seen her hunting-flasks – had she one, or a pair of them?'

Bunny's heart was racing. Sir Charles sat upright, though his tired white face still wore a look of scorn. For a maddening moment Beatrice stood silent, her china blue eyes fixed and stupid.

'The shelf above the wash-basin,' she said at last, 'was cluttered up with 'is shaving-tackle and medicines – aperients mostly. She kept 'er things on the dressing-table: not the chest of drawers with the little round mirror on it – 'e used that for 'is combs and brushes – but the proper dressing-table. There was 'er tortoise-shell set there – brushes and an 'and-glass and a powder-box, but no flasks. Ah, it was on the marquetry chest of drawers that she kept 'em, along with 'er 'unting-whip from India; that was gold-mounted and too good to be left in the 'arness-room unless it was locked up at night, which Miss Patricia wouldn't agree to.'

'You say "she kept *them*". Do you mean there were two of them?'

'That's right. Awkward things they are, out of their cases. She used to stand them up, but me and Sylvia were afraid of them toppling over, and we always laid them down again.'

'I want you to cast your mind back to yesterday morning. How many flasks were on the chest of drawers then?'

Beatrice reflected, 'Let me see . . . Mr Scampnell, 'e was going to the meet by car with young Margot, so 'e was out of the room earlier than usual, and after we'd made the beds we finished the whole room off before we started on the others. Sylvia did the wash-basin and then ran the 'oover over the carpet while I dusted, and we was talking about the inconvenience caused by people dawdling in their bedrooms instead of coming down to breakfast at the right time. No, there wasn't any flasks on the marquetry chest of drawers; the 'unting-whip 'ad gone, and all I 'ad to do was to pick up a photo of some blacks 'olding an 'orse and it was a clear sweep for the duster.'

'Thank you, Miss Blythe,' said Price. 'That's very valuable. Now I trust that you will be good enough to afford us additional assistance. In your opinion, were Mr and Mrs Scampnell a happy couple?'

Beatrice said carefully, 'I never saw 'im raise 'is 'and to 'er, that I *can* say; but I've 'eard 'im say nasty things both to 'er face and be'ind 'er back – 'orrible sarky things. " 'Ere comes the Unspeakable" I've 'eard 'im say to Miss Margot, and I've 'eard 'im call 'er a stingy old bitch and an ugly 'orse-mad old skinflint – to 'er face that was. She could be spitey, too, but in a more lady-like fashion. I've 'eard 'er say, "All this comes of marrying into the middle-classes," and – if you'll excuse me, Sir Charles – I've 'eard 'er call 'im a bloody little tradesman.'

'Goodness!' said Bunny. 'All that behind such a very smug façade!'

'Of course, she 'ad the money,' said Beatrice. ' 'E's only got a kind of pension – at least, that's the conclusion we come to in the 'all.'

'The money probably goes to the stepdaughter,' Price thought aloud. 'I wonder . . . Is there anything else you can tell us, Miss Blythe? What were Mr Scampnell's relations with Miss Hudson, for instance? Can you help us there?'

'I've never 'eard 'im speak of 'er except once, when 'e said something to Mrs Scampnell about "your 'orse-faced pal", but Miss Elizabeth spoke to me of 'im and of Miss Margot several times. She thought Miss Margot was a nice little thing, though she 'adn't no guts – if you'll excuse me, Sir Charles. Once, after Miss Elizabeth 'ad 'ad words with Miss Lisa, she was talking about modern children and their going on and criticizing Miss Lisa for not calling 'er ladyship Mother or Mummy, and then she went on about Miss Margot calling 'er stepfather Scamp, as she did, and many's the laugh we've 'ad over it in the 'all. I'd say that Miss Elizabeth liked

Miss Margot as much as she liked anybody outside the Family and that Marvin – what their row at the end was about I *don't* know.'

Price snapped, 'A row? What row?'

'I don't know anything about it first 'and,' said Beatrice, 'but it was discussed in the 'all.'

Sir Charles said, 'A great many things that would be better not repeated seem to be discussed in the hall.'

'And thank God for that,' said Bunny. 'Beatrice, who did know about it first hand?'

'Young Kate,' said Beatrice without enthusiasm, and to Price she explained, 'the kitchen-maid, my sister's youngest girl.' Then she turned to Sir Charles, 'Of course, in the old days the under-servants weren't allowed to speak at table until the upper servants 'ad withdrawn, but me and Mr Benson and Mrs Capes decided that, within reason, we in the 'all should adapt ourselves to the spirit of the times.'

'That was very wise of you,' said Bunny, 'but I expect you suffer for it: young people are such bores.'

Price said, 'I'll see the girl; but at present I'd like to concentrate on these flasks. Have you been in the room this morning?'

'No,' answered Beatrice, 'I 'aven't. I took Mr Scampnell 'is early morning tea, but we moved 'im into the little green room last night. 'Er ladyship thought it would be better for 'im.'

'Well, thank you very much, Miss Blythe. You've been of great assistance. I think that's all for just now.' When Beatrice had left the room, Price went on, 'If there's any significance in this matter of the flasks, I should hardly expect to discover the second in its customary location. But I'd like to make sure. Would you entertain the idea of visiting the room and just glancing on the chest of drawers, Lady d'Estray? The guests will be rising and, under the circumstances, it will occasion less comment than if I were observed in the passages. I presume you can find some excuse for entering the room if you are questioned?'

'Oh yes. I can bring out some linen ...'

144

'And while the guests are breakfasting, I can make a thorough search of all three bedrooms.'

'I shouldn't think you'd find anything. If I'd got anything incriminating I should get rid of it down the drain – no, a flask wouldn't go, would it? – well, into a rabbit hole or the river. I suppose there's just a chance they may not have thought of throwing it out until I asked about it; if so, they'll have it on them until they go for a nice Sunday walk through Bottom Wood or by the river . . .'

Sir Charles said, 'You were asked to go upstairs and look in the room, Barbara – you can safely leave the rest to the Detective-Inspector.' And when Bunny had gone he said, 'You no longer suspect my wife, I take it?'

'It is our unpleasant duty to suspect everyone until we make an arrest,' Price told him, 'but in point of fact I am glad to be able to inform you that I now regard Lady d'Estray, like your good self, as far down among the "improbables".'

'Then you think there's something in this Scampnell business?'

'Before hazarding an opinion I should require a great deal more evidence than I have to date. In the case of the flasks, there may be some perfectly simple explanation.'

While they talked, Bunny, joined by Babette on the west wing staircase, had reached the large room looking south over the formal garden, which Cecily Scampnell and her husband had occupied. In size and brightness it was equal to the Roses' room on the other side of the main staircase, but the Roses had a private bathroom, contrived by Bunny from a windowless slip of a room, matched, on the Scampnells' side, by the 'upstairs pantry'. Both rooms were charmingly furnished with late eighteenth-century pieces and modern beds, and when Bunny had learned what Cecily's tastes were she had gone round the house collecting sporting prints, which she had substituted for water-colour landscapes by a Victorian Lady d'Estray. Cecily had brought photographs, mostly of India, and hunting trophies – masks and brushes – which she had hung herself, with small regard for the old Chinese wallpaper. A masculine room, thought Bunny, as she drew back the faded, yellow damask curtains; if you didn't know the Scampnells, you'd guess at a domineering husband, but the accent on sport was Cecily's . . . how had he felt about it, the little man from the suburbs of the industrial town in the Midlands? Was he, as few are, truly meek-hearted? Or did he, like so many, hide behind a mask of amiability the cankerous malignity of the domestically oppressed?

On the marquetry chest of drawers there was nothing but a pair of silver candlesticks belonging to the house: there was no flask among the variety of patent remedies on the shelf above the wash-basin or on the dressing-table, devoid of any aid to beauty beyond one bowl of powder, an elaborate old-fashioned manicure set and a selection of stout grey hair-nets. So that's that, thought Bunny, and looked round for the linen she had intended to carry out with her, but the too-efficient Beatrice must have taken it all away last night, she discovered; even the counterpanes on the twin beds had been replaced by dust-sheets, on one of which Babette now lay, her eyes affectedly closed and her tongue showing. Bunny prodded her and signalled to her to follow; then, since her only excuse now for entering the room was to air it, and that would sound remarkably unconvincing to anyone who knew her, she opened the door as soundlessly as possible and peered out into the corridor. It was deserted, but there had been a sound somewhere . . . the closing of a door on her right . . . the locked door into the east wing, which was only opened when an extra piece of furniture was needed, or on warm bright days when Beatrice opened the windows.

Bunny thought: the east wing . . . Of course. Why on earth didn't we think of it? It's a wonderful place to hide in . . . some outsider may have been hiding there for days . . . the disgruntled groom whom someone had thought of in the first place. That there were policemen almost within call didn't occur to her; all the events of her life had conspired to teach her self-reliance. She turned the handle of the door. It opened.

Somewhere down by her ankles Babette snuffled. She'll patter and snort and give me away, thought Bunny, pushing

146

her back into the corridor and shutting the door between them. The bitch gave one searing scratch on the mahogany, and then Bunny could hear no more of her. Lisa had called her, perhaps, or she had caught sight of Captain.

The first-floor corridor in the east wing, like that in the west, ran the length of the building and was lit by a window at the end, which looked southwards, and an east window over the stairs. It was well lighted, but now pale blinds were drawn down over the windows; the morning was dark, and in the white twilight there was nothing sinister, but a kind of eerie elegance, in the long vista of tall, closed doors. Bunny stood listening. Though the rooms on her left looked over a screen of chestnuts to the stableyard, no cheerful sounds of morning penetrated to the corridor: the silence was profound. There were eight doors on her right and four on her left, and in any of these rooms the murderer might move at will; a sigh, a sniff, a footstep, the rustle of garments would be inaudible through the solid mahogany. A systematic search must, she felt, betray her; she couldn't hope to open and shut a dozen doors quite noiselessly; it would be best to take up some strategic position and watch until the adversary revealed himself. The staircase with its sheltering curves and command of three floors seemed indicated. Quite silent in her rope soles, she trod the threadbare Persian rugs which carpeted the corridor. When she reached the staircase a small sound brought her, heart in mouth, to a standstill. Somewhere above her on the second floor a tap was dripping.

There was no bathroom in this east wing of the house; she had planned to convert some of the smaller rooms if the guest-house business proved successful enough to warrant the opening and modernizing of the wing. On the second-floor landing there was, however, a cold-water tap above an old-fashioned sink, where housemaids' pails could be emptied and filled. Bunny tried to remember what grounds she had for assuming that the water had been turned off in the wing; in none of her raids on the furniture had she heard a tap dripping, nor had there been any talk of trouble with frozen pipes during the frosts of the previous winter. If the water had never been turned off, a perished washer might account for the dripping; if it had been turned off . . . and turned on again by someone who had no legitimate business in the east wing . . .

The second floor was darker than the first; the windows were smaller and the drawn blinds dark blue. On the landing you turned left, and the sink stood under the staircase which led to the attics; in the west wing the space had been used for the bathroom which served the nurseries, this being the only improvement in the house that had been made by Hermione d'Estray. Flattening herself against the wall, Bunny peered cautiously round the corner. Margot Rattray was kneeling at the cupboard under the sink. On the floor beside her gaped a brown zip-fastened handbag. She was wearing her Sunday dress, a wool frock of a dull middle-blue. There was a row of covered buttons down the back, and a belt of the same material as the dress, which tied in a meagre bow. Bunny observed, too, that Margot wore bedroom slippers of the moccasin type and a charm bracelet, which tinkled as her hands moved. So that's it, thought Bunny, and, I'd better get back, for what in heaven's name can one say? but before she had taken a step, Margot's head turned, the bobbed hair swinging. She jumped to her feet with something between a gasp and a sigh.

Bunny felt no fear. You couldn't be afraid of Margot, dumpy in the dull little blue dress she had chosen because it was cheap and wouldn't show the dirt. But she felt embarrassed: what *could* one say? Apologetically she explained, 'I heard a noise and, as this wing is supposed to be shut up, I came to investigate.' That was terribly feeble, she thought: I must be tougher. 'What the hell are you doing here?'

Margot whispered, 'You interfering painted-up old hag! Why didn't you die last night?' She took a step nearer. 'Damn you! why didn't you die?'

Bunny said, 'You mustn't talk like that . . . we always thought you were such a nice girl . . . ' Keeping her eyes on Margot's she stepped back into the corridor. 'Even Elizabeth always said what a nice girl you were.'

'*That* silly old cow,' said Margot. '*She* died because she stuck her nose in. Oh, I don't need poison. Just let me get my hands round your scrawny throat.' With outstretched hands and crooked fingers, she sprang.

Bunny dodged for the staircase. She's got weight and youth, but I'm nimbler, flashed through her mind. But she was too late. Margot had hold of her sweater, and the best she could do was to wriggle round and strike a swinging buffet at the bent bobbed head. Margot laughed savagely and caught her by the throat. Bunny remembered that you brought your knee up into your adversary's stomach, and tried it, but with Margot's weight against her she lost her balance and fell backwards, striking her head against the bannisters of the landing. The sudden blackness around her solved all problems. Gladly, gratefully, she plunged down and down.

*

Price broke the silence.

'Lady d'Estray has been gone for rather a long time, Sir Charles. Do you think she can have mistaken my instructions?'

'They were clear enough. But she's very absent-minded; it's quite on the cards that she's meandered off and started something else,' said Sir Charles, rising. 'I'll go and look for her.'

'I'll come with you,' said Price, following him out. 'She may have run into something. It's quite ten minutes since she left us,' he added uneasily.

'Writers,' pronounced Sir Charles, as he crossed the hall, 'are queer people. She has probably opened a book and got engrossed in it. What's that?' he said, halting abruptly. 'Bath water,' said Price. 'No, that other noise,' said Sir Charles and then, 'Oh, it's that dog,' he said, as he reached the gallery, and Price, catching up with him, could see the Boxer bitch running to and fro, jumping against the door at the end of the passage to the accompaniment of a crescendo of

149

unearthly howls. 'It's not gone mad, has it?' asked Price, nervously.

'No,' said Sir Charles, 'no. I think my wife must have gone through to the east wing and shut the dog out. It's curious . . . perhaps she had one of her brain-waves about the furniture.' Then Babette, aware of the men, gave up her assault on the door and bounded towards them. Price recoiled, but Sir Charles said, 'Well, Babette, where's Missis?' and Babette ran back to the door.

Sir Charles went up to it, turned the handle and opened the door a few inches. In a flash the lithe tawny body was through.

'Babette!' called Sir Charles, and 'Barbara!' and, followed by Price, stepped into the east wing. Babette was nowhere to be seen now, but they could hear the scrabble of her feet on the stairs and a high shrill scream and the sound of a fall. Then Price was running up the stairs two at a time and, as well as the noise he made, Sir Charles could hear the dog snarling, and then he, too, was on the landing and there was Babette standing like a statue, her forepaws on the chest of a woman, who lay with her hands over her face and whimpered with fear. Crumpled against the bannisters, Bunny gasped painfully. Sir Charles went to her.

'What's happened, Barbara?'

Bunny croaked, 'Heard her. . . . Followed her in. . . . Found her at the sink there. . . . She tried to strangle me. . . . Babette came. . . . '

Price was snapping his fingers and making chirping noises at the Boxer, but he was utterly ignored. Sir Charles shouted, 'Come here, Babette,' but with no more success. 'Babette,' whispered Bunny, and Babette bounded to her. Margot Rattray sat up. The bitch growled, but quietened when Bunny passed an arm round her neck.

Margot rose to her feet and smoothed her skirt. 'That dog's dangerous: it ought to be destroyed,' she said.

Price did not contradict her. He said, 'Miss Rattray, I must ask you what you are doing in this part of the mansion?'

Margot moistened her pale lips with her tongue. 'When I opened my bedroom door to go downstairs to breakfast, I saw Lady d'Estray unlock the door and pass through, so I followed her. I've had my suspicions all along, but of course since my mother's death I feel much more strongly. I found Lady d'Estray at the sink and she attacked me, and naturally I defended myself and I was getting the best of it – which isn't surprising considering her age and skinniness – when that dog appeared and she set it on me. I make no accusations, but her flying at me like that speaks for itself, doesn't it?'

Sir Charles's face was grey. 'Barbara, this isn't your story?'

'It's damn . . . lie,' croaked Bunny.

Price said, 'Lady d'Estray is in no state to be questioned. We must get her into bed, Sir Charles. I'll take Miss Rattray through and send someone back to help you, but I'd be obliged if you would keep that dog under control until we have left the wing. Come along, Miss Rattray.'

When they had gone Bunny struggled to her feet. 'I can get back under my own steam. It's only my throat that hurts now.' Grasping the bannisters, she got to the head of the stairs. 'I feel a bit giddy,' she said, with her hand to her forehead.

'Wait until someone comes,' Sir Charles advised her.

'If you'll give me a hand . . . ' and then, as he made no movement, 'What's the matter, Charles?' A glance at his frozen face informed her. 'Oh, I see. You believe the Rattray.'

'No,' said Sir Charles, 'no. But you and she tell quite different stories. It's all got to be sorted out, you see . . . '

The reeling stairs were kinder than his company. In a sitting position, with Babette, who thought it a game, frolicking beside her, Bunny went down them. In the corridor, a constable was telling Henry Scampnell, 'Now you go back, sir, and leave it to us. If Miss Rattray dropped her bag, we'll find it.' Scampnell turned and hurried away, and the constable, watching him said, 'Come sneakin' in 'ere, 'e did, most suspicious. Lookin' for summat other than 'is daughter's 'andbag, if you arsks me. Can I give you an 'and, my lady?'

Bunny said, 'I'm quite all right now, only I'm so cold,' and when they were out of the east wing she asked Sir Charles to send a double whisky to her bedroom. He went down the main staircase, hoping that the Roses were still at breakfast or already deep in the Sunday papers in the drawing-room. The dining-room door was, in fact, open, and from the hall he could hear Sybella's voice asking, 'What was going on this morning, Benson?' to which Benson replied, 'Just the police making some further enquiries, madam. Shall I bring you some more toast, or will that be enough for you, sir?'

Sir Charles waited till Benson came out and then ordered the double whisky. 'Her ladyship's had a bad shock,' he felt bound to explain. Then he went to the library and sat down by the fire and set his weary mind to work again. Less than half an hour ago, Price had placed Bunny among his 'improbables', but now . . . Who was the more likely to have known of the sink on the second storey? – he had forgotten it himself, but she was always in and out of the east wing looking for pictures or pieces of furniture . . . who could have become possessed of the key of the wing without attracting comment? . . . who had the wits to fake an attack on herself in order to avert suspicion? . . .

An hour or more of miserable thinking brought him to no happier conclusion than that which had caused him to shrink from touching his wife when she had asked for his help on the east-wing staircase; it was with relief that he heard the door open: this was Price, surely, and an end, however horrible, in sight. But it wasn't Price; it was Patricia, tall, fair, fresh and wholesome, but with a faint line of anxiety on her brow. Coming across the room to him, she said, 'I'm afraid I've given church a miss this morning. Has anything else happened, Daddy? There's a rumour that the police are in the east wing.'

Sir Charles told her.

'Margot – but that's rot,' said Patricia. 'She'd nothing

against Cousin Elizabeth, and people don't murder their mothers.'

'Husbands do murder their wives, though, Pat, and it was Scampnell we were thinking of when the matter of the flasks was considered, though I can't imagine what *he* could have had against Elizabeth.'

'In the flask business, Margot must have been an accessory, and she's never even had the nerve to ride – I can't see her getting involved in a murder. If the story about the flasks came from Lisa, it may be a pure invention.'

Sir Charles sighed. 'Then I'm afraid we're back where we were after that first talk we had, Patricia.'

'Cheer up, Daddy. We must hear something definite soon; the police must have got some clues from this dust-up in the east wing. A car load of plain-clothes men arrived just before I came in here, and Margot's had a long interview with Price in the study.'

Almost querulously Sir Charles said, 'The suspense is horrible. I want it to end, but I'm afraid of the ending.'

'Never mind, Daddy. Whatever it is, we'll face it together.' Father and daughter turned as the door opened, but it was only Benson bringing a tray with two glasses and a sherry decanter. 'Any news, Benny?' asked Patricia. 'Well, miss,' he replied, 'they've been taking finger-prints – Beatrice's and her ladyship's and Sylvia's. Mr Scampnell and Miss Rattray have gone off with the Superintendent in a police car. The Detective-Inspector is in the east wing now, but I couldn't say what he's doing there.'

Sir Charles asked him, 'What about the key of the east wing, Benson? I thought you kept it.'

'In the pantry, Sir Charles. There are hooks on the inside of the door of the glass cupboard and, though there are a great many keys that I can't put a name to, where it is possible each hook is neatly labelled. A mistake it seems now, though it has often proved a convenience.'

Wearily, as though he were sick of the whole business, Sir Charles said, 'And who besides yourself knew about them?'

'Her ladyship, Beatrice, Sylvia, perhaps, and young Eric. But, if I may say so, Sir Charles, this does not necessarily point to a member of the Family or the staff. The guests were in the habit of visiting the pantry to deposit their hunting-flasks, which has often been done while I was at supper or even after I had retired for the night.'

'Of the people who had hunting-flasks two happen to be dead, Benson. Young Marvin has an alibi, and young Rose has very wisely kept away since Miss Elizabeth's murder. Mr Rose had no motive for killing either of the ladies.'

'But it would be quite natural,' Benson said, 'for Mrs Scampnell to ask her husband or her daughter to run down with her flask if she had forgotten it. In the hall we consider Miss Margot a very inquisitive young lady. She offended Mrs Capes once by penetrating into our quarters and entering the kitchen without knocking.'

'What did she want?' asked Patricia.

'A cloth to wipe up some ink, I believe, Miss Pat. When Mrs Capes suggested that she should have rung the bell, she said that she wished to save us trouble. Mrs Capes was extremely annoyed.'

'Well, I sincerely hope we shall hear something definite before tonight,' said Sir Charles, 'or everyone will be feeling nervous at bedtime. I wonder the Roses haven't cleared out, but I suppose the police won't let them.'

'I believe that is so, Sir Charles,' said Benson. 'Mrs Rose seems particularly overwrought, and since Mrs Scampnell's death she has refused to move about the house or to sit in any of the reception-rooms without her husband. Now she favours the theory of a homicidal maniac, who has inhabited the east wing for some time without our knowledge.'

'I wish it were so,' said Sir Charles wistfully.

Benson withdrew. Patricia stayed chatting with her father, and presently Hugo came in and asked who had been arrested: the kennel boy had seen a man and a young woman in a police car on the Harborough road. 'It must have been the Scampnells,' said Patricia. 'Benny told us they had gone

to the police station, but he didn't say they'd been arrested.'
'That's just like people,' said Sir Charles testily. 'Surely
you know, Hugo, that before a person can be arrested a
warrant is necessary? I expect the Scampnells have gone to
the police station to make a formal statement. Where have
you been all morning?'

'Down at the kennels. I went down at half past six this
morning, so I really haven't a clue as to what's been happening.'

'And you "couldn't care less", I suppose,' said Sir Charles
angrily. 'We're in terrible trouble here: we've had two
murders in the house; the murderer is still at large, and all
you do is to make off at dawn to the kennels. Where's your
sense of responsibility? You might be a child, Hugo.' Hugo
said, 'Well, I'm sorry if I was wanted, but I've a bitch whelp-
ing, and it's hounds, not my stepmother's paying guests,
for which I'm responsible.' 'It's not only the paying guests
who are involved,' said Sir Charles, and Patricia, getting
up and linking arms with her brother, said, with the rather
obvious tact which her mother had used, 'We've ten
minutes before lunch, and I've got to go across to the stables
for something – if you'll come with me, I'll put you wise,
Hugo.'

They went out together, and for the first time for days Sir
Charles ceased to think of the murders and thought of his
elder son, who at four-and-twenty wanted nothing in the
world but to hunt foxes round Bottom Wood and over Aston
Wold and up and down the vale of Rushbrook. Since the
Conquest, when they had made their name and got their
land, the d'Estrays had done nothing spectacular; the sol-
diers retired as Colonels, the Indian Civil Servants with
C.S.I.s, the colonial governors with C.M.G.s; in the Church
they had risen to be rural deans and minor canons; nevertheless they had lived on a plane that Hugo was forsaking as he
swept out kennels, skinned carcases, mixed puddings with
only a couple of idiot boys to serve under him. Sir Charles
d'Estray was, in fact, too old and too obstinate and not
courageous enough to acknowledge that the bloodless revolu-

tion of the English was already history: even with paying guests in his house, he didn't see himself as a hotel-keeper: that was his wife's affair. . . .

The gong rang for luncheon. Bunny had asked for a tray for herself and Lisa; and apparently the Scampnells were still at the police station, for only the Roses appeared and, paralysed with embarrassment, remarked – Stanley in an unnaturally gruff and hearty voice and Sybella in a nervous gabble – on the weather, the tenderness of the roast chicken, and the sporting news: luncheon over, they retired to their bedroom. Sir Charles, grateful to the call of duty, set off in a slight drizzle to the home farm to inspect repairs; Captain went with him, but Babette ignored his whistle, preferring, he disapprovingly conjectured, to stuff indoors. On his return, when he had shed his mackintosh and was heading for the library, Benson came through the hall and told him, 'The Detective-Inspector rang up, Sir Charles, and will be here at five o'clock or soon after. Her ladyship is in the library. Shall I serve tea now?' Sir Charles glanced at his watch. 'Five and twenty to. Yes, bring tea in now and we'll get it over. Is Mr Hugo about?' 'I believe he's in the stable with Miss Pat, Sir Charles. I'll let them know.' 'Thank you, Benson, but, look here – surely this is your Sunday off?' 'I could hardly go out at a time like this, Sir Charles,' said Benson. 'I suggested that the boy should go in my place, but even he preferred to remain.' 'Out of loyalty or curiosity, d'you think?' Sir Charles asked him. 'I think out of loyalty,' replied Benson, 'but out of loyalty to Miss Lisa rather than to ourselves.' Sir Charles muttered, 'Hmph', and went on to the library, where he found Bunny crouching over the fire with Babette lion-like at her feet. She turned her head as he entered, but neither smiled.

'As you've come downstairs, I conclude you're better,' he said without warmth.

As coldly she answered him, 'Thank you, yes.'

He picked up a newspaper, and they stayed silent till Benson came in with the tea-tray. Hugo and Patricia followed him. 'How are you, Bunny?' Hugo asked kindly. 'Pat told me as much as she knew about your adventures this morning. So it was Margot . . . '

Bunny, with a malevolent glance at Sir Charles, said, 'You've only my word for it.'

'Good enough,' said Hugo soothingly.

'For you perhaps,' said Bunny.

Patricia, with heightened colour, explained, 'Well, you see, you've told us what happened in the east wing this morning, but you haven't told us why Margot poisoned Cousin Elizabeth. Even the motive for Mrs Scampnell's murder's gone now; we all thought she was murdered because she had a clue, but it's quite obvious that she wouldn't have sneaked on her own daughter.'

'From prefect to policewoman,' said Bunny.

'Really, Barbara,' said Sir Charles. 'Pat,' he went on, seeing his daughter's mouth open, 'don't let yourself be provoked into saying something that you may regret later. The Detective-Inspector will be here very shortly, and please God he'll have some news for us – this uncertainty is appalling. Will you pour out the tea, Barbara?'

'Patricia can,' said Bunny, finding herself suddenly averse to any action which displayed her as Lady d'Estray. 'You remember,' she excused herself, 'that I was half-throttled this morning.'

So Patricia sat down and dispensed tea in a quick efficient way, which seemed to condemn Bunny's usual absent-minded dithering over milk and sugar, and Hugo talked to his father about Elizabeth Hudson's horse: Patricia thought that Marvin would sell it and Hugo might suggest to Lord Badgemoor that he buy it for the Hunt, but it was getting on in years and a good home with some doting woman might be better for it. 'Wouldn't the old chap be useful to you, Pat?' asked Sir Charles. 'I can't think what possessed Elizabeth to leave him to young Marvin,' Hugo said. 'The poor devil had to pretend to be horsey; he'd have lost his job otherwise.' Sir Charles said coldly, 'What job?' and Hugo didn't answer, but Patricia said, 'I'd like to buy Brutus, of course, but shall we want even the horses that we've got? Won't the murders put people off coming here as paying guests – what do you think, Bunny?'

Bunny shrugged. 'I haven't a clue. Considering how people read crime fiction, one would think that they might be attracted. Why not exploit it – revise the booklet and put, along with baths and table wines, "murder included"?'

Sir Charles said, 'Barbara, I wish . . .' but a light knock on the door interrupted him. He said irritably, 'Come in' and in came Price. 'Pardon me if I intrude,' he said as all heads turned to him, 'but, in view of the substantial progress I have made in my investigations, there are one or two points that I would like to talk over with you. I feel sure that you, too, will be interested to hear the latest developments.'

'Will you have some tea?' asked Bunny, feeling the teapot. 'We can ring for some fresh, but actually it's quite hot.'

'Thank you, Lady d'Estray, but I partook at the police station.'

'Cigarette?'

'The Detective-Inspector doesn't smoke,' said Sir Charles impatiently. 'Sit down, Price. I'm thankful to hear that you're making progress.'

Price chose a chair outside the ring that the d'Estrays had made round the fireside, and, sitting up straight, alert, and neat, with his knees together and his hands clasped, he began: 'Lady d'Estray's excursion into the east wing, imprudent and ill-advised though it was, has led us to the evidence required to confirm the suspicions I voiced to you, Sir Charles, in the study earlier today. When, after leaving the wing, I questioned Miss Rattray, she insisted that it was she who followed Lady d'Estray there, that Lady d'Estray attacked her, and that any injuries sustained by Lady d'Estray had been inflicted by her – Miss Rattray – solely in self-defence. This, on the face of it, was a perfectly feasible explanation, and I could scarcely have requested Miss Rattray to have accompanied me to the police station had she not displayed considerable confusion when questioned with reference to the hunting-flasks. I trapped her by pretending to accept her story and then asking her how she imagined that Lady d'Estray had disposed of the second flask; she made various suggestions, following which I enquired why she had previously informed Lady d'Estray that Mrs Scampnell had only one. She was taken aback, hesitated, and finally asserted that the story Lady d'Estray had told me was a fabrication. I left her on the pretext of taxing Lady d'Estray with the untruth if she were well enough to see me; actually I saw Henry Scampnell, who assured me that his wife had only one flask, as his daughter had informed Lady d'Estray. In the light of subsequent events the matter of the flasks seems insignificant, but it was the disparity between the two statements which convinced me of the Scampnells' guilt, for if Henry Scampnell did not act in collusion with his step-daughter, he was at least an accessory before and after the fact. I invited him to accompany his stepdaughter to the police station, and in a very short time I had ascertained that Miss Rattray's finger-prints had been found on the cupboard under the sink in the east wing, though the utensils and the spirit stove and the second hunting-flask, which I found inside the cupboard, had been wiped clean. Some minute shreds of a vegetable substance, which I have despatched to the laboratory, will, I anticipate, prove the presence of the root from which the guilty party distilled the poison. I am on my way now to the Chief Constable's to procure a warrant for the arrest of Margot Rattray and her step-father, but my case would be very much stronger if I had a suggestion to make as to motive. The general impression seems to be that Mrs Scampnell held the purse-strings, and your housemaid, Blythe, asserts that the family life was not so harmonious as it appeared on the surface to be. Can none of you add to this? For instance, have you ever noticed anything to indicate that the daughter or the husband was short of money?'

Bunny said hesitatingly, 'When you come to think of it, the show *was* run for and on behalf of Cecily Scampnell. They lived here for the riding and hunting, but only Cecily rode; there was absolutely nothing for Henry and Margot to do. Surely they would have been happier in London, within reach of concerts and films. Cecily hated London. . . . But I suppose Margot could have found herself a job, if she had really wanted to go. She's well over age – what could have kept her here?'

'That's obvious,' said Patricia. 'Anybody in their senses would rather live here, even if they were kept short of money, than sit in a stuffy office all day and pig it in some frightful flatlet or bed-sitting room.'

'Well, that's a moot point,' said Bunny. 'Me, I think there must have been a great deal more in the Scampnell set-up than met the eye. I wonder if Margot and her Scamp were lovers?'

'*Don't* be revolting,' said Patricia.

Sir Charles said, 'You're letting your imagination run away with you.'

'And *what* an imagination!' said Patricia.

'Shut up, Pat. You haven't an imagination of any sort,' said Hugo.

Patricia said, 'I'm glad I haven't if that's the kind of idea it produces.'

Price said, 'It's not a very nice idea, I grant you, Miss d'Estray. But, human nature being what it most regrettably is, it's possible, and it certainly ties up with the information given by the housemaid – that Miss Rattray and her stepfather laughed and mocked at the deceased together. And that reminds me – I've not yet had time to interview the kitchenmaid, who, I believe, overheard something in the same line. Would it be convenient for me to see her now, Lady d'Estray?'

'Of course,' said Bunny. 'Ring, please, Charles. It's Mrs Capes' afternoon off, so Kate will be available.'

Patricia said, 'I think it's awful to listen to what kitchenmaids have overheard.' She asked Price, 'Is that how detectives always build up their cases?'

'It's very seldom,' he answered, 'that servants' gossip is available. Not everyone has the means to employ a domestic staff, Miss d'Estray.'

'Well, we only have them because we keep a hotel,' said

Patricia. 'I suppose when there aren't any, you go snooping round the neighbours?'

'That,' said Price, 'is our duty.'

'Oh, Benson,' said Bunny. 'Will you ask Kate to come? We understand she's got something to tell the Inspector.' When Benson had gone again, she added, 'Would you like to see her alone?'

'Not unless you feel she might speak more freely in the absence of her employers, Lady d'Estray.'

Patricia said, 'It's not my cup of tea – I'm off anyhow,' and Hugo muttered that he must ring up about a carcase. Bunny said, 'You'll scare the kid, Charles, but I think I might be of use – when we can escape from Mrs Capes, Kate and I discuss her boy-friends.' 'I don't know why I should scare her more than you, Barbara,' said Sir Charles. 'I've known her since she was a tiny tot down at Dog Cottages. However, I've letters to write. I'll come back later.' He went out as the kitchenmaid entered.

Kate Treadwell was a slight, sandy girl of seventeen, who this afternoon had taken advantage of the cook's absence to pile her curls even higher than usual and adorn them with a number of plastic slides of different designs and colours. She had used an orange lipstick and petunia nail-varnish and she smelled overpoweringly of Californian poppy.

'Hullo, Kate! Come in,' said Bunny. 'Hullo, my lady,' Kate responded warmly. 'This is Detective-Inspector Price, Kate.' 'Good afternoon, sir,' said Kate, looking at Bunny.

'Good afternoon, Kate. I understand from Miss Blythe that last Sunday you happened to overhear a conversation between Miss Margot Rattray and the late Miss Hudson. Will you tell us about it?'

Kate, patting her curls, said, 'I wasn't listening. I'd been washing up the oddsies and then I rinsed through the tea-towels and then I went to 'ang them out on the line in the yard, and it was just about the time they come back from church and I could 'ear Miss 'Udson talking. I wasn't listening . . .'

'Just a moment,' said Price. 'Where exactly is the yard you refer to?'

Bunny said, 'If you're facing the house, on the right side of it there's a wall with an arched gateway in it. The gateway leads into the yard – the tradesmen's vans go in that way and the kitchen quarters open out into it. If one wants a little exercise after church, one comes back through the woods and to get to the house one passes the gateway.'

'I see. And are you sure it was Miss Hudson's voice you heard, Kate? Think carefully.'

'I 'eard her first, and then I see 'er go by – 'er and Miss Rattray. Rowing they was. Miss 'Udson says, "It's disgustin'. Besides the relationship, 'e's years older than you are." Miss Rattray she says, "If anything's disgustin', it's the way you've spied on me." Miss 'Udson says, "I've told you before – it was a pure chance that I 'eard what I did. Now, Margot, don't be a silly girl," and after that I couldn't 'ear no more – they went on past the gate and their voices faded away.'

'And what interpretation did you put upon this conversation, Kate?'

'Pardon?'

'What did you think they were rowing about?' Bunny said.

'Well,' said Kate, ' 'aving 'eard the word disgustin', I thought it must be something in the way of sex, but when I mentioned it to the others, they come down on me like a ton of bricks, and my Auntie, she said that what Miss 'Udson was referring to was the disrespectful way that Miss Margot went on with 'er stepfather – calling 'im Scamp and all that. I didn't think so. I thought both Miss 'Udson and Miss Margot sounded too wild, but it's no use arguing with the old brigade, so I kept my mouth shut.'

'Thank you, Kate. That's a great help to me,' said Price, and when the girl had gone out and Sir Charles had reappeared, he pronounced, 'She was right, of course. Miss Hudson must have discovered and was expressing her disapproval of Miss Rattray's intrigue with her stepfather. Miss Rattray resented her remarks . . . not a very convincing motive. . . .'

'But don't you see,' Bunny burst out, 'if Elizabeth had been alive when Cecily was murdered, she would have been able to point to the culprits at once? She *had* to die first. The poison was brewed for Cecily, but it was no use killing Cecily while Elizabeth was alive to tell us that Margot and Scamp were in love. What's foxed us all along was our *idée fixe* that Cecily was killed because she knew something about Elizabeth's murder – whereas it was really the other way round: Elizabeth would have known something about Cecily's murder. We got our tenses mixed. . . . '

'That's all pure supposition, Barbara,' said Sir Charles.

'It's supposition,' said Price, 'but it's also the logical explanation of Miss Hudson's murder. The Scampnells no doubt anticipated our error; it was obvious that we should form the conclusion that we did – that Mrs Scampnell knew too much – and that in consequence we should look for Miss Hudson's enemies rather than for Mrs Scampnell's – Margot Rattray spared no pains to draw my attention to the slight domestic friction between Miss Hudson and yourself, Lady d'Estray.'

'She was clever,' said Bunny. 'I doubt whether the business of the flasks would have led to much. It was just a little sound – the shutting of a door – which betrayed her. It's always the silly little things that matter. . . . '

'And it was extremely fortunate that you were upstairs at the precise moment when the door closed,' Price told her. 'We found an empty workbag near the sink, which indicates that Miss Rattray was tidying up there. Half-an-hour later, even in the event of our attention being drawn to the east wing, we should have found nothing.' He rose. 'I must be wending my way now. I've a couple of men still searching the Scampnells' rooms, so I shall be calling back later.'

As the door closed behind him, Sir Charles said, 'Thank God. Thank God, it's over.'

'But it isn't,' said Bunny. 'This has *happened*. It isn't one of your detective stories: you can't shut the book with a snap when you've found out who dunnit; there's no well-trained author in charge to spare you the anti-climax.'

'Well, naturally,' said Sir Charles, 'we haven't heard the last of it. There's the trial to come, and I daresay there'll be a lot of unwelcome publicity. What I meant was that we've finished with the terrible suspense and suspicion . . . '

Before she laughed, cried, or started to throw around the Minton tea-service, Bunny, murmuring something about a rest before dinner, fled the room.

CHAPTER EIGHT

IT was already spring there. Mimosa was flowering; on the terrace the air was sweet with the scent of it and the scent of the pine-woods on the headland, thrust out into the shining blue waters of the bay. If you climbed the inconsequent little paths up the hillside behind the village and looked from some vantage point into the wild and riven heart of the Esterels, there was a streak of snow to be seen here and there on the higher ranges, and beyond them, secure as yet from the flow of springtide, the white mountains of Dauphiny and Savoy. In England, thought Bunny, coming out on the terrace, leaning on the balustrade and looking down into the water – in England it would be raining, a cold rain that at Aston would blow across the Park and beat on the windows of the dining-room, where Patricia, with a cold in her head and chilblains on her toes, and Sir Charles, with a twinge in his back and a letter from his bank manager in his pocket, would be eating eggs and bacon in the silence which it's best to keep at an English breakfast-table. Her mind went back to her first mornings at Aston, when, determined to carry out her intention of providing a background of English home life for her daughter, she had risen from her bed punctually at half past seven, dressed herself in a tweed skirt, laced-up shoes, a 'twin-set', and a string of pearls, and descended into the icy dining-room, where, over congealing kippers, tasteless tea, and toast that made your gums bleed, she was ignored by Charles and Hugo, put right by Patricia, and crushed on every subject she introduced by Elizabeth Hudson. The first time that she had had breakfast brought to her bedroom, Sir Charles had sent Nanny to take her temperature, so she had had to admit that she was, as he later summed it up, reverting to her sloppy continental habits. What bliss it was now, Bunny thought, looking across the placid bay to the village, the row of humble little shops, the white church of St Laurent, the Poisson d'Or, standing in a semi-circle round the harbour, gay with the emerald, saffron, scarlet and sky-blue and turquoise-blue of

the fishing-boats, beached for repainting on the strip of sand –
what bliss it was to come back to your own design for living,
to your gimcrack villa, your slipshod existence, your friends
without background, as Charles had phrased it in the course
of their parting scene in the Residents' Lounge of the old-
established hotel in Kensington, where they had stayed during the trial. Apparently he had never dreamed that she
might leave him; she'd had reason to complain of his lack of
faith, he admitted, but he had apologized handsomely, and
suspecting your wife of murder had never been mooted as
grounds for divorce, even by that A. P. Herbert fellow. But
Bunny wouldn't argue, or, as he put it, listen to reason; she
had simply said that she had lost the affection and respect
which, as he'd known, was all that she'd felt for him. And on
the evening of the day when the death sentence was passed on
Margot Rattray and her accomplice, and only half-an-hour
after the scene in the Residents' Lounge, Bunny had slipped
out of the hotel, and it wasn't until Sir Charles got back to
Aston and learned that Lisa had left the same day and taken
Babette with her, that he realized this was no tantrum, but
the end of his marriage. He had written then, but of things
which to her had no meaning; he could have wrung her heart
if he had said he missed her, but he wrote of gossip in the
county, of the laughing-stock she'd made him, of dragging his
name in the mud and setting a bad example to the lower
classes. She hadn't replied: you couldn't reply to Winchester
and New College, and beneath all that there was no one but
the Judas she had surprised at her cupboard. She hoped that
he'd not write again . . . and down the steps came Lisa, carrying a letter, the square solidity of which proclaimed the
country of its origin, even to Bunny's myopic eyes across the
terrace.

'For you, from England,' said Lisa.

'Put it down somewhere,' said Bunny fearfully.

'I wondered if it was to say that they've sent off Romanée
Conti. They must have got the cheque by now,' said Lisa
wistfully.

'All right. Let me look,' said Bunny.

The d'Estrays, Elizabeth Hudson included, had done their best to cure her of her silly habit of puzzling over envelopes when it was the work of a second to tear them open and resolve the problem. She looked at the postmark and said, 'London, E.C. . . . forwarded from Aston . . . typed . . . it doesn't look very inviting, does it?' and then she turned it over and read from the back, '*Derwent, Derwent and Battismore.* Weren't they the Scampnells' solicitors?'

'Yes, they were. Oh, do open it. Perhaps the Scampnells have left you a fortune to make up for trying to murder you,' said Lisa, hopping with excitement.

'I think murderers' estates are confiscated, aren't they?' said Bunny, and she opened the letter and there were several sheets of thin lined paper and a covering letter from Derwent, Derwent and Battismore, baldly stating that 'the enclosed' had been received by them for forwarding. 'The enclosed' was written in a clear, thick, square handwriting, which was unfamiliar to Bunny, so she turned to the signature, which, without preamble, was 'Margot Rattray'. Date and address had also been omitted, and the letter sharply began:

LADY D'ESTRAY,

I know you told us all to call you Bunny, but it is such a ridiculous name for a woman of your age, and anyhow, now that you know that I did my best to finish you off, I don't suppose you would be so keen on it. I am writing to you against all the rules and regulations because at my trial my lawyers would hardly let me say anything, when I tried to explain I was told just to answer the questions, and I am sure people got the wrong impression and thought I was just a frightened person muddling along, whereas really those last days at Aston were simply glorious, and if I had the chance to live them again I should act in exactly the same way. You may be very clever and able to write books and get yourself talked about, but you'll never know what it is to have the power and the courage to get rid of those who stand between you and your happiness; you didn't think of killing that cow of a Hudson, you only whined when she bullied you; but I killed her as soon as she annoyed *me*. Though you've got brains, you haven't got my strength of character; you just drift along – you don't *act*, like me.

I'm a very extraordinary person. Most people think they love their mothers, even if they really hate them; but I'm clear-sighted, I can face facts and I've always known that I hated mine. When I was told that she had remarried, I hated her more than ever – nothing's sillier than the way that middle-aged women go on thinking that they're attractive to men. Scamp fell madly in love with me at first sight. He wasn't in love with her at all – who could be? – but she ran after him quite shamelessly and practically tricked him into marrying her. Out of loyalty to her, Scamp didn't speak for ages, but one day he let something slip, which showed me that he loved me, and I realized that all the time I'd been in love with him. Let me tell you, Lady d'Estray, that when a person of my strength of character falls in love it's not the namby-pamby kind of a thing *you're* used to – it's a grand passion sweeping everything else aside. Scamp and I couldn't just run away together because she had control of my father's money, and though Scamp got a stingy salary from his directorship, his family are Quakers, and if there had been a "scandal" they would have forced him to resign from the Board. You couldn't expect two people madly in love to live the rest of their lives at your dreary guest house and watch her spending money right and left on horses and hunting so that soon there would have been hardly anything left for us to inherit, even if – as we always hoped – she was killed in a hunting accident.

It was my idea to kill her. In spite of his great love for me Scamp was shocked at first, but I managed to talk him round. Elizabeth Hudson, who was always gassing away about botany, told me about the dropwort when I was out for a walk with her, and I went back in the dark and dug it up and at night in your upstairs pantry I prepared it on Mother's picnic stove. That was on Saturday night, and on Sunday the Hudson grabbed me when we came out of church and made me walk home with her. The spying devil had found out that

Scamp and I were in love, and she gave me a lecture and said that unless I promised to give him up and go away and get a job she would tell her dear Cecily – as if one could stop the earth moving round the sun or water flowing downhill, as I told her. I promised to think over what she said and give her my decision on Monday. At first I was taken aback, for obviously if I killed Mother that night and the doctor smelt a rat and the police were called in, Elizabeth would tell them about me and Scamp and they would guess at once who had done it. An ordinary person would have given up the plan – Scamp wanted to – but I simply decided to kill Elizabeth and get her out of the way before killing Mother. Actually it was a stroke of genius, because everyone, including you, who are supposed to be so clever, was silly enough to look for someone with a motive for killing Elizabeth, and you thought Mother was killed because she knew something about Elizabeth's murder, instead of the other way round. All the poison I got ready for Mother I had to use for Elizabeth; fortunately I had some of the roots left, and I hid them in the east wing – I had had the key of the door for ages, because Scamp and I used to go there when Mother was out riding, and you thought we were having a nice walk in Bottom Wood. What a mistake! After all the fuss about the Hudson, I hid the stove in the east wing, too, and I got the rest of the poison ready there, when you were all asleep and snoring. As you heard at my trial, Mother had always had two hunting-flasks – they were a relic of those days in India that she used to tell us about until we could have screamed with boredom – and so, of course, it was child's play for me to change the flask I had got ready for the one she had, when she came upstairs from breakfast to put the finishing touches to her ridiculous and most unbecoming hunting clothes. Everything went like clockwork and, as I'd expected, that half-witted detective was racking his feeble brains to find out who could have tampered with the flask while it was in the dining-room, and then you came and asked us whether Mother had had a pair of flasks, and that upset poor Scamp; he had had a tiring day, and of course men are more highly strung than women are. He said he wouldn't be able to sleep for worrying, so I said I'd put some of the poison into the cup of Ovaltine, which you had been silly enough to mention – you see, my Lady d'Estray, if you are really strong you have no troubles or worries. I made no more fuss about killing the people who were in my way than you would about stepping on a beetle. I knew you would be ages in your bath – you always are – so I had plenty of time to slip into the east wing and get the poison and, of course, I had a good excuse ready in case I met anyone as I went to your bedroom. The only trouble I had was with Scamp. He was against killing you at first – he said that you were the one the detective suspected and if you were dead he would begin to look round for another suspect, and then I got the magnificent idea of the confession. While you were lying and soaking in your bath, I slipped along the passage and emptied a jolly good dose of my patent medicine into your Ovaltine, and much later I took your typewriter into the east wing and Scamp and I typed your confession. I enjoyed that. If I had been able to travel about and see things as you have I daresay I should have written as well or better than you can; my work would have been stronger than yours, anyway, because I could have written of the passionate feelings of men and women, instead of a lot of silly nonsense about flowers and kids and cats. If you had drunk your Ovaltine, everyone would have believed that you were responsible for the poisonings, and Scamp and I would have gone away to the wonderful life we had planned for ourselves in South Africa; but through no cleverness of your own, but just because you are so fussy about food and the Ovaltine wasn't hot enough, you didn't drink it, and so you have spoilt two lives and brought to an end one of the greatest love-stories of the world – a much greater one than you, with your shallow mind, could even begin to write. One consolation is that with all your faults you are intelligent enough to realize what you've done, and I hope and believe that the rest of your trivial future will be poisoned by the thought that however many books you write or husbands you marry, you will never experience – because you're incapable of it – the crowded hours of glorious life for which I am now perfectly content to pay the penalty.

Bunny, as she had finished reading each page of the cheap writing-paper, had handed it to Lisa, and as she waited for Lisa to finish, too, she was wondering whether Margot had felt relieved when she had heard that the death sentences had been reduced to imprisonment for life, or if she had felt cheated of the climax of the drama she had devised. Then Lisa, sighing and shuffling the pages together, said, 'Poor thing! There go we, if it wasn't for our glands.'

'Come off it, Lisa,' said Bunny. 'That letter: it's like a medieval stained-glass window depicting some descent to hell – it's crowded with the old, old sins, the good old simple scarlet sins: Envy and Greed, Pride, Hatred, Malice, Lust. Margot was wicked.'

But Lisa, true to her generation, murmured, 'Glands . . . '

A CATALOG OF SELECTED DOVER
BOOKS IN ALL FIELDS OF INTEREST

THE ART NOUVEAU STYLE, edited by Roberta Waddell. 579 rare photographs of works in jewelry, metalwork, glass, ceramics, textiles, architecture and furniture by 175 artists—Mucha, Seguy, Lalique, Tiffany, many others. 288pp. 8⅜ × 11¼.
23515-7 Pa. $9.95

AMERICAN COUNTRY HOUSES OF THE GILDED AGE (Sheldon's "Artistic Country-Seats"), A. Lewis. All of Sheldon's fascinating and historically important photographs and plans. New text by Arnold Lewis. Approx. 200 illustrations. 128pp. 9⅜ × 12¼.
24301-X Pa. $7.95

THE WAY WE LIVE NOW, Anthony Trollope. Trollope's late masterpiece, marks shift to bitter satire. Character Melmotte "his greatest villain." Reproduced from original edition with 40 illustrations. 416pp. 6⅛ × 9¼.
24360-5 Pa. $7.95

BENCHLEY LOST AND FOUND, Robert Benchley. Finest humor from early 30's, about pet peeves, child psychologists, post office and others. Mostly unavailable elsewhere. 73 illustrations by Peter Arno and others. 183pp. 5⅜ × 8½.
22410-4 Pa. $3.50

ISOMETRIC PERSPECTIVE DESIGNS AND HOW TO CREATE THEM, John Locke. Isometric perspective is the picture of an object adrift in imaginary space. 75 mindboggling designs. 52pp. 8¼ × 11.
24123-8 Pa. $2.75

PERSPECTIVE FOR ARTISTS, Rex Vicat Cole. Depth, perspective of sky and sea, shadows, much more, not usually covered. 391 diagrams, 81 reproductions of drawings and paintings. 279pp. 5⅜ × 8½.
22487-2 Pa. $4.00

MOVIE-STAR PORTRAITS OF THE FORTIES, edited by John Kobal. 163 glamor, studio photos of 106 stars of the 1940s: Rita Hayworth, Ava Gardner, Marlon Brando, Clark Gable, many more. 176pp. 8⅜ × 11¼.
23546-7 Pa. $6.95

STARS OF THE BROADWAY STAGE, 1940-1967, Fred Fehl. Marlon Brando, Uta Hagen, John Kerr, John Gielgud, Jessica Tandy in great shows—*South Pacific, Galileo, West Side Story*, more. 240 black-and-white photos. 144pp. 8⅜ × 11¼.
24398-2 Pa. $8.95

ILLUSTRATED DICTIONARY OF HISTORIC ARCHITECTURE, edited by Cyril M. Harris. Extraordinary compendium of clear, concise definitions for over 5000 important architectural terms complemented by over 2000 line drawings. 592pp. 7½ × 9⅜.
24444-X Pa. $14.95

THE EARLY WORK OF FRANK LLOYD WRIGHT, F.L. Wright. 207 rare photos of Oak Park period, first great buildings: Unity Temple, Dana house, Larkin factory. Complete photos of Wasmuth edition. New Introduction. 160pp. 8⅜ × 11¼.
24381-8 Pa. $7.95

LIVING MY LIFE, Emma Goldman. Candid, no holds barred account by foremost American anarchist: her own life, anarchist movement, famous contemporaries, ideas and their impact. 944pp. 5⅜ × 8½. 22543-7, 22544-5 Pa., Two-vol. set $13.00

UNDERSTANDING THERMODYNAMICS, H.C. Van Ness. Clear, lucid treatment of first and second laws of thermodynamics. Excellent supplement to basic textbook in undergraduate science or engineering class. 103pp. 5⅜ × 8.
63277-6 Pa. $5.50

CATALOG OF DOVER BOOKS

SURREAL STICKERS AND UNREAL STAMPS, William Rowe. 224 haunting, hilarious stamps on gummed, perforated stock, with images of elephants, geisha girls, George Washington, etc. 16pp. one side. 8¼ × 11.   24371-0 Pa. $3.50

GOURMET KITCHEN LABELS, Ed Sibbett, Jr. 112 full-color labels (4 copies each of 28 designs). Fruit, bread, other culinary motifs. Gummed and perforated. 16pp. 8¼ × 11.   24087-8 Pa. $2.95

PATTERNS AND INSTRUCTIONS FOR CARVING AUTHENTIC BIRDS, H.D. Green. Detailed instructions, 27 diagrams, 85 photographs for carving 15 species of birds so life-like, they'll seem ready to fly! 8¼ × 11.   24222-6 Pa. $2.75

FLATLAND, E.A. Abbott. Science-fiction classic explores life of 2-D being in 3-D world. 16 illustrations. 103pp. 5⅜ × 8.   20001-9 Pa. $2.00

DRIED FLOWERS, Sarah Whitlock and Martha Rankin. Concise, clear, practical guide to dehydration, glycerinizing, pressing plant material, and more. Covers use of silica gel. 12 drawings. 32pp. 5⅜ × 8½.   21802-3 Pa. $1.00

EASY-TO-MAKE CANDLES, Gary V. Guy. Learn how easy it is to make all kinds of decorative candles. Step-by-step instructions. 82 illustrations. 48pp. 8¼ × 11.   23881-4 Pa. $2.50

SUPER STICKERS FOR KIDS, Carolyn Bracken. 128 gummed and perforated full-color stickers: GIRL WANTED, KEEP OUT, BORED OF EDUCATION, X-RATED, COMBAT ZONE, many others. 16pp. 8¼ × 11.   24092-4 Pa. $2.50

CUT AND COLOR PAPER MASKS, Michael Grater. Clowns, animals, funny faces...simply color them in, cut them out, and put them together, and you have 9 paper masks to play with and enjoy. 32pp. 8¼ × 11.   23171-2 Pa. $2.25

A CHRISTMAS CAROL: THE ORIGINAL MANUSCRIPT, Charles Dickens. Clear facsimile of Dickens manuscript, on facing pages with final printed text. 8 illustrations by John Leech, 4 in color on covers. 144pp. 8⅜ × 11¼.   20980-6 Pa. $5.95

CARVING SHOREBIRDS, Harry V. Shourds & Anthony Hillman. 16 full-size patterns (all double-page spreads) for 19 North American shorebirds with step-by-step instructions. 72pp. 9¼ × 12¼.   24287-0 Pa. $4.95

THE GENTLE ART OF MATHEMATICS, Dan Pedoe. Mathematical games, probability, the question of infinity, topology, how the laws of algebra work, problems of irrational numbers, and more. 42 figures. 143pp. 5⅜ × 8½. (EBE)   22949-1 Pa. $3.50

READY-TO-USE DOLLHOUSE WALLPAPER, Katzenbach & Warren, Inc. Stripe, 2 floral stripes, 2 allover florals, polka dot; all in full color. 4 sheets (350 sq. in.) of each, enough for average room. 48pp. 8¼ × 11.   23495-9 Pa. $2.95

MINIATURE IRON-ON TRANSFER PATTERNS FOR DOLLHOUSES, DOLLS, AND SMALL PROJECTS, Rita Weiss and Frank Fontana. Over 100 miniature patterns: rugs, bedspreads, quilts, chair seats, etc. In standard dollhouse size. 48pp. 8¼ × 11.   23741-9 Pa. $1.95

THE DINOSAUR COLORING BOOK, Anthony Rao. 45 renderings of dinosaurs, fossil birds, turtles, other creatures of Mesozoic Era. Scientifically accurate. Captions. 48pp. 8¼ × 11.   24022-3 Pa. $2.50

THE BOOK OF WOOD CARVING, Charles Marshall Sayers. Still finest book for beginning student. Fundamentals, technique; gives 34 designs, over 34 projects for panels, bookends, mirrors, etc. 33 photos. 118pp. 7¾ × 10⅝.   23654-4 Pa. $3.95

CARVING COUNTRY CHARACTERS, Bill Higginbotham. Expert advice for beginning, advanced carvers on materials, techniques for creating 18 projects— mirthful panorama of American characters. 105 illustrations. 80pp. 8⅜ × 11.
                                                                                              24135-1 Pa. $2.50

300 ART NOUVEAU DESIGNS AND MOTIFS IN FULL COLOR, C.B. Grafton. 44 full-page plates display swirling lines and muted colors typical of Art Nouveau. Borders, frames, panels, cartouches, dingbats, etc. 48pp. 9⅜ × 12¼.
                                                                                              24354-0 Pa. $6.95

SELF-WORKING CARD TRICKS, Karl Fulves. Editor of *Pallbearer* offers 72 tricks that work automatically through nature of card deck. No sleight of hand needed. Often spectacular. 42 illustrations. 113pp. 5⅜ × 8½.   23334-0 Pa. $3.50

CUT AND ASSEMBLE A WESTERN FRONTIER TOWN, Edmund V. Gillon, Jr. Ten authentic full-color buildings on heavy cardboard stock in H-O scale. Sheriff's Office and Jail, Saloon, Wells Fargo, Opera House, others. 48pp. 9¼ × 12¼.
                                                                                              23736-2 Pa. $3.95

CUT AND ASSEMBLE AN EARLY NEW ENGLAND VILLAGE, Edmund V. Gillon, Jr. Printed in full color on heavy cardboard stock. 12 authentic buildings in H-O scale: Adams home in Quincy, Mass., Oliver Wight house in Sturbridge, smithy, store, church, others. 48pp. 9¼ × 12¼.   23536-X Pa. $4.95

THE TALE OF TWO BAD MICE, Beatrix Potter. Tom Thumb and Hunca Munca squeeze out of their hole and go exploring. 27 full-color Potter illustrations. 59pp. 4¼ × 5½. (Available in U.S. only)   23065-1 Pa. $1.75

CARVING FIGURE CARICATURES IN THE OZARK STYLE, Harold L. Enlow. Instructions and illustrations for ten delightful projects, plus general carving instructions. 22 drawings and 47 photographs altogether. 39pp. 8⅜ × 11.
                                                                                              23151-8 Pa. $2.50

A TREASURY OF FLOWER DESIGNS FOR ARTISTS, EMBROIDERERS AND CRAFTSMEN, Susan Gaber. 100 garden favorites lushly rendered by artist for artists, craftsmen, needleworkers. Many form frames, borders. 80pp. 8¼ × 11.
                                                                                              24096-7 Pa. $3.50

CUT & ASSEMBLE A TOY THEATER/THE NUTCRACKER BALLET, Tom Tierney. Model of a complete, full-color production of Tchaikovsky's classic. 6 backdrops, dozens of characters, familiar dance sequences. 32pp. 9⅜ × 12¼.
                                                                                              24194-7 Pa. $4.50

ANIMALS: 1,419 COPYRIGHT-FREE ILLUSTRATIONS OF MAMMALS, BIRDS, FISH, INSECTS, ETC., edited by Jim Harter. Clear wood engravings present, in extremely lifelike poses, over 1,000 species of animals. 284pp. 9 × 12.
                                                                                              23766-4 Pa. $9.95

MORE HAND SHADOWS, Henry Bursill. For those at their 'finger ends," 16 more effects—Shakespeare, a hare, a squirrel, Mr. Punch, and twelve more—each explained by a full-page illustration. Considerable period charm. 30pp. 6½ × 9¼.
                                                                                              21384-6 Pa. $1.95

CATALOG OF DOVER BOOKS

JAPANESE DESIGN MOTIFS, Matsuya Co. Mon, or heraldic designs. Over 4000 typical, beautiful designs: birds, animals, flowers, swords, fans, geometrics; all beautifully stylized. 213pp. 11⅜ × 8¼. 22874-6 Pa. $7.95

THE TALE OF BENJAMIN BUNNY, Beatrix Potter. Peter Rabbit's cousin coaxes him back into Mr. McGregor's garden for a whole new set of adventures. All 27 full-color illustrations. 59pp. 4¼ × 5½. (Available in U.S. only) 21102-9 Pa. $1.75

THE TALE OF PETER RABBIT AND OTHER FAVORITE STORIES BOXED SET, Beatrix Potter. Seven of Beatrix Potter's best-loved tales including Peter Rabbit in a specially designed, durable boxed set. 4¼ × 5½. Total of 447pp. 158 color illustrations. (Available in U.S. only) 23903-9 Pa. $10.80

PRACTICAL MENTAL MAGIC, Theodore Annemann. Nearly 200 astonishing feats of mental magic revealed in step-by-step detail. Complete advice on staging, patter, etc. Illustrated. 320pp. 5⅜ × 8½. 24426-1 Pa. $5.95

CELEBRATED CASES OF JUDGE DEE (DEE GOONG AN), translated by Robert Van Gulik. Authentic 18th-century Chinese detective novel; Dee and associates solve three interlocked cases. Led to van Gulik's own stories with same characters. Extensive introduction. 9 illustrations. 237pp. 5⅜ × 8½. 23337-5 Pa. $4.50

CUT & FOLD EXTRATERRESTRIAL INVADERS THAT FLY, M. Grater. Stage your own lilliputian space battles.By following the step-by-step instructions and explanatory diagrams you can launch 22 full-color fliers into space. 36pp. 8¼ × 11. 24478-4 Pa. $2.95

CUT & ASSEMBLE VICTORIAN HOUSES, Edmund V. Gillon, Jr. Printed in full color on heavy cardboard stock, 4 authentic Victorian houses in H-O scale: Italian-style Villa, Octagon, Second Empire, Stick Style. 48pp. 9¼ × 12¼. 23849-0 Pa. $3.95

BEST SCIENCE FICTION STORIES OF H.G. WELLS, H.G. Wells. Full novel The Invisible Man, plus 17 short stories: "The Crystal Egg," "Aepyornis Island," "The Strange Orchid," etc. 303pp. 5⅜ × 8½. (Available in U.S. only) 21531-8 Pa. $4.95

TRADEMARK DESIGNS OF THE WORLD, Yusaku Kamekura. A lavish collection of nearly 700 trademarks, the work of Wright, Loewy, Klee, Binder, hundreds of others. 160pp. 8¾ × 8. (Available in U.S. only) 24191-2 Pa. $5.95

THE ARTIST'S AND CRAFTSMAN'S GUIDE TO REDUCING, ENLARGING AND TRANSFERRING DESIGNS, Rita Weiss. Discover, reduce, enlarge, transfer designs from any objects to any craft project. 12pp. plus 16 sheets special graph paper. 8¼ × 11. 24142-4 Pa. $3.50

TREASURY OF JAPANESE DESIGNS AND MOTIFS FOR ARTISTS AND CRAFTSMEN, edited by Carol Belanger Grafton. Indispensable collection of 360 traditional Japanese designs and motifs redrawn in clean, crisp black-and-white, copyright-free illustrations. 96pp. 8¼ × 11. 24435-0 Pa. $3.95

CHANCERY CURSIVE STROKE BY STROKE, Arthur Baker. Instructions and illustrations for each stroke of each letter (upper and lower case) and numerals. 54 full-page plates. 64pp. 8¼ × 11. 24278-1 Pa. $2.50

THE ENJOYMENT AND USE OF COLOR, Walter Sargent. Color relationships, values, intensities; complementary colors, illumination, similar topics. Color in nature and art. 7 color plates, 29 illustrations. 274pp. 5⅜ × 8½. 20944-X Pa. $4.95

SCULPTURE PRINCIPLES AND PRACTICE, Louis Slobodkin. Step-by-step approach to clay, plaster, metals, stone; classical and modern. 253 drawings, photos. 255pp. 8⅛ × 11. 22960-2 Pa. $7.50

VICTORIAN FASHION PAPER DOLLS FROM HARPER'S BAZAR, 1867-1898, Theodore Menten. Four female dolls with 28 elegant high fashion costumes, printed in full color. 32pp. 9¼ × 12¼. 23453-3 Pa. $3.50

FLOPSY, MOPSY AND COTTONTAIL: A Little Book of Paper Dolls in Full Color, Susan LaBelle. Three dolls and 21 costumes (7 for each doll) show Peter Rabbit's siblings dressed for holidays, gardening, hiking, etc. Charming borders, captions. 48pp. 4¼ × 5½. 24376-1 Pa. $2.25

NATIONAL LEAGUE BASEBALL CARD CLASSICS, Bert Randolph Sugar. 83 big-leaguers from 1909-69 on facsimile cards. Hubbell, Dean, Spahn, Brock plus advertising, info, no duplications. Perforated, detachable. 16pp. 8¼ × 11. 24308-7 Pa. $2.95

THE LOGICAL APPROACH TO CHESS, Dr. Max Euwe, et al. First-rate text of comprehensive strategy, tactics, theory for the amateur. No gambits to memorize, just a clear, logical approach. 224pp. 5⅜ × 8½. 24353-2 Pa. $4.50

MAGICK IN THEORY AND PRACTICE, Aleister Crowley. The summation of the thought and practice of the century's most famous necromancer, long hard to find. Crowley's best book. 436pp. 5⅜ × 8½. (Available in U.S. only) 23295-6 Pa. $6.50

THE HAUNTED HOTEL, Wilkie Collins. Collins' last great tale; doom and destiny in a Venetian palace. Praised by T.S. Eliot. 127pp. 5⅜ × 8½. 24333-8 Pa. $3.00

ART DECO DISPLAY ALPHABETS, Dan X. Solo. Wide variety of bold yet elegant lettering in handsome Art Deco styles. 100 complete fonts, with numerals, punctuation, more. 104pp. 8⅛ × 11. 24372-9 Pa. $4.50

CALLIGRAPHIC ALPHABETS, Arthur Baker. Nearly 150 complete alphabets by outstanding contemporary. Stimulating ideas; useful source for unique effects. 154 plates. 157pp. 8⅜ × 11¼. 21045-6 Pa. $5.95

ARTHUR BAKER'S HISTORIC CALLIGRAPHIC ALPHABETS, Arthur Baker. From monumental capitals of first-century Rome to humanistic cursive of 16th century, 33 alphabets in fresh interpretations. 88 plates. 96pp. 9 × 12. 24054-1 Pa. $4.50

LETTIE LANE PAPER DOLLS, Sheila Young. Genteel turn-of-the-century family very popular then and now. 24 paper dolls. 16 plates in full color. 32pp. 9¼ × 12¼. 24089-4 Pa. $3.50

CATALOG OF DOVER BOOKS

TWENTY-FOUR ART NOUVEAU POSTCARDS IN FULL COLOR FROM CLASSIC POSTERS, Hayward and Blanche Cirker. Ready-to-mail postcards reproduced from rare set of poster art. Works by Toulouse-Lautrec, Parrish, Steinlen, Mucha, Cheret, others. 12pp. 8¼× 11. 24389-3 Pa. $2.95

READY-TO-USE ART NOUVEAU BOOKMARKS IN FULL COLOR, Carol Belanger Grafton. 30 elegant bookmarks featuring graceful, flowing lines, foliate motifs, sensuous women characteristic of Art Nouveau. Perforated for easy detaching. 16pp. 8¼ × 11. 24305-2 Pa. $2.95

FRUIT KEY AND TWIG KEY TO TREES AND SHRUBS, William M. Harlow. Fruit key covers 120 deciduous and evergreen species; twig key covers 160 deciduous species. Easily used. Over 300 photographs. 126pp. 5⅜ × 8½. 20511-8 Pa. $2.25

LEONARDO DRAWINGS, Leonardo da Vinci. Plants, landscapes, human face and figure, etc., plus studies for Sforza monument, *Last Supper*, more. 60 illustrations. 64pp. 8¼ × 11⅛. 23951-9 Pa. $2.75

CLASSIC BASEBALL CARDS, edited by Bert R. Sugar. 98 classic cards on heavy stock, full color, perforated for detaching. Ruth, Cobb, Durocher, DiMaggio, H. Wagner, 99 others. Rare originals cost hundreds. 16pp. 8¼ × 11. 23498-3 Pa. $3.25

TREES OF THE EASTERN AND CENTRAL UNITED STATES AND CANADA, William M. Harlow. Best one-volume guide to 140 trees. Full descriptions, woodlore, range, etc. Over 600 illustrations. Handy size. 288pp. 4½ × 6⅜. 20395-6 Pa. $3.95

JUDY GARLAND PAPER DOLLS IN FULL COLOR, Tom Tierney. 3 Judy Garland paper dolls (teenager, grown-up, and mature woman) and 30 gorgeous costumes highlighting memorable career. Captions. 32pp. 9¼ × 12¼. 24404-0 Pa. $3.50

GREAT FASHION DESIGNS OF THE BELLE EPOQUE PAPER DOLLS IN FULL COLOR, Tom Tierney. Two dolls and 30 costumes meticulously rendered. Haute couture by Worth, Lanvin, Paquin, other greats late Victorian to WWI. 32pp. 9¼ × 12¼. 24425-3 Pa. $3.50

FASHION PAPER DOLLS FROM GODEY'S LADY'S BOOK, 1840-1854, Susan Johnston. In full color: 7 female fashion dolls with 50 costumes. Little girl's, bridal, riding, bathing, wedding, evening, everyday, etc. 32pp. 9¼ × 12¼. 23511-4 Pa. $3.95

THE BOOK OF THE SACRED MAGIC OF ABRAMELIN THE MAGE, translated by S. MacGregor Mathers. Medieval manuscript of ceremonial magic. Basic document in Aleister Crowley, Golden Dawn groups. 268pp. 5⅜ × 8½. 23211-5 Pa. $5.00

PETER RABBIT POSTCARDS IN FULL COLOR: 24 Ready-to-Mail Cards, Susan Whited LaBelle. Bunnies ice-skating, coloring Easter eggs, making valentines, many other charming scenes. 24 perforated full-color postcards, each measuring 4¼ × 6, on coated stock. 12pp. 9 × 12. 24617-5 Pa. $2.95

CELTIC HAND STROKE BY STROKE, A. Baker. Complete guide creating each letter of the alphabet in distinctive Celtic manner. Covers hand position, strokes, pens, inks, paper, more. Illustrated. 48pp. 8¼ × 11. 24336-2 Pa. $2.50

CATALOG OF DOVER BOOKS

KEYBOARD WORKS FOR SOLO INSTRUMENTS, G.F. Handel. 35 neglected works from Handel's vast oeuvre, originally jotted down as improvisations. Includes Eight Great Suites, others. New sequence. 174pp. 9⅜ × 12¼.
24338-9 Pa. $7.50

AMERICAN LEAGUE BASEBALL CARD CLASSICS, Bert Randolph Sugar. 82 stars from 1900s to 60s on facsimile cards. Ruth, Cobb, Mantle, Williams, plus advertising, info, no duplications. Perforated, detachable. 16pp. 8¼ × 11.
24286-2 Pa. $2.95

A TREASURY OF CHARTED DESIGNS FOR NEEDLEWORKERS, Georgia Gorham and Jeanne Warth. 141 charted designs: owl, cat with yarn, tulips, piano, spinning wheel, covered bridge, Victorian house and many others. 48pp. 8¼ × 11.
23558-0 Pa. $1.95

DANISH FLORAL CHARTED DESIGNS, Gerda Bengtsson. Exquisite collection of over 40 different florals: anemone, Iceland poppy, wild fruit, pansies, many others. 45 illustrations. 48pp. 8¼ × 11.   23957-8 Pa. $1.75

OLD PHILADELPHIA IN EARLY PHOTOGRAPHS 1839-1914, Robert F. Looney. 215 photographs: panoramas, street scenes, landmarks, President-elect Lincoln's visit, 1876 Centennial Exposition, much more. 230pp. 8⅜ × 11¼.
23345-6 Pa. $9.95

PRELUDE TO MATHEMATICS, W.W. Sawyer. Noted mathematician's lively, stimulating account of non-Euclidean geometry, matrices, determinants, group theory, other topics. Emphasis on novel, striking aspects. 224pp. 5⅜ × 8½.
24401-6 Pa. $4.50

ADVENTURES WITH A MICROSCOPE, Richard Headstrom. 59 adventures with clothing fibers, protozoa, ferns and lichens, roots and leaves, much more. 142 illustrations. 232pp. 5⅜ × 8½.   23471-1 Pa. $3.95

IDENTIFYING ANIMAL TRACKS: MAMMALS, BIRDS, AND OTHER ANIMALS OF THE EASTERN UNITED STATES, Richard Headstrom. For hunters, naturalists, scouts, nature-lovers. Diagrams of tracks, tips on identification. 128pp. 5⅜ × 8.   24442-3 Pa. $3.50

VICTORIAN FASHIONS AND COSTUMES FROM HARPER'S BAZAR, 1867-1898, edited by Stella Blum. Day costumes, evening wear, sports clothes, shoes, hats, other accessories in over 1,000 detailed engravings. 320pp. 9⅜ × 12¼.
22990-4 Pa. $10.95

EVERYDAY FASHIONS OF THE TWENTIES AS PICTURED IN SEARS AND OTHER CATALOGS, edited by Stella Blum. Actual dress of the Roaring Twenties, with text by Stella Blum. Over 750 illustrations, captions. 156pp. 9 × 12.
24134-3 Pa. $8.50

HALL OF FAME BASEBALL CARDS, edited by Bert Randolph Sugar. Cy Young, Ted Williams, Lou Gehrig, and many other Hall of Fame greats on 92 full-color, detachable reprints of early baseball cards. No duplication of cards with *Classic Baseball Cards.* 16pp. 8¼ × 11.   23624-2 Pa. $3.50

THE ART OF HAND LETTERING, Helm Wotzkow. Course in hand lettering, Roman, Gothic, Italic, Block, Script. Tools, proportions, optical aspects, individual variation. Very quality conscious. Hundreds of specimens. 320pp. 5⅜ × 8½.
21797-3 Pa. $4.95

HOW THE OTHER HALF LIVES, Jacob A. Riis. Journalistic record of filth, degradation, upward drive in New York immigrant slums, shops, around 1900. New edition includes 100 original Riis photos, monuments of early photography. 233pp. 10 × 7⅞. 22012-5 Pa. $7.95

CHINA AND ITS PEOPLE IN EARLY PHOTOGRAPHS, John Thomson. In 200 black-and-white photographs of exceptional quality photographic pioneer Thomson captures the mountains, dwellings, monuments and people of 19th-century China. 272pp. 9⅜ × 12¼. 24393-1 Pa. $12.95

GODEY COSTUME PLATES IN COLOR FOR DECOUPAGE AND FRAMING, edited by Eleanor Hasbrouk Rawlings. 24 full-color engravings depicting 19th-century Parisian haute couture. Printed on one side only. 56pp. 8¼ × 11. 23879-2 Pa. $3.95

ART NOUVEAU STAINED GLASS PATTERN BOOK, Ed Sibbett, Jr. 104 projects using well-known themes of Art Nouveau: swirling forms, florals, peacocks, and sensuous women. 60pp. 8¼ × 11. 23577-7 Pa. $3.50

QUICK AND EASY PATCHWORK ON THE SEWING MACHINE: Susan Aylsworth Murwin and Suzzy Payne. Instructions, diagrams show exactly how to machine sew 12 quilts. 48pp. of templates. 50 figures. 80pp. 8¼ × 11. 23770-2 Pa. $3.50

THE STANDARD BOOK OF QUILT MAKING AND COLLECTING, Marguerite Ickis. Full information, full-sized patterns for making 46 traditional quilts, also 150 other patterns. 483 illustrations. 273pp. 6⅞ × 9⅝. 20582-7 Pa. $5.95

LETTERING AND ALPHABETS, J. Albert Cavanagh. 85 complete alphabets lettered in various styles; instructions for spacing, roughs, brushwork. 121pp. 8¾ × 8. 20053-1 Pa. $3.95

LETTER FORMS: 110 COMPLETE ALPHABETS, Frederick Lambert. 110 sets of capital letters; 16 lower case alphabets; 70 sets of numbers and other symbols. 110pp. 8⅛ × 11. 22872-X Pa. $4.50

ORCHIDS AS HOUSE PLANTS, Rebecca Tyson Northen. Grow cattleyas and many other kinds of orchids—in a window, in a case, or under artificial light. 63 illustrations. 148pp. 5⅜ × 8½. 23261-1 Pa. $2.95

THE MUSHROOM HANDBOOK, Louis C.C. Krieger. Still the best popular handbook. Full descriptions of 259 species, extremely thorough text, poisons, folklore, etc. 32 color plates; 126 other illustrations. 560pp. 5⅜ × 8½. 21861-9 Pa. $8.50

THE DORÉ BIBLE ILLUSTRATIONS, Gustave Doré. All wonderful, detailed plates: Adam and Eve, Flood, Babylon, life of Jesus, etc. Brief King James text with each plate. 241 plates. 241pp. 9 × 12. 23004-X Pa. $8.95

THE BOOK OF KELLS: Selected Plates in Full Color, edited by Blanche Cirker. 32 full-page plates from greatest manuscript-icon of early Middle Ages. Fantastic, mysterious. Publisher's Note. Captions. 32pp. 9¾ × 12¼. 24345-1 Pa. $4.50

THE PERFECT WAGNERITE, George Bernard Shaw. Brilliant criticism of the Ring Cycle, with provocative interpretation of politics, economic theories behind the Ring. 136pp. 5⅜ × 8½. (Available in U.S. only) 21707-8 Pa. $3.00

THE RIME OF THE ANCIENT MARINER, Gustave Doré, S.T. Coleridge. Doré's finest work, 34 plates capture moods, subtleties of poem. Full text. 77pp. 9¼ × 12. 22305-1 Pa. $4.95

SONGS OF INNOCENCE, William Blake. The first and most popular of Blake's famous "Illuminated Books," in a facsimile edition reproducing all 31 brightly colored plates. Additional printed text of each poem. 64pp. 5¼ × 7. 22764-2 Pa. $3.50

AN INTRODUCTION TO INFORMATION THEORY, J.R. Pierce. Second (1980) edition of most impressive non-technical account available. Encoding, entropy, noisy channel, related areas, etc. 320pp. 5⅜ × 8½. 24061-4 Pa. $4.95

THE DIVINE PROPORTION: A STUDY IN MATHEMATICAL BEAUTY, H.E. Huntley. "Divine proportion" or "golden ratio" in poetry, Pascal's triangle, philosophy, psychology, music, mathematical figures, etc. Excellent bridge between science and art. 58 figures. 185pp. 5⅜ × 8½. 22254-3 Pa. $3.95

THE DOVER NEW YORK WALKING GUIDE: From the Battery to Wall Street, Mary J. Shapiro. Superb inexpensive guide to historic buildings and locales in lower Manhattan: Trinity Church, Bowling Green, more. Complete Text; maps. 36 illustrations. 48pp. 3⅞ × 9¼. 24225-0 Pa. $2.50

NEW YORK THEN AND NOW, Edward B. Watson, Edmund V. Gillon, Jr. 83 important Manhattan sites: on facing pages early photographs (1875-1925) and 1976 photos by Gillon. 172 illustrations. 171pp. 9¼ × 10. 23361-8 Pa. $7.95

HISTORIC COSTUME IN PICTURES, Braun & Schneider. Over 1450 costumed figures from dawn of civilization to end of 19th century. English captions. 125 plates. 256pp. 8⅜ × 11¼. 23150-X Pa. $7.50

VICTORIAN AND EDWARDIAN FASHION: A Photographic Survey, Alison Gernsheim. First fashion history completely illustrated by contemporary photographs. Full text plus 235 photos, 1840-1914, in which many celebrities appear. 240pp. 6½ × 9¼. 24205-6 Pa. $6.00

CHARTED CHRISTMAS DESIGNS FOR COUNTED CROSS-STITCH AND OTHER NEEDLECRAFTS, Lindberg Press. Charted designs for 45 beautiful needlecraft projects with many yuletide and wintertime motifs. 48pp. 8¼ × 11. 24356-7 Pa. $2.50

101 FOLK DESIGNS FOR COUNTED CROSS-STITCH AND OTHER NEEDLECRAFTS, Carter Houck. 101 authentic charted folk designs in a wide array of lovely representations with many suggestions for effective use. 48pp. 8¼ × 11. 24369-9 Pa. $2.25

FIVE ACRES AND INDEPENDENCE, Maurice G. Kains. Great back-to-the-land classic explains basics of self-sufficient farming. The one book to get. 95 illustrations. 397pp. 5⅜ × 8½. 20974-1 Pa. $4.95

A MODERN HERBAL, Margaret Grieve. Much the fullest, most exact, most useful compilation of herbal material. Gigantic alphabetical encyclopedia, from aconite to zedoary, gives botanical information, medical properties, folklore, economic uses, and much else. Indispensable to serious reader. 161 illustrations. 888pp. 6½ × 9¼. (Available in U.S. only) 22798-7, 22799-5 Pa., Two-vol. set $16.45

DECORATIVE NAPKIN FOLDING FOR BEGINNERS, Lillian Oppenheimer and Natalie Epstein. 22 different napkin folds in the shape of a heart, clown's hat, love knot, etc. 63 drawings. 48pp. 8¼ × 11. 23797-4 Pa. $1.95

DECORATIVE LABELS FOR HOME CANNING, PRESERVING, AND OTHER HOUSEHOLD AND GIFT USES, Theodore Menten. 128 gummed, perforated labels, beautifully printed in 2 colors. 12 versions. Adhere to metal, glass, wood, ceramics. 24pp. 8¼ × 11. 23219-0 Pa. $2.95

EARLY AMERICAN STENCILS ON WALLS AND FURNITURE, Janet Waring. Thorough coverage of 19th-century folk art: techniques, artifacts, surviving specimens. 166 illustrations, 7 in color. 147pp. of text. 7⅞ × 10¾. 21906-2 Pa. $9.95

AMERICAN ANTIQUE WEATHERVANES, A.B. & W.T. Westervelt. Extensively illustrated 1883 catalog exhibiting over 550 copper weathervanes and finials. Excellent primary source by one of the principal manufacturers. 104pp. 6⅛ × 9¼. 24396-6 Pa. $3.95

ART STUDENTS' ANATOMY, Edmond J. Farris. Long favorite in art schools. Basic elements, common positions, actions. Full text, 158 illustrations. 159pp. 5⅜ × 8½. 20744-7 Pa. $3.95

BRIDGMAN'S LIFE DRAWING, George B. Bridgman. More than 500 drawings and text teach you to abstract the body into its major masses. Also specific areas of anatomy. 192pp. 6½ × 9¼. (EA) 22710-3 Pa. $4.50

COMPLETE PRELUDES AND ETUDES FOR SOLO PIANO, Frederic Chopin. All 26 Preludes, all 27 Etudes by greatest composer of piano music. Authoritative Paderewski edition. 224pp. 9 × 12. (Available in U.S. only) 24052-5 Pa. $7.50

PIANO MUSIC 1888-1905, Claude Debussy. Deux Arabesques, Suite Bergamesque, Masques, 1st series of Images, etc. 9 others, in corrected editions. 175pp. 9⅜ × 12¼. (ECE) 22771-5 Pa. $5.95

TEDDY BEAR IRON-ON TRANSFER PATTERNS, Ted Menten. 80 iron-on transfer patterns of male and female Teddys in a wide variety of activities, poses, sizes. 48pp. 8¼ × 11. 24596-9 Pa. $2.25

A PICTURE HISTORY OF THE BROOKLYN BRIDGE, M.J. Shapiro. Profusely illustrated account of greatest engineering achievement of 19th century. 167 rare photos & engravings recall construction, human drama. Extensive, detailed text. 122pp. 8¼ × 11. 24403-2 Pa. $7.95

NEW YORK IN THE THIRTIES, Berenice Abbott. Noted photographer's fascinating study shows new buildings that have become famous and old sights that have disappeared forever. 97 photographs. 97pp. 11⅜ × 10. 22967-X Pa. $7.50

MATHEMATICAL TABLES AND FORMULAS, Robert D. Carmichael and Edwin R. Smith. Logarithms, sines, tangents, trig functions, powers, roots, reciprocals, exponential and hyperbolic functions, formulas and theorems. 269pp. 5⅜ × 8½. 60111-0 Pa. $4.95

HANDBOOK OF MATHEMATICAL FUNCTIONS WITH FORMULAS, GRAPHS, AND MATHEMATICAL TABLES, edited by Milton Abramowitz and Irene A. Stegun. Vast compendium: 29 sets of tables, some to as high as 20 places. 1,046pp. 8 × 10½. 61272-4 Pa. $19.95

REASON IN ART, George Santayana. Renowned philosopher's provocative, seminal treatment of basis of art in instinct and experience. Volume Four of *The Life of Reason*. 230pp. 5⅜ × 8. 24358-3 Pa. $4.50

LANGUAGE, TRUTH AND LOGIC, Alfred J. Ayer. Famous, clear introduction to Vienna, Cambridge schools of Logical Positivism. Role of philosophy, elimination of metaphysics, nature of analysis, etc. 160pp. 5⅜ × 8½. (USCO) 20010-8 Pa. $2.75

BASIC ELECTRONICS, U.S. Bureau of Naval Personnel. Electron tubes, circuits, antennas, AM, FM, and CW transmission and receiving, etc. 560 illustrations. 567pp. 6½ × 9¼. 21076-6 Pa. $8.95

THE ART DECO STYLE, edited by Theodore Menten. Furniture, jewelry, metalwork, ceramics, fabrics, lighting fixtures, interior decors, exteriors, graphics from pure French sources. Over 400 photographs. 183pp. 8⅜ × 11¼. 22824-X Pa. $6.95

THE FOUR BOOKS OF ARCHITECTURE, Andrea Palladio. 16th-century classic covers classical architectural remains, Renaissance revivals, classical orders, etc. 1738 Ware English edition. 216 plates. 110pp. of text. 9½ × 12¾. 21308-0 Pa. $11.50

THE WIT AND HUMOR OF OSCAR WILDE, edited by Alvin Redman. More than 1000 ripostes, paradoxes, wisecracks: Work is the curse of the drinking classes, I can resist everything except temptations, etc. 258pp. 5⅜ × 8½. (USCO) 20602-5 Pa. $3.95

THE DEVIL'S DICTIONARY, Ambrose Bierce. Barbed, bitter, brilliant witticisms in the form of a dictionary. Best, most ferocious satire America has produced. 145pp. 5⅜ × 8½. 20487-1 Pa. $2.50

ERTÉ'S FASHION DESIGNS, Erté. 210 black-and-white inventions from *Harper's Bazar*, 1918-32, plus 8pp. full-color covers. Captions. 88pp. 9 × 12. 24203-X Pa. $6.50

ERTÉ GRAPHICS, Erté. Collection of striking color graphics: *Seasons, Alphabet, Numerals, Aces* and *Precious Stones*. 50 plates, including 4 on covers. 48pp. 9⅜ × 12¼. 23580-7 Pa. $6.95

PAPER FOLDING FOR BEGINNERS, William D. Murray and Francis J. Rigney. Clearest book for making origami sail boats, roosters, frogs that move legs, etc. 40 projects. More than 275 illustrations. 94pp. 5⅜ × 8½. 20713-7 Pa. $2.25

ORIGAMI FOR THE ENTHUSIAST, John Montroll. Fish, ostrich, peacock, squirrel, rhinoceros, Pegasus, 19 other intricate subjects. Instructions. Diagrams. 128pp. 9 × 12. 23799-0 Pa. $4.95

CROCHETING NOVELTY POT HOLDERS, edited by Linda Macho. 64 useful, whimsical pot holders feature kitchen themes, animals, flowers, other novelties. Surprisingly easy to crochet. Complete instructions. 48pp. 8¼ × 11. 24296-X Pa. $1.95

CROCHETING DOILIES, edited by Rita Weiss. Irish Crochet, Jewel, Star Wheel, Vanity Fair and more. Also luncheon and console sets, runners and centerpieces. 51 illustrations. 48pp. 8¼ × 11. 23424-X Pa. $2.50

YUCATAN BEFORE AND AFTER THE CONQUEST, Diego de Landa. Only significant account of Yucatan written in the early post-Conquest era. Translated by William Gates. Over 120 illustrations. 162pp. 5⅜ × 8½. 23622-6 Pa. $3.50

ORNATE PICTORIAL CALLIGRAPHY, E.A. Lupfer. Complete instructions, over 150 examples help you create magnificent "flourishes" from which beautiful animals and objects gracefully emerge. 8⅛ × 11. 21957-7 Pa. $2.95

DOLLY DINGLE PAPER DOLLS, Grace Drayton. Cute chubby children by same artist who did Campbell Kids. Rare plates from 1910s. 30 paper dolls and over 100 outfits reproduced in full color. 32pp. 9¼ × 12¼. 23711-7 Pa. $3.50

CURIOUS GEORGE PAPER DOLLS IN FULL COLOR, H. A. Rey, Kathy Allert. Naughty little monkey-hero of children's books in two doll figures, plus 48 full-color costumes: pirate, Indian chief, fireman, more. 32pp. 9¼ × 12¼. 24386-9 Pa. $3.50

GERMAN: HOW TO SPEAK AND WRITE IT, Joseph Rosenberg. Like *French, How to Speak and Write It.* Very rich modern course, with a wealth of pictorial material. 330 illustrations. 384pp. 5⅜ × 8½. (USUKO) 20271-2 Pa. $4.75

CATS AND KITTENS: 24 Ready-to-Mail Color Photo Postcards, D. Holby. Handsome collection; feline in a variety of adorable poses. Identifications. 12pp. on postcard stock. 8¼ × 11. 24469-5 Pa. $2.95

MARILYN MONROE PAPER DOLLS, Tom Tierney. 31 full-color designs on heavy stock, from *The Asphalt Jungle, Gentlemen Prefer Blondes*, 22 others. 1 doll. 16 plates. 32pp. 9⅜ × 12¼. 23769-9 Pa. $3.50

FUNDAMENTALS OF LAYOUT, F.H. Wills. All phases of layout design discussed and illustrated in 121 illustrations. Indispensable as student's text or handbook for professional. 124pp. 8⅛.× 11. 21279-3 Pa. $4.50

FANTASTIC SUPER STICKERS, Ed Sibbett, Jr. 75 colorful pressure-sensitive stickers. Peel off and place for a touch of pizzazz: clowns, penguins, teddy bears, etc. Full color. 16pp. 8¼ × 11. 24471-7 Pa. $2.95

LABELS FOR ALL OCCASIONS, Ed Sibbett, Jr. 6 labels each of 16 different designs—baroque, art nouveau, art deco, Pennsylvania Dutch, etc.—in full color. 24pp. 8¼ × 11. 23688-9 Pa. $2.95

HOW TO CALCULATE QUICKLY: RAPID METHODS IN BASIC MATHE-MATICS, Henry Sticker. Addition, subtraction, multiplication, division, checks, etc. More than 8000 problems, solutions. 185pp. 5 × 7¼. 20295-X Pa. $2.95

THE CAT COLORING BOOK, Karen Baldauski. Handsome, realistic renderings of 40 splendid felines, from American shorthair to exotic types. 44 plates. Captions. 48pp. 8¼ × 11. 24011-8 Pa. $2.25

THE TALE OF PETER RABBIT, Beatrix Potter. The inimitable Peter's terrifying adventure in Mr. McGregor's garden, with all 27 wonderful, full-color Potter illustrations. 55pp. 4¼ × 5½. (Available in U.S. only) 22827-4 Pa. $1.75

BASIC ELECTRICITY, U.S. Bureau of Naval Personnel. Batteries, circuits, conductors, AC and DC, inductance and capacitance, generators, motors, trans-formers, amplifiers, etc. 349 illustrations. 448pp. 6½ × 9¼. 20973-3 Pa. $7.95

CATALOG OF DOVER BOOKS

TOLL HOUSE TRIED AND TRUE RECIPES, Ruth Graves Wakefield. Popovers, veal and ham loaf, baked beans, much more from the famous Mass. restaurant. Nearly 700 recipes. 376pp. 5⅜ × 8½. 23560-2 Pa. $4.95

FAVORITE CHRISTMAS CAROLS, selected and arranged by Charles J.F. Cofone. Title, music, first verse and refrain of 34 traditional carols in handsome calligraphy; also subsequent verses and other information in type. 79pp. 8⅜ × 11. 20445-6 Pa. $3.50

CAMERA WORK: A PICTORIAL GUIDE, Alfred Stieglitz. All 559 illustrations from most important periodical in history of art photography. Reduced in size but still clear, in strict chronological order, with complete captions. 176pp. 8⅜ × 11¼. 23591-2 Pa. $6.95

FAVORITE SONGS OF THE NINETIES, edited by Robert Fremont. 88 favorites: "Ta-Ra-Ra-Boom-De-Aye," "The Band Played On," "Bird in a Gilded Cage," etc. 401pp. 9 × 12. 21536-9 Pa. $12.95

STRING FIGURES AND HOW TO MAKE THEM, Caroline F. Jayne. Fullest, clearest instructions on string figures from around world: Eskimo, Navajo, Lapp, Europe, more. Cat's cradle, moving spear, lightning, stars. 950 illustrations. 407pp. 5⅜ × 8½. 20152-X Pa. $5.95

LIFE IN ANCIENT EGYPT, Adolf Erman. Detailed older account, with much not in more recent books: domestic life, religion, magic, medicine, commerce, and whatever else needed for complete picture. Many illustrations. 597pp. 5⅜ × 8½. 22632-8 Pa. $7.95

ANCIENT EGYPT: ITS CULTURE AND HISTORY, J.E. Manchip White. From pre-dynastics through Ptolemies: scoiety, history, political structure, religion, daily life, literature, cultural heritage. 48 plates. 217pp. 5⅜ × 8½. (EBE) 22548-8 Pa. $4.95

KEPT IN THE DARK, Anthony Trollope. Unusual short novel about Victorian morality and abnormal psychology by the great English author. Probably the first American publication. Frontispiece by Sir John Millais. 92pp. 6½ × 9¼. 23609-9 Pa. $2.95

MAN AND WIFE, Wilkie Collins. Nineteenth-century master launches an attack on out-moded Scottish marital laws and Victorian cult of athleticism. Artfully plotted. 35 illustrations. 239pp. 6⅛ × 9¼. 24451-2 Pa. $5.95

RELATIVITY AND COMMON SENSE, Herman Bondi. Radically reoriented presentation of Einstein's Special Theory and one of most valuable popular accounts available. 60 illustrations. 177pp. 5⅜ × 8. (EUK) 24021-5 Pa. $3.95

THE EGYPTIAN BOOK OF THE DEAD, E.A. Wallis Budge. Complete reproduction of Ani's papyrus, finest ever found. Full hieroglyphic text, interlinear transliteration, word-for-word translation, smooth translation. 533pp. 6½ × 9¼. (USO) 21866-X Pa. $8.95

COUNTRY AND SUBURBAN HOMES OF THE PRAIRIE SCHOOL PERIOD, H.V. von Holst. Over 400 photographs floor plans, elevations, detailed drawings (exteriors and interiors) for over 100 structures. Text. Important primary source. 128pp. 8⅜ × 11¼. 24373-7 Pa. $5.95

CATALOG OF DOVER BOOKS

SOURCE BOOK OF MEDICAL HISTORY, edited by Logan Clendening, M.D. Original accounts ranging from Ancient Egypt and Greece to discovery of X-rays: Galen, Pasteur, Lavoisier, Harvey, Parkinson, others. 685pp. 5⅜ × 8½.
20621-1 Pa. $10.95

THE ROSE AND THE KEY, J.S. Lefanu. Superb mystery novel from Irish master. Dark doings among an ancient and aristocratic English family. Well-drawn characters; capital suspense. Introduction by N. Donaldson. 448pp. 5⅜ × 8½.
24377-X Pa. $6.95

SOUTH WIND, Norman Douglas. Witty, elegant novel of ideas set on languorous Meditterranean island of Nepenthe. Elegant prose, glittering epigrams, mordant satire. 1917 masterpiece. 416pp. 5⅜ × 8½. (Available in U.S. only)
24361-3 Pa. $5.95

RUSSELL'S CIVIL WAR PHOTOGRAPHS, Capt. A.J. Russell. 116 rare Civil War Photos: Bull Run, Virginia campaigns, bridges, railroads, Richmond, Lincoln's funeral car. Many never seen before. Captions. 128pp. 9⅜ × 12¼.
24283-8 Pa. $6.95

PHOTOGRAPHS BY MAN RAY: 105 Works, 1920-1934. Nudes, still lifes, landscapes, women's faces, celebrity portraits (Dali, Matisse, Picasso, others), rayographs. Reprinted from rare gravure edition. 128pp. 9⅜ × 12¼. (Available in U.S. only) 23842-3 Pa. $7.95

STAR NAMES: THEIR LORE AND MEANING, Richard H. Allen. Star names, the zodiac, constellations: folklore and literature associated with heavens. The basic book of its field, fascinating reading. 563pp. 5⅜ × 8½. 21079-0 Pa. $7.95

BURNHAM'S CELESTIAL HANDBOOK, Robert Burnham, Jr. Thorough guide to the stars beyond our solar system. Exhaustive treatment. Alphabetical by constellation: Andromeda to Cetus in Vol. 1; Chamaeleon to Orion in Vol. 2; and Pavo to Vulpecula in Vol. 3. Hundreds of illustrations. Index in Vol. 3. 2000pp. 6⅛ × 9¼. 23567-X, 23568-8, 23673-0 Pa. Three-vol. set $36.85

THE ART NOUVEAU STYLE BOOK OF ALPHONSE MUCHA, Alphonse Mucha. All 72 plates from *Documents Decoratifs* in original color. Stunning, essential work of Art Nouveau. 80pp. 9⅜ × 12¼. 24044-4 Pa. $7.95

DESIGNS BY ERTE; FASHION DRAWINGS AND ILLUSTRATIONS FROM "HARPER'S BAZAR," Erte. 310 fabulous line drawings and 14 *Harper's Bazar* covers, 8 in full color. Erte's exotic temptresses with tassels, fur muffs, long trains, coifs, more. 129pp. 9⅜ × 12¼. 23397-9 Pa. $6.95

HISTORY OF STRENGTH OF MATERIALS, Stephen P. Timoshenko. Excellent historical survey of the strength of materials with many references to the theories of elasticity and structure. 245 figures. 452pp. 5⅜ × 8½. 61187-6 Pa. $8.95

Prices subject to change without notice.

Available at your book dealer or write for free catalog to Dept. GI, Dover Publications, Inc., 31 East 2nd St. Mineola, N.Y. 11501. Dover publishes more than 175 books each year on science, elementary and advanced mathematics, biology, music, art, literary history, social sciences and other areas.